It was Dolly Allen, my editor.

'Are you awake?'

'Just. Did you find another incorrect citation that you felt couldn't wait?'

'No, something rather worse. Gordon Fairly has been found dead.'

I woke up quickly. 'That's shocking, of course. But, if I may ask, why did you feel you had to tell *me*?'

'Murdered.'

'Did you say what I think?'

'Yes. Gordon Fairly was murdered this morning. Scotland Yard are talking with Gerard and the firm's solicitors now. A Chief Inspector Stewart. David Chaldecott, of all people, appears to be the chief suspect.'

I was trying to take it all in. For some reason the sentence *No one gets murdered in the morning* was running through my mind.

I must have said it out loud, because Dolly answered firmly, '*He did.*'

IT CAN'T BE
MY GRAVE

Look for these Tor books by S.F.X. Dean

BY FREQUENT ANGUISH
CEREMONY OF INNOCENCE
SUCH PRETTY TOYS
IT CAN'T BE MY GRAVE

S.F.X. DEAN
IT CAN'T BE MY GRAVE

A TOM DOHERTY ASSOCIATES BOOK

IT CAN'T BE MY GRAVE

Copyright © 1983, 1984 by S.F.X. Dean

Reprinted by arrangement with Walker and Company

First Tor printing: April 1987

A TOR Book

Published by Tom Doherty Associates, Inc.
49 West 24 Street
New York, N.Y. 10010

ISBN: 0-812-50188-8
CAN. ED.: 0-812-50189-6

Library of Congress Catalog Card Number: 84-13192

Printed in the United States of America

0 9 8 7 6 5 4 3 2 1

for Michael and Betty Higgins

the actor edges
an abyss every scene

applause is the kiss
for the terror in technique

each reaches for the ache
in the other

like a lover

FS

CHAPTER 1

After more than a year away from it, London felt good. Of all the great cities in the world perhaps only this one has kept its soul. No American city has managed it, and if any in Europe have, they've escaped my notice. But London has its integrity. Filth, crime, pollution of every known variety, and poverty never really out of sight — though that was always true of all cities, and Shakespeare's London had those things in plenty — but always something else in addition.

London keeps a human scale and a collective consciousness of being ten thousand villages of small public societies. Whatever the sociologists make of it, here is a city which has kept going while it was still possible there to be human and to belong to a group of friends connected to reality through this place. You can get that in a small town in the States, or on a good university campus, but never within any other American corporation. London is a thousand 'locals', and I could be away for ten years and walk back into mine with a sense that, in some respect at least, I'd come home.

Of all the pubs in this city of pubs, the St James's Tavern on Great Windmill Street was my home away from home. It wallows in the smelly heart of dirty old Soho, a big, crowded, raging, noisy place full of smoke and music and theatre people. Nothing about it is like my usual surroundings, so perhaps some alter ego, some shadow self, was let free when I entered. I sipped my pint at a back table and listened to the cheerful uproar and basked in London.

Hugh James walked in just before eleven, his entrance a

drama and his passage around the circular bar a noisy procession.

The bar-tender had a pint in hand for him by the time he reached the service bar and he swept it up and saw me at the same time.

'Kelly, you dreary scholar, what the hell are you doing away from the books in this iniquitous sinkhole?'

He slammed his mug down and leaned over to embrace me in a sweaty, smoky, enthusiastic bearhug. I got his coat button up my nose. We had not seen each other for five years, but it might have been five weeks.

'James, your damn button's up my nose, how are you? I knew if I sat here long enough your fine figure would darken the sky.'

Everyone called him by his surname, always had, fellow actors, critics, and fans.

He settled next to me on the flattened red cushions of the bench and sighed. He sighed as he did everything else, theatrically. He looked tired, as a man should who had just come off stage after three hours of hard work, but otherwise he seemed unchanged in any essential way.

James and I had been at Oxford together thirty-odd years before, when I was a visiting Fellow from America and he was briefly ambitious to be a playwright and literary light. We had spent a year arguing and boozing and partying together—what the English call getting a University education—before he quit to become an actor and I returned home to become a professor. We had met five or six times since without ever having exchanged a written line—that was not Hugh James's style—and whenever he appeared, it seemed to me that he had never been away. He had the gift of being immediately and entirely present wherever he was, nothing held back, a kind of stage presence that worked as well in a crowded bar as on stage.

I told him he looked a little weary, but in good fettle.

'You're a liar.' He glared at me and crossed his arms, swelling his chest menacingly. 'Look again. Pay particular attention this time to signs of encroaching senility.'

He posed grimly. I studied him.

'Sorry, same old James. Ugly as sin, as unevenness of bone structure and a coarse animal vitality which passes for attractive on stage, the same blatant drinking lines in the small veins of the nose that you displayed when you were twenty, the eyes bloodshot and sunken, a slight tendency to spit when talking — really, James, you haven't changed a bit.'

'You're practising deceit, Neil,' the famous voice mounted through the words to a roar, although I was just a foot away. 'You are trying to protect me from the truth, and there is no meaner charade. Don't, for God's sake, lie to me, Neil. Look, you damned idiot!'

He grinned a horrible, toothy smile at me and rolled his eyes.

'Ah. You have new false teeth.'

'I knew it.' He covered his face with his thick workman's hands. 'You saw them the instant I entered this bower. You spotted them across the room and bent your head in horror. You ducked to try to avoid contact with me. You said to yourself, "Oh God, will you look at old James over there, with his china teeth screaming Senility! at me." I got them two months ago. Aren't they wonderfully ghastly? I clack on stage. I'm looking for a part as a Spanish dancer so that I can accompany myself.'

'All right, I did. They are really awful, James.' He hadn't changed at all. We both laughed at him.

'I knew it. The damn things sit there in the bedside glass, you know, the smile of the skull, prophesying death and all that old horror. Theatre manager wants to change my billing to read "Hugh James and his Shop Teeth". Buy me a drink.'

'You're in a new play, why don't you buy me one?'

He perked up immediately. 'You see me?'

'Don't flatter yourself. I arrived in town two hours ago. Saw your famous name in the funnies. Should I? Is it any good?'

'I'm marvellous. The play's negligible.' He leaned to whisper in a perfectly audible voice, 'And doomed. But I am superb. A triumph of craft takes a weakly written part and forges from it a characterization of more than human power. Yes, you could say I'm good.'

He commanded two more pints with a magisterial gesture over the heads at the bar, and while we toasted his newest triumph he told me his wildly prejudiced version of the current London theatre season. He levelled the new Barbican, demolished several older establishments between Piccadilly and the Strand, left a dozen reputations bruised, and one, Charles Leonard's, in ruins.

'If Leonard is that bad, James, old pal, how do you explain that he is director of London's biggest hit of the moment and the author of another that's been running for two years?'

He studied me from the side of his eyes, eloquent nose twitching.

'How long has that Agatha Christie shambles been running? Ten years? Thirty? Three hundred? And may I call your pitiful attention to *No Sex, Please, We're British* while you're on the town? The world's longest-running bare asinine play? Fifty years has it been exposing itself to this city? Come off it, Neil, whoever married longevity to merit in this potato race?'

We talked about his job, my extended two-year sabbatical holiday from mine and my plans in London. At least he asked me what they were, but, characteristically, did not wait to hear my answer before making new ones for me. My friend was a man of headlong enthusiasms, not given to the common decencies of conversational exchange.

'You're staying with us while you're here, of course.'

'Thanks, but no. I have a perfectly good room over in South Kensington.'

'Tourists,' James expostulated. 'You'll be swimming in bloody tourists. No, no, I won't have it. Sheila will kill me if I let you do that. You must stay with us. Settled, by God.' He beamed at me as if it really had been settled.

'You're too used to getting your own way. Being a matinée idol for so long has made you a spoiled child.'

'Yes, that's true. It's wonderful how people of all sorts knuckle under to my charm and male force.'

'Well, not me. South Ken will do fine.'

'Are you defying me, Kelly?'

'Who is Sheila? Yes, I am.'

'Forget bloody Sheila. I won't be defied by a man who owes me everything. A man for whom I . . .'

'You what?' I was curious what fantasy he might concoct to justify my having a sense of obligation to him.

He looked grievously wounded, but smiled gamely. Out of ideas, apparently. He waved away a lifetime of moral obligations with a hairy paw. 'Ingratitude, how sharper, etcetera. Sheila?' He brightened considerably and took a drink. 'You'd like to meet Sheila, would you, you raging ingrate? Not on your life. Not for a million quid. Do you think I would expose her, gentle soul that she is, sweet girl, love of my loins, tripes and heart, to the likes of you, morally low, socially negligible, intellectually effete? Yes, by God, I will. You're just the ticket to make her appreciate the contrasts between us and so increase her admiration for me, something I had heretofore imagined impossible. Sheila is my wife, you clod.'

He peeked rather shyly from behind his pint as he drank, a boyish and wholly endearing glance.

'You haven't!'

'I have. Haven't what? Married? I by God have!'

'You? Who swore in this very pub eight? nine? years ago in the hearing of dozens of us that you would never?'

'That was years ago.' He brushed it aside. 'Besides, that was in reference to what's her name, Elena, that bitch.'

'Elena my foot. She might have been the proximate cause, but you were renewing your vows that night. I refuse to believe it. No church would bless it, no city licensing authority would sanction it, and no woman in her right mind would go through with it.'

He thumped the table and grabbed our drinks to keep them upright. 'It's true, goddammit. And in a church, since you mention it. I go to church as often as you do these days, I dare say. Twice last holy week, Holy Thursday and Easter Sunday. I was dizzy with devotions. I stank of incense.'

'And did all your dire prophecies come true? Were all the monstrous portents borne out? Or were you wrong, O great one?'

'I may have exaggerated the negative possibilities of marriage. It's actually rather pleasant.' He lifted his glass.

'You said, may I remind you — ' and I recited to him from vivid memory, ' "Shall I let the sweet small moments of silent communion bulk slowly into giant silences? That woman's body, skin like the petals of flowers, harden and swell into a bloated Yorkshire pudding, lopsided and tough? The fire of my youth, my golden, hilarious and irresponsible youth, sour?" '

'I mixed that metaphor — my fire sour?'

'You did. My recall is total, "Shall I," you said, "turn slowly into a chained, lurching caricature of myself, dropsical and farting, big-veined and comic? No. No once," you said, "No twice. And no a thousand times. I'd, as the song says," you said, "rather die than say yes." '

He winked. 'Yes, well, one says things and then one thinks them over and modifies them.'

We both enjoyed a good laugh and toasted the news.
'When?'

'Oh, almost a year now. It's quite nice, really.'

'Best thing in the world for you. You do seem tamer,
now that I consider it.'

'Christ, don't say that.' He shushed me and glanced
over his shoulder. 'I have a reputation to maintain, you
know. Start saying that, and with the show staggering
towards an early grave and the china teeth and all, they'll
be calling me "poor old James".'

'The play?' Actors will often say nothing good about a
play when it's running well and nothing bad when it's
failing.

He shrugged and made interlocking circles on the table
with his glass. 'They posted the closing notice tonight.
After next Friday's performance. Fourteen performances.'
He snorted derisively. 'And for that I passed up two other
things that might just go on forever. Not one, two. Ah
well, what else is new, eh?'

'I'm glad it's your profession and not mine.'

'I think you've said that before, you mincing pendant.
Let me see, the show you're in has been running for
what — two hundred years?'

'And it will be there when I get back. If I ever do.
What's next for you?'

He sighed gustily. 'God knows.' He buried his face in
his Guinness, looked up as if he was about to say
something dramatic, then sighed again and let it pass
unsaid.

He had the talent all good actors have of casting a pall
of gloom by his sadness and warming a whole room with
his pleasure. The temperature at our table dropped
about ten degrees.

'Is Sheila an actress?'

'Who? Oh, her. Yes. I suppose you could say that. As
good as I am, actually. Hasn't had the chances she

deserves. Bit old for ingenues now, and rather too specially good-looking for general character parts. She'd make a hell of a Lady Macbeth. Does a nice comic turn, too, nice bones. It was her bones got me first, I tell her that. We're waiting for her now, you'll see. She's the sister-in-law in that Ayckbourn thing they've revived at the Apollo. Damn thing runs all night.' He checked his watch.

We both stopped talking to listen to the guitar-player. James looked at his watch again. I pointed to it.

'That's something else.'

He brushed me away again. 'I know, I know.'

'Time was *your* servant, you used to say, not you its.'

'Gift from Sheila, actually. Damned useful invention. I recommend it.'

'I think you've become an orderly citizen, my fat friend.'

He growled with disgust. 'Yer daft. Let me hear the man play.'

'Orderly, regular, married, worried about jobs—why, James, you've become like the rest of us. I like it. Welcome to the human race.'

'Keep it,' he mouthed sideways. 'My shirts may be clean now—that's one more advantage to domesticity, she takes my shirts to the laundry—but underneath beats the same wild heart of a bird. No change at all, none.'

But there was no fire in it. The old lion was growling from memory, not rage. My friend was middle-aged, he was married, and he was worried, and perhaps it was time to stop ragging him as though we were both undergraduates, rehearsing for our imagined bohemian futures.

Our conversation was continually interrupted by a stream of his friends, dropping by his shoulder for a quick *sotto voce* exchange of commiseration about the play or a friendly insult or two. Nothing had sharp edges at the St James's, which perhaps is why James called it his patron pub. He could blur out into several dimensions, keep three conversations going at once, laugh at one man's joke and simultaneously toss rude remarks at another table.

Now, abruptly, he focused himself and stood to sweep up in his hug a woman who had come edging through the mob towards us.

'Here she is, my wench of a wife and darling girl.'

He kept her under one arm with her feet off the floor to introduce her to me. She bore it all with the patience of experience.

'Sheila, love, this is Neil Kelly, an American of scholarly pretentions and no discernible talent, whom I put through Oxford by writing all his papers for him. Neil, this great hulk of a woman is Sheila.'

He put her down and she shook hands, smiling. She was just over five feet tall and could not have weighed more than one hundred and ten.

'Hello, Neil. I've heard of you from the Rugger King here, and I'm pleased to meet you.'

She had an actress's voice, full and resonant, pitched just below the din in the place. If her face was not pretty, it was memorable, a far better thing for a serious actress, with a wide, mobile mouth and slightly protuberant eyes, huge green eyes. Her hair was a short shock of brown, shapeless. I thought of Judy Garland and of Piaf and I had a sudden image of this waif in centre stage commanding an audience with that husky voice and enormous eyes.

'Hello, Sheila—James?'

'No. I was already Sheila Edwards when I met this oaf, and when you've spent ten years getting your name drummed into people's heads the way we have to in this business, you don't throw away the advantage for the sake of a romantic gesture.' She edged into the seat next to her husband, giving him the hip vigorously.

'She has no heart, is the truth,' James said, shoving

over. 'All brains and bulk, but no real heart at all.'

Now he kissed her face tenderly and got a hug for his effort.

Someone from the bar lifted a small drink of some kind—what the English call a martini, from the look of it—over several heads to her place. As she drank it and waved thanks Hugh James took a back seat for a moment to her in the centre of the circle, then he asked her how it had gone tonight.

She made a *comme ci, comme ça* gesture. 'Slow. Thanks to Philip. He got a laugh from some claque of idiots in the stalls with that awful hamming he does in the first act and that got him started. He dragged everything out to twice its length. Della wanted to kill him.'

They exchanged backstage gossip about her play for two minutes, letting her unwind from her job just the way any ordinary citizen must too, griping and sloughing off the annoyances. It occurred to me that she already knew about his show closing, but was waiting for him to mention it. A passing acquaintance patting James on the shoulder and saying in a stage brogue that 'he was that sorry for his throuble, the darlin' play dead so young' finally introduced the subject.

Sheila admitted that someone named Sid had told her already. 'Next Friday?'

James lifted his glass. 'It was doomed from the start. Cheer up, we'll find one better.'

'We've got one better,' she said emphatically.

James looked at me. 'Shop. Do people in the faculty lounge talk shop all the time? It's the curse of this lot.' He gestured disgustedly around the room. Sheila took his large hand in her tense, small one.

'Don't mind me,' I said. 'If this has become a wake for James's play, so be it. We all know he won't be out of work for long.'

It was true, and we all knew it with some satisfaction.

In a profession with an average unemployment figure around ninety per cent, James had somehow, by a combination of virtuosity and sheer hard work which he made look like playing around, always managed to be employed. When he wasn't on stage he was on the TV screen, and often enough he was seen in juicy character roles in British and American films. He had that unbeatable combination of talents in the bone and luck which only the most successful practitioners of any art have.

'Brace yourself,' Sheila told him. 'Us too. Closing notice posted tonight. They want the Apollo for that American thing Kerbrook is hot on. He says with two other Ayckbourns in London we're starting to die.'

James took a drink and belched. 'Christ.'

Now I felt that I had really walked into a wake. Even for a buoyant optimist, two unemployment notices for one family in one evening was a bit hard to take. A rare silence had us all glancing at each other. Sheila broke the spell.

She spoke to James, but pointed her thumb at me. 'Ask him. Have you asked him yet?'

'Him?' James's look was eloquent with disgust. 'What in hell does he know?'

'He might. You said he was some kind of scholarly genius.'

Never to me he hadn't.

'She's a liar,' he growled at me. Turning to her he said, 'Let it go, forget about it, all right? Tomorrow we'll think about whatever.'

'Coward.' She prodded him in the ribs. 'Gutless sissy.' She elbowed him in the side. 'Pusillanimous pussy.' She stuck out her tongue at him.

He dismissed her with an airy wave. 'Never marry, Neil, I warn you. Tell me instead about what terribly intellectual book you're writing these days.'

Sheila gave him one more shot in the ribs for good measure. Marriage prospers when a shared language arises and flourishes.

'Wrote. I finished it ten months ago, after nearly three years of work. Not writing a thing at the moment. I'm on a prolonged holiday.'

There was no need I could see for going into detail about the hellish year before, when I had left Devon and gone off to hike through Yorkshire and Scotland. Only in the cold north had I found myself able to work again and finish my book on John Donne. I had been on the verge of chucking it, but I was glad now that I hadn't. It had been the work I needed to restore my sanity, and it had paid me well.

'James says you're an expert on the sixteenth century.'

'I thought I told you to shut up,' he hissed at her.

'Ignore him,' she said to me. 'He's pissed off because he thought *he* was going to get all the sympathy tonight, and I've horned in on it. We'll ignore him and you tell me about the sixteenth century.'

The guitar-player and a pianist had got together now, and the encouragement from the bar was deafening.

'More the seventeenth, actually,' I roared. 'But the book is about Donne.'

'We're both pig-ignorant actors. Wasn't he a poet?'

James bellowed loud enough to be heard above both the din and the music. 'Speak for yourself, you abysmal child of the Bermondsey gutters. I was explaining John Donne to this Yank poseur when he was still breathing heavily from reading Henry Wadsworth Longfellow. Was he a poet? Jesus, that I should live to hear my wife sound so stupid.'

Sheila kissed his ear and grinned. 'James hates it when I show how dumb I am. I embarrass him. I quit school at eleven — they said there was no hope for me — and I really don't know anything. Don't ask me what makes a radio work or how cars run or who Einstein was or anything, really. I can learn a part in half the time it takes Falstaff here, though, can't I Fatty, eh? Tell me about Donne. I'm a sponge if I pay attention, even if I don't understand it.'

'I'll do better than that. I'll give you a copy tomorrow.'

She clapped her hands. 'I love getting presents. Is it a bestseller? Will you make a packet on it?'

James groaned and shook his head. 'More of your ignorance showing, love. No one makes a packet on scholarship. Better ask him if it's been well-reviewed in the learned journals.'

'Actually James,' I shouted with some embarrassment, 'I've made a packet on it. It has also been favourably reviewed in a couple of learned journals, if that helps, but against all reason, there appears to be something of a new John Donne boom in America. The book was grabbed first by a very rich book club, then by a trendy producer for a movie with a very trendy actor to star in, and now they are preparing a mini-series for TV. I'm rather rolling in it at the moment, to my own complete astonishment. And Donne's, I'm sure, wherever he is. I even broke a vow and flew back to New York for the publication party. I felt like Harold Robbins.'

The movie and TV part of it interested both of them. For half an hour they cross-examined me about the casting and scriptwriting decisions, frequently breaking into private arguments, sometimes approving what I had authorized because I had been unable to prevent it.

The book was just about to be published in London, and I had come back to attend the legal and ceremonial activities attendant on the launching of an expensive publishing venture. It was the least I could do, and the inflexible rule for dealing with publishers, as Winston Churchill or Harold Robbins or someone once remarked, is always to do that and not one damned thing more.

The pair with the piano and guitar were bringing the

house down now with some very Nashville-sounding Country and Western.

'Let's clear out of here and go home,' James boomed above the din. 'It's beginning to sound like some damned Yank honkytonk. You're coming too, so move,' he said to me over his shoulder.

Sheila linked her arm in mine as we stood up.

'Isn't he sweet? Isn't he subtle, gracious and charming? Do come. Oh, don't not come just because James has invited you with an ultimatum, or at least, if you're going to not come, come and have some coffee or supper even if you can't stay. It's only over in Hampstead.' She leaned to whisper in my ear. 'It will cheer him up, I think.'

It was hard to be disagreeable with her.

We went by Tube. Neither James nor Sheila would keep a car in London, although each admitted to keeping one at their place down in Kent.

They lived out in a pleasantly middle-class, gardened kind of street, not far from the house bearing the blue circular plaque on its front announcing quietly that Sigmund Freud had lived and died there.

Sheila, who really had come up from the London slums on the strength of her energy and talent, found the idea of being a housewife was her greatest thrill. She told me that at first it was all guilty pleasures, and she wondered if other housewives felt the same way shopping for fish and doing the laundry. Then she laughed at herself, admitted that she had been amazed to find that other women felt that way when they slipped away from the laundry for a theatre matinée.

For James, Hampstead might have been Soho or his country estate; he was happiest when he was being his disorderly, grumbling self wherever he was.

'Where's the damned bottle of Mumm's I was saving, Sheil?'

'Look in the cupboard behind the empties.'

He dug out the prized bottle and held it reverently.

'God, what a way to treat decent champagne. She won't throw away empty bottles, you know. If Freud still lived up the street I'd have him explain that to me. She keeps a hundred empty wine bottles in that cupboard, and then sticks our only decent wine in there along with them. Ignorant.'

'I told you I was ignorant,' she called happily from the next room.

He unwired the cork and thumbed it up slowly.

'When we both can't get a job any more because you're too fat and I'm too thin, we're going to open a bistro across the river. We'll need those bottles to put the candles in,' Sheila explained archly. 'Someone has to think of these things.'

'Class will tell,' James intoned, pouring. 'Here, Kelly, cool if not cold, and in a claret glass if not in a goblet. To your marvellous book. May you fool everyone and make millions. What's the title of the damned thing?'

'*The Lives of John Donne.*'

He winced. 'God, sounds clever. I hate it already.'

'Do you know the play *Arden of Faversham*, Neil?' Sheila asked suddenly.

James rolled his eyes up to heaven. 'Good Christ, here we go again.'

Arden of Faversham? Was she joking? I could remember reading it in graduate school, in about nineteen fifty-two. I suppose that's where anyone who encountered it at all read it. I had never heard of it being actually produced on stage. A forgotten Elizabethan play, author unknown. Much mayhem, some broad comedy, lots of morality laid on at the end.

I kept stalling and racking my brain while I drank my champagne. 'I probably read *Arden of Faversham* the last time thirty-five years ago. No, wait, a student did a thesis on the problem of its authorship about fifteen years ago, and I had to re-read it then, along with all the secondary stuff about it. Let's say I know about it, but I'd hate to have to pass an exam on it without a chance to bone up.'

She was watching me intently, like a hungry student. 'Who do you think wrote it?'

I sipped some more champagne. 'Well. There's a fair chance that Thomas Kyd—'

James emitted a tremendous raspberry. 'Oh, Neil, come off it. Kyd my arse. Marlowe wrote it, and if you think about it, it will be obvious. God, you academic types. Here, have one of these things.' He took a tray of hot sandwiches from Sheila and gave me one.

Sheila took her own, two. 'Don't let Fatso here start on Christopher Marlowe, either, Neil. Don't you honestly think, when you think about it, that Shakespeare wrote it?'

James burned his tongue on his sandwich and waved at her disgustedly as he gulped wine.

The question was perfectly fair, since more learned scholars than the three of us had been arguing those same names for several centuries, trying to match up the important play with its probable author.

'Well, there are some circumstantial problems if you think Shakespeare, even a young Shakespeare, was the author, Sheila . . .'

James took another huge bite of his sandwich and smiled benignly on both of us. Through a full mouth he said quite distinctly—an actor's trick—'Besides, we all know that Lucy Goodman wrote it, don't we?'

I looked at him blankly. 'I gather I'm supposed to look at you blankly now and say, "Lucy *Who?*" '

'You heard me, you Yank pretender. The famous Shropshire playwright Lucy Goodman, fifteen-sixty to fifteen ninety-six? What's more—' he brandished half a sandwich daintily—'I know a chap who is willing to bet two million pounds on it.'

Then we all sat down and they told me about Gordon
Fairly.

Sir Gordon Fairly had a great deal of money, having
built himself what can only properly be called a financial
empire, with its base in a tangle of holiday camps and
travel agencies, and its dizzy heights in the high skies of
airlines and cable television. Like many another self-
made man, he had conceived a passion for genealogy
when his knighthood came through. He had managed to
unearth a branch of his family in the Deritend slums of
Birmingham and have them traced through birth and
baptismal records back to a family farm in remotest
Shropshire.

In Shropshire, still abbreviated by all right-thinking
Englishmen to Salop, the line ended, but rather
spectacularly, in a sixteenth-century great-grandmother,
an elusive creature named Lucy Goodman. She might or
might not have gone to London to write plays, something
totally unheard of in those days, and theoretically
impossible. England had a woman chief executive then,
but in the theatre even women's roles were played by male
actors, so firm was the prohibition against women in the
milieu of Shakespeare and Jonson. A Mary Sidney,
Countess of Pembroke, might write a strictly classical
playlet from the French for her own group's amusement,
but it was well established that there were no women in
the rough and tumble world of London theatre.

Sir Gordon Fairly wanted to build a repertory theatre
in the Clee Hills of Salop as a memorial to Lucy
Goodman, England's lost woman playwright. Indeed, he
wanted James to establish the company there to act in
Arden every season, along with other plays by obscure or
suspected women playwrights.

Sheila was bouncing with excitement. Obviously the
idea was a grand one to her.

'Think of it, Neil, if he's right. A woman playwright

entirely unknown before, and good enough, even if she only wrote the one play, for the scholars to think perhaps Shakespeare or Kit Marlowe wrote it.'

She was full of Fairly's plans; James was pretending to be asleep on the sofa, his wine glass balanced on his belly.

There was, apparently, a notebook of Lucy Goodman's still in possession of the family, and in it Fairly was convinced that he had found the original notes for *Arden*.

It was as thrilling an idea as Sheila thought it to be. Someone had written *Arden*, and that person had genuine if not yet fully mature gifts. It was based on an actual set of events which had occurred in Kent, where the wife of Arden had conspired with her young lover and two hired thugs to kill her husband as he played backgammon in his own home. It had been published in 1592, and Fairly was convinced that other evidence in the family records proved that Lucy Goodman had given a copy of the play to a certain Elizabeth Throckmorton, who was a lady-in-waiting to Elizabeth I.

'An inscribed copy, mind you,' Sheila added, deftly catching James's glass as it slipped from his stomach when he sighed. 'I think that if she did, and it was her own play, she was trying to get it to the attention of Queenie herself, maybe so she could have permission to dedicate it to her?'

'If she did, it's too bad, isn't it, that she chose Bess Throckmorton as her go-between.'

Sheila was astonished and fascinated. 'You know her? You really are an expert on them, aren't you? James, wake up, you fool, do you realize that your friend here *knows* this Throckmorton character?'

He looked at me out of one open, suspicious eye.

'It's not all that much of a feat or a secret, you know. Bess Throckmorton married Sir Walter Raleigh. She was quite a famous woman in her own right. And quite a woman. I suppose she's best known for retrieving his head after he was executed and carrying it around in her purse for the next twenty-nine years.'

'Oh God.' James put a pillow over his face.

'I love her,' Sheila crowed. 'Wait till Gordon hears all this.'

'Surely Gordon Fairly knows all this if he's had researchers working on it. Any competent historian could piece that together for him.'

'Don't talk to Gordon about researchers. Apparently some phoney tried to sell him a fake coat of arms he said the Goodmans had been given by James I, and he paid him a thousand quid and found out it was all a con. He hates them all now. He's got this wacky daughter who went to Cambridge, but she won't do it for him, poor man, and he's that frustrated trying to get her to take over the project. She's into Women's Lib.'

'I should think this was right up her street. A chance to prove that a woman was among the great playwrights of the greatest age of English theatre.'

'You'd think so, wouldn't you? But apparently she told Gordon she wasn't interested in liberation for one woman in the sixteenth century, she wanted it for all women now.'

James interrupted with a yawn. 'Besides, there is one small detail: the alleged inscribed copy of the alleged play given to the alleged lady-in-waiting, eh?'

It was a consideration. 'But you will admit, James, that if Fairly can produce that, he'll have something rather special,' I argued.

'Aye, there's the rub, as we say in the theatre, eh?' He took off his shoes and socks and wiggled his toes luxuriously. 'Who's for bed, woman? "Would she dance *The Shaking of the Sheets*, for that's the dance her husband means to lead her." ' He waggled his thorny eyebrows like a vaudeville villain.

Sheila was picking up his jacket and putting it on a hanger, and replied almost absent-mindedly, 'Thomas

Heywood, Act One, *A Woman Killed with Kindness*, sixteen-seven.'

'Witch.' He threw a sock at her. 'You read my mind.'

'I read books, you Varsity oaf. You ought to try it.' She stage whispered to me, 'He tries to catch me, but he never does. I know everything he knows.'

'She sucks my blood. Neil will tell you that we University fellows have put all that memory stuff behind us. We have passed on to the higher wisdom.'

She heaved a sofa pillow at him. 'It's lucky for you then that I'm sweet-tempered.'

'Don't believe her.' He fired the pillow back at her and ducked behind the sofa.' She's sweet-tempered up to a point. Ask any director who's ever worked with her. She's rather a famous bitch if you get her goat. Ask Charles Leonard, for example.'

Sheila was haughtily ignoring him, straightening out the cushions and speaking only to me.

'Charles was asking for it. If he had not provoked me by picking on poor Jeannie Hillings, I'd never have laid a hand on him.'

'A log,' James said distinctly from behind the sofa.

'I beg yours.'

'It was a log you laid on him. On his head. From the fireplace on the set of *St Joan*.'

'A tiny splinter of kindling.' She held her fingers a few inches apart.

'Ten stitches.'

'He was soft in the head anyway, that one.' She was beginning to get shrill and she was shouting at the sofa.

James apparently could read the storm signals in her tone. He appeared with aplomb from behind his hiding-place. 'Neil, you get the sofa-bed you're sitting on, so just say when you're ready for bed. All this crap about Fairly of Faversham can get awfully boring if Toodles there gets her bloody teeth into it all night.'

'I really am a bit travel weary. That train from Edinburgh was brutal. I take it, then, if I'm allowed one final bit of curiosity, that Fairly definitely hasn't yet got his hands on the so-called presentation copy of the play, the signed one?'

Sheila was shining-eyed with excitement. 'Not because he hasn't been spending a packet to find it. Some keeper of documents at the British Museum, which is about the only institution he trusts since he's a Governor of it or something, told him that there might be a reference to it in a letter from the Earl of Essex, if you please, before he got *his* block chopped off, and another reference to a mysterious L.G.'

'God,' James groaned, 'we've been over this with Gordon a dozen times. He's like any other fanatic, he won't even hear the evidence against his pet theory.'

It was Sheila's turn to snort. 'Like any other fanatic with four hundred million quid, you mean. And ready to hand over two million just for openers. What do you really think, Neil?'

'I'm not sure whether you're asking me if you should do the play, or if Lucy Goodman wrote it, or even if Lucy Goodman even existed. I think I'll take refuge in scholarly prudence and promise to sleep on it and announce my infallible answers to all these questions in the morning. I'm really exhausted, if you don't mind, James.'

'Mind?' He looked astonished at the suggestion. 'Mind being booted out of my own living-room just after I've come home from work? This is like seven o'clock in the evening to most people, you know. Mind? Of course not, we love it. We enjoy going to bed in the middle of the day so that you can stick to your sybaritic schedule of eighteen hours' sleep a night. Mind . . . ?'

Sheila punched him in the gut and hauled him by the

hand after her from the room. She reappeared to toss me a towel and tell me there was a ground-floor loo all to myself before throwing a kiss and shutting the door.

CHAPTER 2

At breakfast I admitted to them both that the sole literary personage I could recall being born in the Clee Hills was A.E. Housman.

'Eighteen-fifty-nine,' Sheila said, nodding agreement.

I must have looked a bit startled by this prompt datum so early in the morning.

'Ignore her. She has a photographic memory,' James said, opening his paper. 'She is dumb, not ignorant, rather like those idiots who win quiz shows.'

Sheila smiled her sunny smile. 'He's jealous because he has all that education and he doesn't have any information. I have to tell him everything. Last year I had to tell him what political party he votes for.'

She put eggs and bacon and toast in front of me and coffee in front of her husband's paper. 'He'll eat when he's ready, you eat now while it's hot.'

She stood sipping from her own coffee cup, reading the back of James's paper and gesturing for me to eat my solitary sumptuous breakfast.

'Actually, not to make too much of it,' she murmured, appearing to read from the *Guardian*, 'there's Thomas Percy, seventeen-twenty-nine and William Langland, circa thirteen hundred.'

'These eggs are perfect. I'll take your word for it. And now we add Lucy Goodman, circa fifteen-sixty, eh? Well, is our robust friend over there behind the paper going to do it?'

James's large hand groped out and took the coffee cup

from sight. He spoke a sentence without revealing himself. 'Lot more to it than that, isn't there?'

Sheila grimaced. 'He means the whole repertory thing. Setting up a company, building a theatre, organizing it — James isn't sure he wants all that.'

'James *is* quite sure,' came from behind the *Guardian*. 'He doesn't.'

'Can't you get someone else, someone whose trade it is to organize and produce and so forth, and you just act and direct? Or is that too simple-minded a layman's question?'

A grampus-like 'Hmph' billowed the paper out. 'It's the bloody revenge of art on life.'

He folded the newspaper into a wreck and considered my place and his own. 'Why has this casual drop-in got an entire English breakfast with the bacon cooked exactly the way I like it and never get it, crisp and curly, and I sit he.e, master at my own table, with a cup of tepid coffee?'

Sheila made a tripping exit and slid back in with a hot plate of bacon and eggs for the master.

'I've been drying it out in the oven, dear.'

He took a piece of my bacon and compared it with his own, ate both. 'Don't do domestic comedy, waif. It isn't you.'

I was learning to time my questions to their routines.

'What does that mean, "the revenge of art on life"?'

'Tell him,' James told her through a cram of egg.

'For two years, until last summer, really, James starred in a series on the telly called *Merman's Mermaid* . . .'

'Isn't that cute to the edge of puking?' James mimed his distress. 'Even after all this time it ruins my digestion to hear that title. Thank God it wasn't picked up for American TV, the hell with the money. That way I'm still respectable in one part of the English-speaking world.'

'. . . about the manager of a theatre company in the provinces — Cornwall, actually — who holds it all together despite drunken actors and actresses with abortions and tragic love-affairs in the company . . .'

'Etcetera, etcetera,' James shouted. 'For God's sake, Sheila, have you no decency? He gets the picture. Don't describe it to the crack of doom. Bloody awful.'

'It was a great popular smash. More important, it was Sir Gordon's favourite show. So one day, out of the blue, you might say . . .'

'If you have a fascination for cliché . . .'

'. . . his solicitor called. Sir Gordon's.'

'And the rest is bloody history. The man is completely deluded. He saw me recite some wretched lines on that wretched show . . .'

'Which paid for this wretched house.'

'Which poured the lolly into my lap, granted, but which I prefer to forget, and which is why I quit the damned thing and sank it, and almost gave my agent, the covetous Sid, an infarction. The point is that this titled oaf with all his millions has convinced himself that only I, the great Merman of the Mermaid, can produce his dream theatre, the Lucy Goddam Goodman Memorial Gift Shoppe in the hidden hills of Salop, heretofore famous only for William Whatshisname and A.E. Whatshisname.'

'Langland,' Sheila said absent-mindedly. 'Housman.'

'I have the solution,' I announced. It seemed to take them a moment to hear me. Both looked at me and said nothing.

'Don't do it,' I said.

No one said anything.

'That's my solution. Let's hear the applause now, folks. You don't want to do it. You apparently don't need the money. Ergo, don't do it. QED.'

'It's not that simple,' James said lugubriously.

'It never is, is it?'

The doorbell rang.

Sheila looked at James. 'That'll be Sid.'

James picked up his   per again with a lordly gesture.
'Of course it is. Tell him to piss off.'

'Tell him yourself,' she said, taking our plates. 'He's
your agent. He's his agent,' she said to me reasonably.
'Mine, too, of course, if it comes to that, but he was his
first.'

I asked them if it was a correct surmise that their agent
wanted them to do the Lucy Goodman thing.

'First that new obscenity by Leonard, then, yes, the
Lucy Goodman thing. Why wouldn't he? There's
thousands in it for him, and all he has to do is sign the
cheques. Go and tell him to piss off, Neil, there's a good
fellow.'

They had bedded and fed me, it seemed the least I
could do, so I went and answered the door.

The man standing there was short and corpulent and
he beamed happily when I appeared. Over his shoulder I
could see a black Daimler, five yards long, parked at the
kerb. The agency business must be very good indeed in
his part of London.

I saw no point in bandying words. 'James says that you
should piss off.'

He laughed hugely and threw up his hands. I thought
promptly of S.Z. 'Cuddles' Sakall, who would hold his
great shaking fat head and stare while the Ritz Brothers
ran riot in all the musicals of my youth.

'He is a great joker, is our James. Are you his man?'

'I am his guest. He did tell me to tell you that. I
suppose if you don't feel like complying, you should come
in.'

'I am Gordon Fairly. Let's go and find the rascal and
see who he thought I was.' He barged past me and into
the house, sniffing the aroma of bacon hungrily.

In a last attempt to rescue my mission, I announced the
new arrival in a proper butler's tone. 'Sir Gordon Fairly.

He refused to piss off.'

James did not miss a chew or a swallow. 'I know who it is, you Yank dimwit. Go away, Gordon. I'm desperately ill and I'm afraid it's contagious.'

The new guest seated himself at the table. 'Ah, good morning, Miss Edwards. My sympathy on the demise of your not very good show. May I have some of that coffee with a small sugar, and cream? I love a free meal.'

Sheila, who was civilized enough to be mildly embarrassed, scooted into the kitchen. Her husband, who was not, read on.

'You might as well come out from behind that rag you abuse your intelligence with, James, and speak to me.' He turned politely to me. 'And if you are not the butler, who are you, sir, if I may ask.'

'I'm Neil Kelly,' I said. 'A visitor. An old friend of the chap behind the rag.'

'And an American, I perceive. What do you do? Are you also an actor? You look too intelligent.'

James threw his paper at the ceiling with an exasperated command. 'Don't answer him. Who is he, this mannerless bastard who swarms into my house and home at the crack of dawn and begins cross-examining my guests at my own table, and why, in the name of God is my wife bringing this intruder coffee while I sit here with an empty cup?'

This time Sheila had the pot in her other hand and poured for him, saying, 'Say when.'

James instead began to launch another barrage of opprobrium against his beaming guest and only too late realized that she meant it, pouring away, the scalding coffee finally flooding his cup and overflowing his saucer until it burned his thumb. The resulting hasty withdrawal of his hand made a messy spill, most of it landing in James's lap.

'Jaysus, I'm burned alive,' he yelped. 'Oh God, that

hurts.' He sprinted for the bathroom, where we heard splashing and cursing for the next two minutes.

'No, I'm a teacher,' I said.

I could see that Sir Gordon approved of my timing.

'And what do you teach, Mr Kelly?'

I told him as briefly as I could. It seemed apparent that, as James had anticipated, he saw my presence there as some sort of omen in favour of the Lucy Goodman project. The huge head wagged from side to side delightedly.

'But you are a man of literature, and of the sixteenth century, moreover. Splendid.' He asked me if James and Sheila had explained the proposed project to me and promptly asked my opinion of it.

'I have none. I haven't seen the evidence.'

He nodded approvingly. 'I take that as an implied request to see the evidence, Mr Kelly. Is it Professor Kelly? Should I be calling you that?' he asked courteously.

'Neil will do fine.'

'Excellent. You Americans are not so enchanted with titles and initials, eh? And you shall call me Gordon.'

Sir Gordon Fairly, sitting there silently crowing over the full breakfast Sheila had set before him, was a type more common in America, perhaps, than in modern England, although he was a common enough sixteenth-century type, to be sure. The *sui generis* tycoon who managed to get a thorough education to go with his acquisitive instincts and love of risk on his way from rags to tycoondom. His lack of any physical impressiveness could have been turned into either a comic defence behind which a ruthless intelligence could mass itself and do mischief, or this—a superb casualness which knew itself and had no need of illusions to support its authority. He asked what he wanted to know and he said what he meant. For most of the people he dealt with he must be a frightening figure, since in his natural commercial habitat the proportion of façade and bluster to intelligence and will must be approximately what it is in any university common room, but raised to a power of ten.

James rejoined us scowling and limping. Sheila smiled at him maternally. If she had wanted Gordon and me to meet without her husband's ham-handed interference, she had accomplished it decisively, if not neatly. It occurred to me that she and Sir Gordon Fairly had more in common than their humble origins and would be natural allies if they chose to cooperate in managing James into this project.

'Ah, Merman, old man. Family jewels still intact, I hope.'

'I'm crippled for life, if that's what you mean. And don't call me that. Turn my stomach on top of everything else. My balls are done for—a minor matter to you, I suppose. Happened to you, you'd just buy yourself a new pair.'

'No one is that rich, James,' he said sadly.

'Gordon has just been asking me if I'd like to examine the evidence for the Lucy Goodman hypothesis.'

James glared at me and shook his uncombed head. 'And you'd do it, too, wouldn't you? Did you tell him that you don't know your arse from his elbow about it?'

He turned on Gordon Fairly.

'The man knows John Donne and he knows sweet F.A. else. Narrowed to a point he is, like any academic too long in the library. Sharpened to a bloody intellectual ice-pick, fit to dig into one problem. You'd trust him with judging your evidence?'

Gordon ate on unruffled. He quoted Santayana suavely, citing the passage describing the Harvard faculty as 'a vast concourse of coral insects, each secreting a single cell and leaving the fossil remnant to enlarge the world'.

'Are you a coral insect sort of scholar, Neil, or is your view a bit more catholic than that?'

Sheila butted in, as I as beginning to realize she always would when she was ready. 'Perhaps the best proof would be Neil's new book. Didn't you say the publication party is today, Neil?'

Gordon was polite, if not enthusiastic. 'Oh, you have a new book. Excellent.'

'Yes, today. Which reminds me. I have to get back to my own shaving things and laundry at my digs and get my day organized.'

I started tying my shoes and making other gestures in the direction of leaving.

'What is the title of your book, Neil? Who's publishing it?'

'*The Lives of John Donne.*'

'The poet,' Sheila put in grandly.

'Dunham is the publisher. The presentation to the press and all that is this afternoon.'

Sheila breathlessly added a top dressing of the American sales figures and film possibilities.

Gordon mopped his plate with a piece of toast and savoured it before replying. 'Very good. In that case I won't have to buy a copy in order to read it, because I already own it. My communications company owns your publisher, therefore . . . I'm afraid, if you look closely at the corporate structure of the thing, *I* am your publisher. So, you will let your publisher drive you back to your hotel, eh, and tell me about this marvellous book Sheila says will make so much money for us both.'

He rose and turned to our sullen host. 'James, I have called a meeting for this afternoon at five. Please be there. Sheila, darling, persuade him and you be there, too. The executive suite on the thirtieth floor of my building in the City. Only my solicitor and a few other concerned persons will be there. James, just for you I have laid in some smoked Scotch salmon and some Russian caviar a communist colleague sent to me as a bribe to get in on my satellite system in Norway.' He chuckled happily and took my arm towards the door.

'If you think I'll be there, you're mad,' James said with snarling finality.

Sheila winked at us.

Gordon stopped and looked serious for a moment. It made his quiet voice rather more frightening than James's shouting. 'James, you are being a bore. I have offered you a business proposition which you must examine because you are not a fool. I have given you my time to an extent that would make some men in this city swoon with envy, and I am telling you that I will give you more. Men don't get an appointment with me just for the asking. My time is carefully allotted to what profits *me* best, financially, or spiritually, or æsthetically. *I* decide. I belong to a Board of Directors to which I must go now for one hour. That is one hour each six months. For that hour of my time they pay me twenty-five thousand pounds. Because I am worth it. Because at our last meeting I saved them fifteen times that by preventing them from the production of a disastrously designed fitting for a nuclear power plant. If you are afraid of the Lucy Goodman project becoming a laughing-stock, don't worry, it will be me they will laugh at. If you think this opportunity will repeat itself, you are wrong. If you can convince me of its impracticability, come and do so, I will listen. But end this foolishness.

'Come, Neil, we'll ride back together and my chauffeur will get a look at you so that he will be able to recognize you when he picks you up after your autograph party this afternoon.'

We left together. It was rather like being swept up in a small, compact, fast-moving cyclone.

I suppose that if you have been in one chauffeured

Daimler furnished with eighteenth-century antiques, you've seen them all.

Sir Gordon and I sat in a small, tasteful room, speeding towards my B & B. The walls were covered in pale fawn silk and indirectly lit. Since the windows were bronzed dark in any case, Gordon had masked them with framed Hogarth drawings. The bar was an exquisite fruitwood miniature sideboard. The largest furnishing was the owner's chair, upholstered in bottle green velvet. I occupied the brown leather club chair.

'My wife will not ride in it,' my host said genially, indicating the rug with a thumbs down sign. 'She says that having a miniature Aubusson woven to fit the floor was tacky.'

There are times to be silent. This seemed to be one.

'The very rich are *not* different from you, Neil, despite what Fitzgerald thought. They play silly games and indulge their vanities and so on, just like professors or actors. The real difference is a pathetic one and has to do with the irony of wealth and power, an irony which often leads rich men to religion in the end. Can you guess what it is?'

'It's obvious that there are simply fewer things — fewer silly indulgences — available to them exclusively.'

He pointed at my nose with a stubby manicured finger. 'Right on the nose. Exclusivity is the key. In the end it isolates us all. My wife and I love each other a great deal, but she must have her own car, furnished in her own way. Her own room, of course, her own country house. We play at being rival powers, except that we both know she is a client state supported entirely by foreign aid. From me.'

I really had no interest in any further exploration of the wonderful world of executive marriage.

'I'm sure, Gordon, that there are magazine feature writers who would give a great deal for this interview . . .'

'But you find it boring as hell, eh? Good for you for saying so.' I earned another approving nod of the great head. I suppose that his daily world had so much insincere flattery in it that even a little rudeness was a relief.

'How long have you actually known Hugh James?' he asked.

'Thirty-odd years. We were at Oxford together.'

'He thinks I'm barmy trying to get him to head up my project. Do you think I'm barmy?'

'What I don't think is that you want him to do it because you saw him play a theatre manager on TV.'

'Ah, you're a sly one. That's what Sheila thinks, too.'

'I think that you had a very thorough job of research done on our mutual friend by some team of bright young men you employ to do that sort of thing, and that it showed in a number of ways that James is indeed a gifted organizer and an imaginative and original artist.' This time I pointed to his nose. 'Who has never chosen to exercise those gifts on any scale.'

He walloped his big hands together with pleasure.

'Right. Got it in one. He's never *chosen*. The TV part was a sport for him, I could see that. The reason he was so good in it was because he could play at doing what he had always really wanted to do, but was afraid to. He *wanted* to play at being an impresario.' He gestured at the room we were riding in. 'Just as I like to play at being a Bourbon or a Romanov in here. That's what I'd really like to be, you know—King. God, that would be fun. I suppose you can find grounds for pity in that, eh? It's the sort of thing the old poets wrote ironic verses about.'

'Irony has always been available as a mask for envy.'

He shook his massive jowls and rolled his eyes in a caricature of woe. 'Sometimes it's not, that's the problem. I'll wager you're thinking of such a poem now and seeing me in its light. Bet?'

I saw no reason not to admit it. 'No bet. I thought of De Vere's poem, *Were I king, I could command content;* do you want to hear all of it?'

'Yes, yes, go on.'

> *'Were I obscure, hidden should be my cares;*
> *Or were I dead, no cares should me torment,*
> *Nor hopes, nor hates, nor loves, nor griefs, nor fears.*
> *A doubtful choice, of these three which to crave,*
> *A kingdom, or a cottage, or a grave.'*

He nodded enthusiastically. 'What is this conceit, do you think, this sheik's dream of a motor-car? Is it my kingdom or my cottage? I don't plan to die here, I can assure you, so it can't be my grave.'

'Without pausing from his own rhetorical question, he added thoughtfully, 'I think Lucy knew him.'

I must have missed a beat.

'De Vere, the Earl of Oxford,' he added. 'Now you will think I'm really obsessed, but it's a fact. As you will see, there's a mention of him in the notebooks. I promise you, when you examine the documentary evidence, scant as it is now, you will be intrigued. *Arden of Faversham* was written by a woman, I am sure of that, sir, and I feel I'm half way to proving that the woman was my ancestor, Lucy Goodman, to whom I am determined that appropriate recognition will come.'

'I think I should enjoy seeing your evidence, Gordon,' I said, surprising myself by the realization that it was true as I spoke the words.

'Good, good. Tell me, Neil, do you have such a fantasy still unfulfilled?'

I examined the Hogarth on my side and answered him over my shoulder. 'Why don't you have that team of bright young men find that out for you?'

The car stopped softly and his driver spoke through the intercom. 'The post is here, Sir Gordon.'

'Excellent. Thank you, Steve.'

He touched something and the Hogarth to his left slid down out of its frame, revealing the head and shoulders of an English mailman on a bike. The sturdy, decent figure and honest red face looked like all the rural postmen in England. He handed five or six letters to Sir Gordon Fairly, saluted with two fingers and pedalled off.

I couldn't very well ignore it, so I asked the obvious question. 'You have your mail delivered to your car?'

He smiled with satisfaction, fanning the letters out in his hand. The window glided silently up again and the car moved almost imperceptibly forward.

'Of couse. It's where I am at this hour.' He dealt the letters into two piles, threw one into the gilt wastebasket and held on to just one. 'I should explain. When I was a very young man I wanted to get post, but I never did. It seemed to me some sort of adventure — as the cowboy says in that American song, "cards and letters from people I don't even know". So I arranged, as soon as I was rich enough, to have a messenger firm send a man to my home to pick up the post from my box each morning and call Steve to find where the car is, then bring it to me. At the office, you know, I never even get to look at the post until it has been handled by seventeen assistants, so this is my morning treat.'

'It looks very much like my mail — three-fourths junk.'

He was delighted. 'It is, it really is. Just like anyone's mail, really, in that respect. Begging letters and so forth. Silly offers to increase my income by starting my own mail order business at home. Ah, but this morning, a letter from my daughter. She lives in Jersey.' He held up a square blue envelope and kissed it. 'That letter alone makes it worth the trick.'

We pulled up with the same soft, quick stop and my door opened. We were in front of my pension.

'Goodbye, Neil Kelly. Oh, and I will, I will. Have my

bright young men find out more about you, fear not.' He
was laughing as he waved me out of the immense car.

Two girls passing stopped to look into the car and then
at me. One of them said, 'You on TV or in the movies?'
She had an unmistakable American accent.

I smiled sadly and shook my head. The other one took
my picture anyway, just in case, I suppose, before I went
into my modest hotel.

CHAPTER 3

Winston Bradley had urged me to let them put me up at
the Stafford, which was just off Green Park and round the
corner from their offices. But I was too experienced in the
ways of publishers to accept that goodie. It would have
meant that I was entirely at their beck and call for
interviews, and other forms of interference in my privacy
ruinous to amusement.

I had chosen instead to take a room at a comfortable,
slightly rundown pension in bed-sit land where I could
come and go without any immediate neighbours knowing
or caring who I might be. It was, in fact, the first place I
had ever stayed in London, years before, and I had both a
sentimental attachment to the neighbourhood and a
perverse pleasure in staying there now that I could easily
afford better. Something like Sir Gordon's self-indulgence
standing on its head, and perhaps a clue to why some men
became academics. Or, as psychiatrists call them,
masochists.

My anonymity had probably been compromised a bit
by having Gordon's sensational Daimler drop me off, but
since the only witnesses were those two girls in Michigan
State sweatshirts and backpacks, probably not by much.

I had never really unpacked properly after arriving the

previous evening, so I did that chore and laundered my travel stuff in the washbasin and spread it on the window-sill to dry. The bathroom on the first landing was unoccupied, so I showered and shaved singing and then lay for half an hour on my bed naked, thinking of nothing. The sofa-bed in James's house had been chiefly remarkable for an intermittent tendency to fold itself up with me in it, and by the time I had figured out that it was unwise to sleep on its left side at all, dawn had arrived.

Anything was better than thinking ahead to the boredom and fakery of a publishing party, so I let James's — and Gordon Fairly's — problem wander through my mind.

It was clear that my old friend was, for the first time since I had known him, beginning to feel the advance of age and some responsibility for planning his life beyond the next job. Taking a wife had done that to more than one man, and reaching fifty had done it when nothing else would. Whether Sheila was consciously guiding him in that direction or not, her presence in his life was obviously the major influence on his new, prudent attitude.

After my short meeting with Gordon Fairly there was no doubt in my mind that he was serious about his Lucy Goodman project and that he would persist. He believed in the historical reality of Lucy Goodman the playwright, and in her authorship of *Arden of Faversham*, and he was not simply a fool being carried along by a blind act of faith. He reminded me rather of those nineteenth-century giants, businessmen and amateurs, who virtually created the modern science of archæology by deciding in their studies that they knew exactly where to find Knossos or the tomb of Agamemnon, and then, in the face of all reason and common sense, going off and doing it.

Arden was real enough. I was going to have to read it

again, and soon, if I was going to be of any use in judging
Lucy Goodman's possible authorship, but I could recall
enough of its provenance to grasp some of the problems
we'd face. It was really a good, solid tragedy, and in its
own way an honest-to-God revolutionary event in English
theatre, the first domestic tragedy. It was not about kings
or nobles, but about a middle-class married couple.
Whoever had written it had ignored all the known rules
for writing a play and had invented an entirely new way
of dramatizing lust and greed, a way neither the Greeks
nor the Romans, the accepted models, had ever thought
of.

The other striking thing about *Arden* was that it was so
well written. Hence, of course, all the theories about
Shakespeare or Marlowe or some other genius having
written it when he was young. Apart from the main plot,
there was a comic sub-plot involving the two hired
assassins, whose names were Black Will and Shakebag,
and it was genuinely low and bawdy and funny. Will?
And Shakebag? Had those been the actual names in the
case or was someone hinting that a certain Will
Shakesomething was having a bit of fun? Or, conversely,
was someone who didn't admire Will Shakesomething
playing a practical joke on him? One way of reading the
play was as a parody of high tragic drama.

I studied the handbill Gordon had slipped to me just
before I left his car. It was a mock-up of the flyer he had
designed for the cover of his project plans, copied from
the frontispiece of the 1592 folio edition of *Arden*.

I groaned and put the thing down. I had to stop thinking of excuses and get ready to go to my own party. I
was letting my mind run away with me, doing just what I
had suspected Gordon Fairly had been doing. It is
altogether too easy to let a hypothesis take root in your
will to believe and then start arranging the evidence to

THE

LAMENTA-
BLE AND TRUE TRA –
GEDIE OF M. AR-
DEN OF FEVERSHAM
IN KENT.

Who was most wickedlye murdered, by
the meanes of his disloyall and wanton
wyfe, who for the love she bare to one
Mosbie, hyred two desperat ruf–
fins Blackwill and Shakbag,
to kill him.

Wherein is shewed the great mal–
lice and dissimulation of a wicked wo–
man, the unsatiable desire of filthie lust
and the shamefull end of all
murderers.

Imprinted at London for Edward
White, dwelling at the lyttle North
dore of Paules Church at
the signe of the
Gun. 1592.

support your bias, rather than staying calm and objective
and making the evidence add up *against* your strictest
doubts. The latter is what scholars are trained and paid

to do, and what I had just spent three years doing for the life of John Donne. Maybe my mind wanted a holiday. I made a mental note not to give myself one if the result was going to be that I made an ass of myself.

I left *Arden of Faversham* and Gordon's Lucy Goodman hypothesis on the window-sill with my other odds and ends needing an airing and went off in the direction of Green Park and the hospitality and commercial friendship of my publishers. If I were to let myself be more than a half-hour late they might turn actively hostile.

I was greeted by the dyspeptic Winston Bradley, Dunham's Editor in Chief, nervously massaging his gut and talking in bursts to a gaunt, sepulchral figure who kept caressing his own throat and pursing his mouth around an ancient meerschaum as he listened. Middle-aged men develop habits pointing to their medical futures, as every decent diagnostician knows; all body language is medical forecast.

'Here comes the sorely missed guest of honour now,' Winston said, extending his arms. 'Neil, good to see you again, old man.'

'Winston, how are you? Am I early? I can leave and come back in an hour if you'd rather.'

'For God's sake, Neil, now that we've got you here, stay. You're damned late as it is. We like our money's worth, you know. There are about thirty inside, we're waiting for one or two more. Say hello to George Adamson. George is directing the ad campaign for us on this one.'

Winston, I knew of old, had a mortal, superstitious fear of ever using the word 'book' when he was talking about books. Just as all professional actors will say 'the Scottish play' or 'you know' rather than ever say *Macbeth* — a superstition as old as English theatre —

Winston avoided calling the objects he edited and sold by their real generic name.

I shook hands with George Adamson and accepted his compliments on 'the product'. Apparently he was tuned to Winston's sensitivity.

'I'm glad you like my book,' I said. 'It's a damned good book, even if I do say so myself. A book which will influence the way people think about Donne, I hope.'

George took the pipe from his mouth carefully while Winston reeled from the body blows I was delivering.

'And one that will sell, if I may say so.' He smiled bonily and puffed out a cloud of pollution, scratching his jaw with the pipestem.

I returned his smile. 'Yes, let's not forget about the dear sales curve, as Sean O'Casey was fond of saying. It is a book that will sell. Has sold. Just think, Winston—' I put my arm around my suffering editor's shoulders. 'Bookstores, bookclubs, book programmes on TV, book review shows on radio, then on to the second-hand bookstores, paperback bookstands, book condensations . . .'

He moved away. 'You're making me ill, Neil. I'd rather have a drunk to deal with than a sadist, any day. Come on, the reason for your coming is in there, and you've delayed the drama of your arrival quite long enough.'

He led us all into the room where the product's campaign rally was being fuelled.

'It's time to make you pay for your sins, you American fiend, with a little stand-up comedy and academic charm. Are you ready?'

One is either ready or not. If you are not drunk, then a suit of armour or an invincible unwillingness to take the proceedings seriously will do on the bestseller publicity circuit. The valley of death is a piece of cake compared with it. The smell of money is the smell of blood to publishers and to those fringe figures of all the arts who are art's chief publicists, and they feed in a frenzy, like those small, needle-toothed fish who can strip the flesh from a man in two minutes.

I had survived the American debut by the simple expedient of answering every question outrageously, and I was confident that I could survive this. I waded in, protected only by my purity of heart and the wilful suspension of my last shred of disbelief.

The first thing to know about publishing parties is that they are a ritual form, not a functional one. They don't sell books. What they do is reassure the people who write and sell books that they are not all insane for doing it. They conform as closely to the American Legion Trophy Night model or Salesman of the Year Banquet model as they can, because that is the proven form. All persons engaged in activities which they suspect in their hearts all others hold in contempt require these confirmations of purpose and this communion. There is everything but the opening prayer and the closing company song. I suppose that somewhere, probably in California, there are even publishers who have those, but not yet, thank God, in London.

I shook hands, I accepted drinks to hold, I posed for photographs, I signed my name to my book. I answered the same questions — I believe there were three of them — approximately one hundred times. If there was the slightest hint of hysteria beyond the norm in the air, I put it down to my long absence from the urban energies of commercial London. After a year wandering in Scotland even Green Park can seem a hell-bent kind of place.

A half-hour into the rites Gerard Chaldecott, the chairman of Dunham's, took me by the arm and led me away from the wilderness of happy talk into a tiny desert of quiet in one corner. When the Chairman indicates that he wishes to be apart from the throng for a moment, the throng always understands. The room magically cleared away from our end.

'How long have you known Gordon Fairly, Neil?' he asked me in an anxious whisper. His grey eyes bulged, showing their red veins, and both his breath and his fussy little moustache smelled of gin.

'Oh, not long, actually. We've spent a little time together talking about the sixteenth century, being rich—that sort of thing.'

He glared at me suspiciously. 'I don't know why I deal with writers at all. You're all too damned clever for my own good.'

Gerard had been saying this to writers for almost fifty years, knowing that he was far more clever than most of them and at least even with the rest.

'Well, I know you know the bugger, because he called me fifteen minutes ago and bawled hell out of me for not having a much grander presentation for the book than this.' He indicated the beautiful room with a glum gesture that seemed to indicate it was an obvious slum.

'Well, Gerard, I think this is just fine, so relax.' I patted his shoulder reassuringly.

'You're missing my point, I'm afraid, Neil, old man.' He sighed and cocked his head. 'Or you're being damned clever again, is that it?'

'I guess I'm just plain missing the point.'

'Sir Gordon's mania for the Elizabethan period was virtually our entire justification for having Dunham run miles over budget on your book. Originally it had been proposed that we make some sort of presentation of it to him—oh, well . . . Good heavens, do you think all this is the normal hoopla to christen a learned—even a *bestselling* learned—biography of a remote literary figure? Not at all. Quite the contrary. I'm afraid it was my son's idea in the main, and one I opposed vigorously, that we let the budget go hang this once in the hope that

Sir Gordon would become some sort of godfather to our folly.'

'Make *him* an offer he couldn't refuse, you mean?'

'David can explain it better than I. As a matter of fact, he used precisely that appalling phrase, whatever it means. But, you see, now, far from either objecting to the book's cost or accepting it because it's his particular interest, he's simply pissed off at me and demanding that I spend more to promote it. And it all has to do with his interest in you somehow.'

'Tell him he's nuts.'

He winced. 'I'm afraid that's not on, all things considered. We shall simply have to accede to his wishes and do all this again. Bigger and better, as you Americans say. At the Savoy.'

'No dice.'

'Eh? What's that?' He growled like a movie gangster. 'Whaddya mean, "no dice"?'

'I'm afraid this is it, publicitywise, Gerard. End of the line, my final gesture of goodwill to the industry which is making me rich and famous. Make the most of this one, because there isn't going to be another, not at the Savoy or anywhere else.'

He looked more miserable. 'Sir Gordon won't like it. He effectively owns this house, you know.'

'I know. And yes, I know. I'll explain to him, fear not. I'm seeing him later, and I'll tell him then.'

He looked mildly astonished and vastly relieved.

'You know him that well, eh? You are? You will, eh? Good, good. Do that.' His look of a man impressed and bucked up changed suddenly to a look of man experiencing nausea. I followed his glance to the doorway.

He hissed in my ear. 'He's sent over William. He told me he would.'

A faintly familiar face materialized in the doorway,

setting off a quick migration of reporters and cameras in that direction.

'William who?' I hissed back at him.

He rolled his bulging eyes. 'God, you writers. I don't know why I deal with writers. *That* is merely the most watched face on British TV. He does that talk show. Everyone, literally everyone, listens to him. The silly shit.'

Since I had watched British TV fewer than six times in two years, and three of those occasions had been rugby matches, I was unsurprised by my own ignorance of the famous one.

The most listened-to voice was apparently about to speak, because a hush fell over the clamouring *papparazzi*. The most admired teeth flashed insincerely and beautifully just once and the words came.

'Hey, where's my old buddy Neil?'

Many heads pivoted to catch my reaction to this incredible accolade from El Supremo. Shrewd old William Whoeverhewas spotted me with an unerring eye in the spotlight, gave a showbiz start, opened his hands to frame his incredibly watched face, and came towards me.

'Neil Kelly, you're looking grand. Absolutely. It's a marvellous, marvellous book. You absolutely must come on the show and tell a breathless British public about it.'

He clasped one of my hands in two of his and turned to the cameras to announce that he predicted that *The Lives of John Donne* would set off a wave of interest in the poet which would dwarf the Evelyn Waugh wave and make everyone forget entirely the Edwardian wave as a whole wholly.

Everyone had a good chuckle at that one. Supremo was obviously in super form. His brand-new old friend Neil Kelly laughed as hard as anyone else.

'What did you say your last name is again?' I asked him.

Except for one brief murderous flash in the famous

blue eyes meant only for me, he joined in the laugh for that, too.

'Wisdom, William Wisdom, you remember, you rascal.'

We had them in stitches. Frick and Frack.

'Oh, *that* William. Wisdom. Bill, how are you? What have you been doing with yourself? Got a job yet?'

My laugh topped his. He unembraced my hand. Gordon Fairly must have a very large hold indeed over this twit if he was as big a noise as he appeared to be and he still had been forced to stop whatever he was doing and toddle over to my autograph party just because he was told to. He was certainly holding in a lot of hostility, to judge from the tension in those neat little hands I had just been holding.

He held out a copy of the book to be signed. It was well-handled and many pages were dog-eared or marked with pencil down the margin. Some committee of his bright young men must have sweated mightily to write a two-hundred-word digest of it for him to read on the ride over.

I wrote on the flyleaf: *I don't know you or like you any better than you know or like me, pal. Cheer up, Sir Gordon will love you for it,* and signed it with a flourish.

A female companion who had trailed the great one into the room, attracting her own admirers by exposing a great deal of breast through an exiguous dress, now made her move into the charmed circle. He introduced her as his friend Cindy.

'Ooh, let me see what he wrote, William,' Cindy squealed. 'I love to see what real authors write. When I had my autograph party, all I could think of to write was *Sincerely, Cindy.*'

He smiled falsely at her and held on to the book. 'It's private. I wouldn't share it for the world.'

She shrugged, apparently used to his pettiness and cold

answers framed in that gleaming grin. She turned to me.

'I wrote a bestseller about dieting. It sold just over fifty thousand in hardback, I got a quarter million for the paperback rights, and it was syndicated in fourteen newspapers.'

At last, someone who talked like a genuine writer.

'Maybe I should add a chapter or two about how John Donne kept himself thin,' I told her.

She laughed agreeably before she was expertly whisked into another smother of drinkers by the Wisdom, shouting over her shoulder, '*My* autograph party was at the Savoy!'

I was just beginning to realize how many people I didn't know at Dunham's, despite my old friendships with Winston and Gerard.

An ugly, pleasant-faced man about five feet tall walked over to me while I was still trying to think of another way of engaging Cindy in more conversation.

'Kelly, does it ever occur to you, you smug bastard, that you are standing in a receiving line aboard the *Titanic?*'

The pleasant-faced ugly little man was shaking my hand enthusiastically as he spoke. I try to rise to all such occasions in the manner of the local population. Englishmen are the greatest send-up artists in the world.

'Has the hotel struck ice? I could use some in this drink.'

'I read your book, Kelly, and if you'll allow me to say so, your style makes the muses weep and wince.'

'Well, thanks for reading it anyway, despite the pain.'

He waved away my gratitude with a dismissive sweep. 'I had to. I'm the one who had to brief the goddam sales force. Write up the summary and so on. You know, explain it to those idiots. I didn't really understand it, you understand, so now they don't understand it either.'

He had a punishing northern burr and he was obviously drunk as an old habit. I wondered mildly what the sales force thought about my book, considering their teacher. But on second thoughts, I've known any number of professors who have explained John Donne to any number of students without understanding one word of him, so perhaps there was no harm done which had not already been done better.

He took a long pull of his whisky. 'I told them your man Donne couldn't keep his doohicky in his pants for the first thirty years, and then couldn't get it out for the next thirty.'

'I've heard worse explanations of Donne, but not, I think, of my book.'

He waved his drink carefully. 'I suppose you think you could do it better,' he burred pleasantly.

David Chaldecott, a junior officer in the firm and the son apparently being groomed for bigger things in the family tradition of publishing, arrived escorting a serious-looking woman, and cut him off disgustedly.

'Go away, Walter, you're full.'

Walter stood to his entire height and spoke with slow dignity. 'I am not full. Gibbous, perhaps. But several small stages yet from full.' He weaved away towards the bar, but not before adding behind his hand to me, 'If the band start playing "Nearer, my God, to Thee", grab a lifejacket.'

The woman with David winked at me and said, 'You've just met Walter Harrison. I assume he told you your book is unintelligible crap. He does that to all our authors. Hello, I'm U.D. Allen.'

Her handshake was quick and nervous, like her smile. She stubbed out a cigarette in a saucer.

'How do you do. Every firm needs a grumpy drunk, I guess. I was afraid when he first spoke that he might be you.'

She had long hair and a too-long face, and she looked tired, but she had what the seventeenth century would have called 'a merry eye', and, as I knew, she had an educated head. She was my editor, although we had never met.

'Sorry about the initials bit. Ursula Dorothea, but I abandoned that mouthful years ago. My friends call me Dolly.' She gave a resigned smile. 'Sorry, but it started in school and there it is.'

'Better than Dot, I suppose. Please call me Neil. The book looks marvellous. The jacket is far more dramatic than the American one.'

'Thanks. George says it has market impactability. I think that's what he said. It sounds awful enough to succeed.'

'And I'd have thought after the American edition that you'd have found far fewer errors and loose ends, but your letters have made it abundantly clear how many loose ends even the redoubtable John Krale in New York left hanging.'

She looked unhappy. 'I've just been told there's another one we missed.' She grabbed a book from the pile. 'Do you want to see how unobservant we both are, or would you rather just drink and nibble those ghastly canapes?'

The morsel I was gnawing didn't seem all that bad. Bacon wrapped around a scallop, I thought. I ingested it and reached for the book.

'I've mastered the skill of eating and reading at the same time. Show me.'

She riffled to the middle of the book and pointed to a passage about 'Songs and Sonnets'. 'There. We both blew it. Where you talk about the Paracelcist motif in the sonnets . . .'

I groaned. 'Don't tell me I left out the Nicholl citation? It was his idea I was stealing there.'

'Oh, you cited him, but the poem you quoted from was "Love's Growth" and you noted it as "Valediction Forbidding Mourning".'

We looked at the wretched, rash, wrong citation together. It will not seem a large matter to those who do not practise the black arts of scholarship, but I felt a familiar pang of unreasonable fury at the error. Scholars, even bestselling ones, wake up at night sweating blood about fumbles like that. It's bad enough when you say something stupid in front of a roomful of inattentive undergraduates—that Samuel Johnson was Ben Jonson or that Shrewsbury is just north of London; it will haunt you for days. If your error gets into print it will haunt you for years. Close readers, little old ladies on Brattle Street and pouncing PhD candidates at Cornell will write to you forever and point to the error with pardonable pride and hints that you might want to mention them in the next edition. When your mistakes get into print, you know how ballplayers feel reading the sports page. There it is, in the box score for all the world to see: *Error, Kelly.*

Dolly Allen had been saying something. David had slipped away.

'Hm?' I grabbed another baconian scallop and pretended I had been distracted by the waiter.

'I said, you're clenching your jaw. The trouble with you is, you think it's your error, whereas I know that it's mine. After all, I'm your editor.'

'Don't be so noble. No author ever really expects his editor to contribute anything to the book.'

She tried one of the canapes and spat it out. 'Look who's being noble now and masking it with a fine show of British rudeness. You do adapt well. Here comes our leader. Stick around and I'll show you how I think you can improve the logic of your argument about contemplation and action in "The Exstasie".'

As she melted away into the mob I called after her.

'Who spotted the error?'

'Walter Harrison.' She lit a fresh cigarette and laughed.

I watched her go, revising my mind about old Walter and admiring her bottom, which was rather nice. If she'd do something different with her hair she'd be an attractive woman.

Gerald Chaldecott was indeed edging towards me. He had with him two younger men, one with the aggressive handsomeness and checked suit of a public relations specialist and the other his son David, being brought back to the Author whether he wanted it or not.

Gerard introduced the aggressive one as Mark Darrow, George Adamson's assistant. He demonstrated his crushing grip, which is what some people do when they have nothing intelligent to say.

He told me that he loved the book and that he thought we'd be setting some sales records with this one and perhaps picking up a few awards along the way. He called that a dynamite combination. He explained hastily that he had never had a chance to read up on the Renaissance and so on at Oxford, 'a bit tied up with reading rugby and rowing and so on, ha ha,' but that it had been an education to leaf through my book.

'Amazing how these Renaissance chappies did it, isn't it? Or wasn't it, rather. All dead now, of course. You don't see that nowadays, I suppose, unless Americans do it, ha ha. I mean, in and out of all those beds, religion, politics, so on. Painted great frescoes, too, I imagine. Composed sonnets, operas, all that. Married, too, wasn't he? Your man Donne?'

'Rather. Nine children.'

'Well, of course, women were more fertile then, don't you think? Chap told me they had to be to keep up with the mortality rate, sickness, so on. Makes sense, don't you think?'

'I guess you can't fool Mother Nature.'

He laughed immoderately. 'Listen, Neil, I think it's just super that William Wisdom is here and that you'll be doing the show with him . . .'

Gerard put his hand on the Darrow bicep, which, predictably, tensed inside the checked sleeve.

'Later, perhaps, Mark. Neil and I have some things to discuss now. David, have you filled Neil in on our negotiations with those American film people?'

Darrow held up a hand in a Hollywood gesture. 'Say no more, G.C., say no more. We'll talk later, Neil, about the Wisdom show and a few other ideas I've got churning. Be thinking about an appearance at Oxford, eh? There must be some group up there who read Literature and so on. Don't react now, just hold the thought. I'll get back to you.'

The two juniors left, one punching the other enthusiastically in the arm.

This time Gerard wanted more privacy than was provided by a cleared out corner. In any case, it had proceeded to that point all parties reach where the press people, except for one or two completely worthless freeloaders, had left and the publisher's friends and employees were beginning to make their stretch run at the free booze. In that phase of convivial decline even the Chairman lost some of his exclusivity and even secretaries dared unspeakable intrusions. As we were slipping through a side door to a private sitting-room Gerard was goosed by a girl in a purple linen suit tied around her ankles. She had an astonishing, towering cloud of rather orange hair.

He dodged the compliment wearily. 'I hate to take away the guest of honour, Neil, but, as you can see, the productive part of the festivities has passed. I hope you don't mind indulging me for a few moments.'

'On the contrary. I consider it a rescue operation.'

'Hm. Yes, some writers like it, some don't. Cindy, at her party, took off all her clothes after the first hour and stood on a table offering to match arses with any woman in the room. There were several takers and it became quite disgraceful.'

'Well, it was a diet book. I suppose that might have been an important selling point. I didn't know that Dunham's had published the famous diet book.'

'No? Oh, rather. Paid the rent for half a year, that appalling little darling.' His baggy eyes gleamed happily for a moment, then clouded again. 'That's how all this difficulty with Fairly's people got started. We're owned now by FairCom, you know, and it's that I wish to put a small bug in your ear about.'

He collapsed with an audible breath of relief on to the yellow sofa and motioned me to a chair beside him.

An exploring couple opened the door opposite, stuck their heads in, saw us and shut it again fast. The girl had a cloud of orange hair; the man was David Chaldecott.

Gerard shook his head disdainfully. 'David should be ashamed of himself. That sort of thing is done upstairs. Oh well, the poor young bugger, I suppose he knows he's never going to run Dunham's now, and he's having what joy he can of it before the axe falls.'

'Gerard, I'm pretty sure you didn't spirit me in here to tell me your family's house rules for sexual shenanigans. What about Fairly or FairCom or whatever?'

He spoke to the ceiling, head back on the sofa cushion, eyes closed. 'The situation is actually quite threatening. To Dunham's, you understand. We are—or were, before the board saw fit to defy me and endorse our absorption by the Fairly group—an old, respected house. That was very much a no-confidence vote in me and my family, actually. No other way to look at it. My great-grandfather, Donald Dunham, began by publishing ordnance maps and navigational charts. A lot of famous voyages depended on Dunham charts in those days. We didn't publish anything literary, you know, until well into the last century, when my great-uncle, William Chaldecott, published several books about travel in America. The trans-Mississippi West and so on. That made our name here in London, and gradually the entire operation shifted here from Edinburgh. As you well know, Dunham's then became a house of literary and scholarly repute equal to any.'

He blinked his eyes and rubbed them wearily. 'My son has put our entire office operations on computer.'

It was difficult to tell if he admired or deplored that more.

'The publishing business is not what it was anywhere any more, you know, Neil.'

'I know a few examples in New York. Good solid old houses taken over by conglomerates of oil companies and God knows what else, and run as a tax loss by corporate types who never read a book, let alone published one. They often go from serious literature to soft-core porn in a few years.'

'Or diet books. I suppose that's the intermediate stage between respectability and soft-core porn. Neil, your lovely book on Donne would never — simply never — have been purchased this past year by Dunham's if it had not had the advantage of the American tie-ins with the subsidiary publicity — films and so on. I mean that. Good as it is — and Neil, believe me, I'm proud to be your publisher for this fine book — I told them to make it a beautiful book and damn the cost this time, you know, because it might just be a swan song for Dunham's, and I wanted us to go out singing beautifully.'

He waved abstractedly at a thought. 'I suppose I'm ready for my retirement to Devon, so it isn't a personal thing. I simply hate to see Dunham's sunk by a chap like this — this unprincipled, jumped-up man Fairly. Granted, he has some sort of amateur's intelligent interest in English literature — some notion his great-grandmother wrote *Hamlet* or something equally preposterous, I'm told—but I think you'll agree, that scarcely makes him a promising patron of serious literature in today's market. One hears the wildest rumours . . . Oh God, I just don't know.'

He actually wept a single tear which coursed slowly down his nose until he dashed it angrily away with a knuckle.

'I'm an old fool, and I shouldn't have taken that last whisky. Sorry.'

I was embarrassed and at a loss for something to say about Gordon Fairly. He wasn't a typical business ignoramus, but I could see Gerard's point of view. He saw Gordon as a pirate swinging aboard his stately old ship, cutlass in hand, ready to hack and loot. Perhaps in his position I'd be shedding a maudlin tear or two myself.

'What is it you'd like me to say to Gordon Fairly, Gerard, assuming I have the chance?'

He waved distractedly again, brushing invisible webs away. 'No, no, Neil, my good fellow. Why should you get heartburn because I can't swallow Fairly? Forget it, please. I should never have started this abominable conversation. I criticize my son David, but the fact is this sort of thing—involving you in what is properly my difficulty—well, this isn't done below the first floor either.'

He stood slowly and buttoned his rumpled jacket and smoothed it. 'I shall appreciate it if you forget that I ever opened the subject with you, Neil. A moment of panic. Some sort of equivalent to Cindy jumping up on the table starkers, I suppose. It is a fact that your book—have I made it clear to you how very proud we all are that your *Lives of John Donne* is a Dunham book?—might well be our last serious contribution to English scholarship or literature. Now, let us leave the dreadful matter there.'

We walked towards the lobby together. There seemed little point in going back into the final scrimmage around the bar. Someone in there was singing 'What Are We Going To Do With Uncle Arthur?'

'Would it help Dunham's, Gerard, do you think, if I were to do all this hoopla—the TV show with Willy Wisdom and the Savoy thing and all that?'

His look was a mixture of hopeful sadness and despairing embarrassment. 'If any word or gesture you could make honestly, Neil—without compromising your own sense of yourself one whit, because God knows my own integrity is in pawn to this fellow already—if it should influence Fairly to reconsider his plans for Dunham's, it would be the finest gift I've ever received.'

It was a hard exit line to follow. We shook hands like two mourners at the death of a mutual friend, no suitable epitaph at hand.

I accepted my coat from the girl deputed to look after them and left while Gerard was gloomily making his way back to the private sitting-room.

CHAPTER 4

The flashiest permanent floating cottage or kingdom in London was waiting for me in St James's Place. The muscular Steve touched his cap and held the living-room door for me to enter. To my relief, no one I could see was watching. I ducked into the club chair again and let myself be wafted, a secret plum in a rich, speedy pudding, to my next entertainment.

'So this is what it feels like to be a millionaire's whore,' I said aloud to myself.

'No woman ever rides in this car, sir,' a shocked but respectful voice said.

I realized it must be my driver. 'Can you hear everything said back here?'

'Only if you've got your elbow on that control button, sir. There's an override on Sir Gordon's chair, but if he's not sitting there, you have the control. Sir Gordon would never let a woman ride in the Daimler, sir, that's all I meant. That's what the Rolls is for, if I may say so. Freddie drives the Rolls.' He laughed a good dirty pub laugh. 'He's no threat at all to the women, is Freddie, if you catch my meaning.'

'The palace eunuch, is Freddie, I take it.'

'That's exactly what Sir Gordon calls him. He—'

'Thank you, Steve. Sorry to interrupt your driving.' I took both my arms off the furniture to shut off any and all units. I had no wish to share palace gossip with the garrulous help. The control I had violated was under my left elbow. For the rest of the ride I sat very still and said nothing aloud.

The Daimler might have been personal and even whimsical, but Gordon Fairly's place of business was all concrete, glass, steel, and efficiency.

Steve delivered me from the vehicle into what I then discovered was an underground parking garage. He said that it would take just a few seconds to phone upstairs for the private elevator to Sir Gordon's suite.

Unhappily, the phone apparently reserved for that purpose was occupied by a cursing young female with the vocabulary of a much older boatswain. She slammed the receiver down and turned wrathfully on the chauffeur, who happened to be standing there when she whirled, hair flying.

'*You!* You Wop bastard, you tell them who I am. I don't know their damn childish code word, and I want to see my father.'

Steve was smiling and at ease under her assault.

'Hello, Carol. It's nice to see you again.'

'Never mind the sarcastic crap, you moron. Get on that

phone and tell that cookie upstairs to send that goddam lift down here.'

'Actually, Carol old dear, I was just going to do that very thing, and you wouldn't even have had to raise your voice. But it's not for you, love. It's for Professor Kelly here. Professor Kelly, may I introduce Carol Fairly, Sir Gordon's daughter?'

She brushed him aside, literally, to confront me. 'No he may not. My name is Ashley. Gordon is my father, but that's a biographical fact, not a definition of who I am. This Dago who thinks he's God's gift to frustrated chicks imagines he can insult me all he wants because he knows that I'm above reporting him to his keeper. How the hell do you rate the private lift? Is my father taking piano lessons? You look like a semi-competent music teacher.'

It was quite an experience meeting her. Whatever she chose to call herself, she had the energy and general social deportment of an angry tigress. It seemed a sudden trick of perspective, but I could see, looking at this rather frail girl in the centre of that small storm of anger she generated, what her father would have looked like if he had been a pretty young woman instead of a corpulent old man.

'I'm Neil Kelly. I'm here because your father was kind enough to ask me to look at his material concerning your several times great-grandmother, Lucy Goodman.'

She threw her hands slowly into the air, lifting her long streaky blonde hair to its full length as she did so, a rather spectacular, if melodramatic effect.

'Jee-sus! You're part of that. You goddam Lucy Goodman groupies, you're like goddam Moonies, you're everywhere, waiting to pick that idiot's pocket, telling him his grandmother wrote Shakespeare's plays or whatever the hell it is you've got him believing.'

Steve stood politely at parade rest, watching. I think he shrugged slightly when I glanced at him. He was obviously familiar with La Ashley's temper and dirty tongue.

'Ashley, I am a Professor of Literature specializing in the period in question, and I happen to be a friend of Hugh James. I have no axe to grind, no thesis to sell, and no preconceptions. I have daughters of my own, who, if their manners were bad enough, might be allowed to howl at me as you are doing. But I don't intend to spend one more minute being screamed at by you in this concrete tomb. If you have problems with your male parent, take them to him, don't expect me to listen to them.'

Steve gave a nod of approval and spoke into the phone. The elevator had obviously been held just a floor above us, because it appeared in less than a second.

She stepped forward. 'I'll ride up with you. Don't worry, I won't speak another word,' she said venomously.

Steve stepped in front of her with his arms crossed. 'Sorry, Carol. I have my orders, and they don't include you, just him.'

The girl was immediately back up to high C. 'Are you telling me, you Wop son of a bitch, that I can't get into my father's lift?'

He smiled. He was, and it clearly gave him great pleasure to do so. 'That's right. Him, but not you.' He turned to me, still blocking her with his body. 'Go ahead, Professor. I'll handle this.'

The furious girl raised herself up on her toes and screeched, 'You, Freddie or whatever the hell your name is, get over here.'

From the driver's window of a silver Rolls-Royce drawn up fifteen feet ahead there now appeared the worried face and cap of the other Fairly chauffeur.

'You brought me here, now tell this idiot to get out of my way. Come on, you cretin, get over here and speak the magic goddam word into this thing, if you know what it is.'

He climbed, with every visible sign of reluctance, out of the pretty car and walked back to where the three of us were enacting our inane tableau. He tipped his cap to me, but spoke to the angry girl.

'Gee, I'm sorry, Miss Fairly, Miss Ashley, but it's like Steve says.' He was a slim, dark, somewhat rabbity-looking individual, either a worried boy or an immature man, his eyes going uncertainly from the muscular chauffeur blocking the elevator to the gesticulating girl.

'Forget Steve, for God's sake. I'm the one you drove here. You know who I am. Give me the damn password and I'll tell them myself.'

Freddie seemed to shrink a little more into his jockey shorts. 'Like I said, miss, I'm only supposed to drive you around front to the commissionaire's booth if I don't have instructions from Sir Gordon about the private entrance.'

'I'll be damned if I'll go in by the tradesmen's entrance and I told you that.' She was still talking at the top of her voice. I wondered how I could get away from her little tantrum and into that elevator without having her physically attack me.

'Does Sylvia have to report to the doorman when she comes here? Are you going to tell me you take Lady Fairly around to the commissionaire?'

'I don't know about that, miss,' the miserable Freddie said. 'I never brought the lady down here.'

'OK, Freddie.' Steve was directing traffic again now in his best bored take-charge manner. 'Wrap it up. If Miss Fairly don't want you to drive her to the front entrance, take the Rolls back to the garage. Leave this to me.'

The wizened little driver looked relieved. He gave Steve a two-fingered salute. 'Gotcha, Steve. He's the boss, miss. Are you sure I can't drive you to the front . . . ?'

'Get out of here, you useless little creep,' she screamed

at him. 'He's the boss? He's a flunky just like you . . .

Steve indicated the elevator to me with his head while she was raging at the feckless Freddie. 'Go ahead, Professor. I'll handle this.'

He closed the door and I was sped upward.

I was met upstairs by an unsmiling woman who told me that she was Sir Gordon's secretary's assistant, and she ushered me to a huge room with a panoramic view of the City. David Chaldecott was standing at the vast window looking out, and a man in black boots, black jeans and an open red silk shirt was supine on the sofa.

David turned when my escort had left, clearly intending that I should be shocked by his being there. 'Are you surprised to find me here, Professor Kelly? I dare say where you come from things are a bit less complicated.'

I was damned if I'd give him the benefit of my surprise. Donnish humour provides a number of formulæ out of such contretemps.

'Noah Webster, Mr Chaldecott, was once interrupted by his wife while he was undressing her maid. She said, "Mr Webster, I am surprised." That patient lexicographer, always a stickler for exactness, said, "No, no, my dear, *we* are surprised. *You* are offended or amazed." '

'I like "stickler" in that anecdote. David wasn't wooing me, I promise you.' The athletic fellow in the silk shirt laughed, not bothering to get up or take his boots off the sofa. 'Hi, I'm Charles Leonard.'

'Ah. The director, playwright, etcetera.'

'That's me. Aging boy wonder of the West End.' He flopped over on to his stomach, gathered himself improbably into a spring and was suddenly, gracefully, doing a handstand on the arm of the seven-foot couch.

'You want a performer of improbable physical feats?' He pointed to himself with one hand while continuing to hold himself erect with the other. 'That's me. I am available for christenings, boat launchings, weddings, and circumcisions. Patriotic occasions a speciality.'

He dismounted lightly to his feet and struck an oratorical pose. 'You weesh,' he gargled in a mournful dialect, 'recitations of ethnic verse, sagas of the sofferings of my pipple, balalaika music provided? Atsa me.'

He shook hands. He had a predictably wiry grip. 'I guess weights, perform minor emergency surgery, write ballads for occasions, and have been known to mix a fair dry martini.'

Charles Leonard was certainly a presence. I said, 'Someone was asking me only today whatever became of the Renaissance man.'

'And here I am.' He threw out his arms in a Bob Fosse gesture. 'Showtime, folks.'

'You'll have to allow for Charles's compulsive personality,' David said over his shoulder. He had turned back to look at the City below. 'Give him a new audience and he's on.'

'David,' Charles said chattily, 'why don't you stick it up your ass? You know you'll enjoy it.'

'Charles will come on in his outworn 'sixties demi-monde style, but he's quite harmless. For all his manifold talents, the amazing thing about Charles is that he has no talent at all for anger. He wouldn't hurt a fly.'

'David means I'm a coward. That's true. But he thinks that means he's safe from harm with me. That's not quite true.'

'If you two gentlemen have a problem between you, I'd suggest that I didn't come here to referee it. I thought there was to be a meeting concerning Sir Gordon's Lucy Goodman project. Has it been cancelled?'

David checked his watch. 'It's not due to start for ten minutes. Relax. There'll be a meeting, all right, and Charles is here for the same reason you and I are, to discuss a project that can make us all a lot more famous—' he goggled his eyes at Charles—'and well off than ten hit plays in the West End, and if he didn't believe that, he wouldn't be here.'

'Does your father know you're here, David?'

Charles crowed. 'He'd have a goddam heart attack if he did.'

'I'm not going to attempt a confessional self-defence—what you Americans call "copping a plea", I believe,' David said without heat. 'I am here because I believe with all my heart that what Sir Gordon is undertaking in his proposed reorganization of Dunham's is by far the best thing that could happen.'

Charles mimed puking on to the carpet.

I thought Charles was right about what Gerard's reaction might be if he did find that his heir was conspiring with Gordon Fairly to reorganize Dunham's.

'Before you say anything else, David, I think you are beginning to cop a plea, as we Americans say. You really don't need to, to me. I'm not your father.'

It occurred to me that this was the second time in fifteen minutes that I had told someone that.

'When Sandra told me that Father had you closeted in that side sitting-room of his, I had to see for myself. I should have known he'd be doing his wounded weary warrior bit, patient eyes closed, waiting for the descent of the uplifted blade from his tormentors. He has a good line in self-pity these days, does my Dad. Between us, his concept of Dunham's is twenty-five years out of date and so is he. I'll bet he asked you to make his case for him to Sir Gordon, the sly old fox.'

'Whatever he said to me I'll continue to treat as a private matter, David.'

He sneered. It was extremely unattractive. I realized that it was the real David. He was a contemptuous young man when he wasn't being solemn. That could be a dangerous combination, contempt fuelled by self-righteousness.

'My father hasn't a clue, Neil. I suppose we'd better both be on a first name basis in this project. Dunham's is small change in Sir Gordon's overall corporate picture, a bagatelle.' His eyes tended to glaze with intensity as he started to talk about large sums of money. I had seen lust do that to a man, but never before covetousness.

'We are dealing here with a transnational conglomerate whose profits before taxation last year amounted to two hundred and sixty million pounds. The total dividend proposed for this year is thirty-seven pence per share — that's a twenty-four per cent increase, my cynical friends, and there are fourteen hundred offices in sixty countries. And the total assets run just slightly under twenty thousand million pounds.'

He was breathing heavily and a sheen of sweat had broken out on his forehead.

'Would you like to guess, Neil, what fraction of one per cent of that total Dunham's entire operation is worth?'

'I'd be glad to if you'll help me compute the value of just the five Nobel laureates published by Dunham's in this century alone.'

He grinned evilly. 'That's easy. They're worth exactly what they bring in in the profits column. Cindy's diet book outsold them all combined.'

'At last, someone who actually knows the price of everything and the value of nothing. I thought you only existed in Wilde's perverse imagination.'

Sheila and James were shown in, preventing any further escalation of the hostilities in the room. They were accompanied by a rather dapper man with extremely intelligent eyes, which darted about, measuring those present. He might have been a professor of philosophy or a worldly cardinal in bespoke flannels.

Sheila started towards me with her guest in tow, but

was waylaid by Charles, who leapt from the sofa with a musical cry, kissed her on both cheeks and gave a quick military salute to James. James looked disgusted and headed for the small bar in the corner. Then he and the worldly cardinal got to arguing about something, and Sheila glanced over at me, shrugged with annoyance, and went over to the bar to make peace.

Charles Leonard materialized at my elbow demanding to know if I had seen his show at Drury Lane. He mimed shock and incomprehension that I hadn't. 'You realize it combines my talents and Sir Gordon's money? He's backed three shows for me now. I think it amuses the devil to be an angel.'

Sir Gordon Fairly's entrance silenced our several conversations. He counted the house with a practised eye as he swept through to take his chair, apologizing briefly for his tardiness without offering any explanation. Perhaps the trace of white anger around his mouth was directed at himself for violating his own firm rule about promptness. Somehow, though, I suspected his daughter Ashley had finally reached him. He was trailed by an anonymous, nearly androgynous middle-aged male carrying a briefcase.

He started with James.

'I am particularly pleased, James, that you were able to join us for this conference. Sheila, good afternoon. And I see that your houseguest and our newest author, the man who solved the enigma of John Donne, is here too. Good. My dear Charles, how good of you to break away from your demanding schedule to be here. Sidney.'

So the worldly cardinal was Sid.

'David will act as recording secretary for us. Harper Pease, my solicitor, will listen and ensure that I do not transgress any of Her Majesty's statutes, or indeed, any more general moral precepts in what I say or do.'

The colourless male smiled bleakly and looked at us

through wintry rimless glasses.

Gordon leaned forward, placed his hands on the table, and began to speak quietly. There was no need for emphasis and he knew it. David scribbled, Harper Pease held a thick pile of papers together alertly, even James seemed to be attentive. Two million pounds ticking away in the near corner resonates like Big Ben in sensitive souls.

'We are here because we are each, in our own way, interested in the possibilities of the Lucy Goodman Theatre project.'

I thought it only decent and honest to demur. 'Not me.'

David was aghast. He swivelled his head to glare at me. 'Sir Gordon was speaking.'

Gordon lifted one finger. Just that, and David subsided with a mumble.

'Neil is quite right. I anticipated his interest. He is here because I asked him to study the documentation concerning the life and work of my brilliant ancestor.'

He inclined his massive head towards me in a tacit apology.

I returned his bow. It was fascinating to watch a man whose control over his associates was sufficiently seigneurial to guarantee that a crooked finger could secure the desired response. I suppose Henry VIII had the gesture in his repertoire, for indicating to a displeasing wife that she should report to the Tower.

He went on at some length to state our proposed common purpose, the creation of the Lucy Goodman Festival and Theatre Centre for the study and production of *Arden* and other possible Goodman works and other works by neglected women playwrights.

'Where's the loo, Gordon?' James rumbled.

David nearly swooned.

This time Gordon actually spoke to him. 'At ease, David. These people are artists, not businessmen.'

James paused theatrically, rising from his chair.

'Blimey, do you actually mean, sir, that businessmen actually don't go to the actual loo? I never knew that.'

'It's through the door next to the bar, James. You will discover that it's fitted with an intercom, because, yes, we City types do occasionally go there, and you will be able to hear what we are saying and even comment if you wish.'

'If there's a one-way mirror that lets you all watch me, for Chrissakes tell me now so that I can piss in style and zip up with a flourish.'

Sheila said drily, 'Leave it shut off. Believe me, it wouldn't be worth the electricity.'

James disappeared into the loo, only to be heard a moment later singing 'Old Man River' over the intercom.

Gordon laughed delightedly and shook his head in disbelief. 'I am obviously being too bullish, too direct. Let us all just mill about a bit. David, push that button and we will have some food and drink to fuel our deliberations.'

The required button must have been pushed, because a section of wall panelling slid back to reveal a much larger table set as a bar and a second table of food, including the promised Russian caviar.

James broadcast his flush and a scurrilous mutter about people who start eating and drinking the minute a peer goes to the House of Lords.

Sheila put her arm around my neck and whispered, 'I am sorry you got dragged into this circus, Neil. Please don't just stay out of politeness to me and James.'

I rose to accompany her to the bar. 'If I look greenish, Sheila, it has nothing to do with this party. You must remember, I've just come from a genuine three-ring circus where I was the man on the flying trapeze, and I don't know if my insides can take any more rich goodies.'

But a man does what he can and endures what he must, as Thucydides remarked to Oscar Wilde, so I took a

small helping of Caspian caviar on a triangle of rye bread
and a glass of Pouilly Fuissé, chilled, and then sat by the
tinted picture window, out of the general hubbub.

London was below me at the end of a perfect spring
day, thick with the golden light and sable shadow which
is the rich people's view of urban pollution.

Sheila brought Sid Dawkins over and introduced us. He
continued to contradict all my ideas about theatrical
agents. He spoke Oxbridge and seemed diffident to the
point of self-effacement.

I explained my preconceptions to him and apologized.
'I thought agents were like bookies—loud suits, plenty of
East End chatter, maybe a Groucho moustache and a big
cigar.'

'That's quite all right, Neil,' he said seriously. 'You're
quite my image of an American professor. Except that
you seem sober.'

Sheila stuck a finger into my ribs and said, 'Gotcha.'
His timing was impeccable.

'Watch out for this mild-mannered feller, Yank. He's
James's and my solicitor, too, and he has bloody ice-water
in his veins and the soul of a nightclub comedian. Full of
witty thrusts, he is.'

We all looked at the view together and agreed that
London was wonderful and the caviar was the best we had
eaten that day. Sheila was shovelling it in by the cracker-
load, with plenty of chopped onion, eyes widening with
delight at every bite.

James ambled into our group, grumbling about bloody
David having the nerve to take him on for bringing Sid.

'I told him that if Gordon needs his Harper, I need my
fiddler. Same thing, isn't it? Keeps me from disgracing
myself, does my man Sid. Foxes the Inland Revenue for
me, sends flowers to my mistresses on their birthdays, *and*
only takes fifty per cent off the top for doing it.'

He hugged the calm Sid with one arm, preventing him

from eating his cracker and caviar, beaming down at him.

Gordon suggested this time, in a reasonable but no-nonsense, tone, that it might be time to talk about the table of organization for the project as a first step for putting ourselves in working order.

I stayed in my seat away from the main table while they sorted themselvs out there into something like a semblance of a real meeting. Charles did choose to sit with his chair backwards to the table.

Gordon began by suggesting that their ultimate goal might be to achieve a comprehensive organization not unlike the Royal Shakespeare Company.

'Cor,' Sheila cooed in her best Liza Doolittle voice, 'that's what Oi wants. Brenda for me patron.'

Sid passed a quick note back over his head to me explaining that 'Brenda' is one name given by irreverent Londoners to the Queen. I hoped that I wasn't going to need a running translation of the whole proceedings.

Charles lifted his chin from his chairback to murmur, 'Except, of course, that we shall do it right.'

James turned on him and Sheila both with a contemptuous blast, as though explaining football to someone who proposes to coach it without ever having played it.

'You bloody amateurs! Don't look at me with those great hurt deer's eyes, woman. Him I don't expect to know his bloody arse from his stupid elbow, but you — you all talk about the bloody RSC as though you knew what it is. Granted, Charles, they do it all wrong. Jesus, the three witches in *Macbeth* this year are three girl undergraduates in jogging suits, for sweet Jesus' sake, doing modern dance. Never mind that. Do you know what it takes even to get a mistake like that on stage? How many heads of departments there are for RSC, eh? You, do you know, Mr Computer? You? Has anyone bothered to study the anatomy of the animal and count its bloody legs before you decide you can invent a better horse than that? Seventeen heads of departments, that's how many. And thirteen staff, just at Stratford, leave the Barbican out of it. Seven full-time administrators. Five Directors. Two Artistic Directors. And a Consultant Director. This is to do bloody Shakespeare, mind you, for whom there's an entire library available in sixty-four languages to help you. Thirty-three actors. Nine Associate Directors. Six Designers. A Music Director. A Voice Director. Do I need to go on?'

Charles blinked his eyes and held up his paws, begging. 'Oh, please, sir, please do go on with this thrilling recitation. Then, sir, will you do the rail schedules from Paddington to Penzance for us, sir?'

Gordon spoke. 'I do know that the board of Governors is too large. It has sixty-six members.'

James bowed sarcastically in his direction. 'And a governing Council of sixteen. It's nice to see that someone here has at least one fact under control. The least important one, but a fact.'

Sid, apparently judging James to have exhausted his rage for the moment, inserted himself into the discussion deftly, compelling everyone to lean forward to hear his quiet voice.

'James, all that is true, but aren't you conjuring up a monster instead of describing the problem we should have to face if the Lucy Goodman Theatre became a reality?'

'No,' James snorted at him, leaving the table to go to the bar for a refill.

Sid's rebuttal continued, just as evenly. 'The original Shakespeare Memorial Theatre opened in eighteen-seventy-nine. That's just a bit over one hundred years ago, if you need help with the arithmetic, James. It did not get a royal charter until nineteen-twenty-five. They didn't get a decent building to play in until nineteen-thirty-two. You're describing an entity which envolved over a century before reaching its present model of organization and saying that we shall have to match that immediately. Nothing of the kind.'

Gordon eyed Sid respectfully. It was a good piece of corrective comment.

'Then I take it, Mr Dawkins, that your advice to James and Sheila is to enter into the preliminary planning stage of this project as though it is a realistic, achievable operation.'

'You're rushing me a bit, Sir Gordon. My advice to my clients will be given to them in due time. I merely wanted this discussion to be guided by historically accurate facts, not a monstrous fantasy.'

He slipped a pair of heavily rimmed glasses on and took his own notes from an inner pocket.

'Since I seem to have the floor for a moment, let me add this. It seems to me that the project will depend heavily upon cooperation and support by the local Council authorities. There is, additionally, no point in bypassing Arts Council support—' he looked at Gordon over his spectacles—'even thought one understands that the figure of eighty-one thousand appears to have been mentioned as an upper limit of probable support, despite your initial projection of a possible two hundred thousand in our first conversation on the subject.'

David was having kittens, but Gordon was unruffled. 'Arts Council or not, local Council or not, we shall go ahead. We will not let them do to us what they did to the Theatre Royal in Plymouth. Naturally, I shall not refuse any support, especially if it promises wider community involvement and hence support, but I have never considered this project contingent on such support.'

Sid smiled winningly, but indicated that he had another question in a way which suggested it was just a throw-in, and would only take a moment to clear up. I have seen that look on the face of a poker-player making a modest raise to keep the sheep in the game for one more round while he carelessly held three aces.

Gordon had, too, I think. He was watching Sid more closely now.

Sid asked him if the article in the *Guardian* last week about FairCom increasing its borrowing limit by £500 million was accurate.

Gordon was suave and just a touch bewildered. 'Mr Dawkins, I cannot see the relevance of your question to this discussion at all. FairCom are on the verge of expanding our network of commercial connections in Israel to include our marketing their engineering products throughout Africa. To do that intelligently we require expanded borrowing limits with the banks. But that has nothing whatever to do with the Lucy Goodman project. Here we are dealing with matters entirely under my personal control and funded out of my personal holdings. Does that answer your question?'

Sid smiled his self-deprecating smile. Perhaps four aces.

'Not quite, I'm afraid. Isn't it true that FairCom's new ties with Israel would land you on the Arab boycott list, and thus seriously endanger your substantial interests in the Gulf through your own petroleum holdings? And if that happens, and the City banks do not support your proposed expansion of borrowing limits, might not the short term impact be disastrous?'

Gordon had obviously played a lot of poker himself, and if anything he seemed stimulated by the cross-examination.

'If and if and if, Mr Dawkins. None of your if's will come to pass, but if they should, sir — this is my if — if they should, then I guarantee you this. If all my industrial and commercial holdings were liquidated at zero net profit tomorrow, the Lucy Goodman project could and would still go ahead, funded entirely out of my personal resources.'

He added one passionate, hoarse avowal. It was impossible to disbelieve in his sincerity. 'This meeting was originally scheduled for tomorrow, because that will be my sixty-fifth birthday, and to begin this project is my birthday present to myself. We are meeting today for the simple reason that tomorrow is matinee day and three of my principals are actors.' He shrugged lightly. 'If I were King maybe I would change the calendar or have matinees on Mondays, but there are limits to my powers. This project will occupy my time increasingly from tomorrow onwards and my other business activities less. It will be my monument when I die, and it will be done right.'

He tapped one stubby finger on the table to emphasize his closing remark, and it had the force of a gavel closing the discussion.

James, doing his speaking through food trick again, commented through a smoked salmon sandwich. 'If there's anyone here fantasizing, it's not me. Christ, you're giving us to yourself as a birthday present?'

Charles spoke, keeping his chin on the back of his chair and moving his mouth like a ventriloquist's dummy, his voice a tiny falsetto. David almost wept at the new *lèse-majesté*.

'I'm only a bit player in this scene, but I'll tell you this much about my friend Charles Leonard.' He suddenly vaulted off his chair and took a fencing pose, speaking like Orson Welles. 'If I am to be the Artistic Director of this project, there will be no need of another. *Le Directeur, c'est Moi!*' He impaled himself with his invisible sword and swaggered back to his seat and swung into it as though it were a saddle.

James leaned across to him with blood in his eye. 'Who in hell told you anything about being Artistic Director, you clown? Gordon, did you tell this road company Douglas Fairbanks that he was to be Artistic Bloody Director?'

That set off a general yelling match involving James, Charles, Sheila, Sid, and Gordon. Harper Pease sat with his hands folded over his briefcase on his lap, listening blankly. Perhaps this sort of thing went on daily in Number One Courtroom at the Old Bailey. David threw down his pen across his notes and covered his eyes.

The nub of the argument was James's assumption that his own proposed title of Managing Director included the duties of Artistic Director and Administrative Manager, while others conceived of the titles as meaning something different.

It occurred to me that, among other things, Gordon had permitted James to make an implied public announcement that he did consider himself Managing Director of the Lucy Goodman project, despite all his earlier protests.

Gordon lifted a hand in his solicitor's direction and Pease produced from his case a ten-page folder. It had the *Arden* frontispiece from the 1592 edition printed on its cover.

It was, as we all might have expected, a table of organization for the project, with each position defined as to duties and limits of responsibility. Gordon had obviously anticipated this preliminary skirmishing about imprecisely defined functions, but since he had previously organized or reorganized some sixty companies much more complex in structure, he was not entirely unaware of what was needed.

Without hiding the pleasure the document gave him he explained it and admitted that there was deliberately just one copy at this stage. Only James was to have it. When James approved of it, Charles would have the right to review it and challenge any section. He would personally direct both processes. When they three agreed, a staff conforming to its provisions would be hired for planning and development, with Charles and James both having a veto over any appointment.

'We appreciate your brief analysis of the RSC, James, truly. Indeed, your awareness of their problems speaks exactly to that administrative instinct in you I'm banking on. But we shall be organized somewhat differently. And I think that you and Charles—we need you both, you know, and you need each other, remember that—will be satisfied.'

The meeting got down to arranging a schedule of further meetings and specifics of places and routing lists for exchanging schedules. *Mutatis mutandis* I might be back in the Faculty Senate at Old Hampton, setting up another committee to review and revise the curriculum.

When the meeting adjourned so that Sheila, James, and Charles could get to their respective nights' work, Gordon asked me to stay behind for some further conversation.

CHAPTER 5

That conversation was to be the subject of some rather relentless review and analysis by me and others afterwards, notably the Murder Squad of New Scotland Yard.

It was, as far as the police were going to be able to determine, the last conversation Sir Gordon Fairly had with anyone outside his family before he was killed.

The murder took place the next morning, while I was still asleep in my South Ken pension, letting the weariness and mild hangover induced by over-indulgence abate.

The process of abatement was interrupted by a knock

on my door. In a London B & B, if you are not expecting
a caller, that usually means that a wandering neighbour
has mistaken your room for the john on that floor or is
simply going blindly along the hall trying each door in
desperate hope.

'It's not the loo. Go away,' I told them.

'Telephone call for you, Mr Kelly,' my landlord's
mournful foghorn voice announced. 'Down in the
ground-floor hall, sir.'

Bloody murder was what I'd have liked to commit on
whoever had dug out my address and saw fit to get me
into another publicity shindig first thing today. I pulled
on the clothes one wears for a trip through the public hall
and went to the phone, stepping barefoot on a badly
driven nailhead in the stair-runner as I descended.

It was Dolly Allen, my editor.

'Are you awake?'

'Just. Did you find another incorrect citation that you
felt couldn't wait?'

'No, something rather worse. Gordon Fairly has been
found dead.'

I woke up quickly. 'That's shocking, of course. But, if I
may ask, why did you feel you had to tell *me*?'

'Murdered.'

'Did you say what I think?'

'Yes. Gordon Fairly was murdered this morning.
Scotland Yard are talking with Gerard and the firm's
solicitors now. A Chief Inspector Stewart. David
Chaldecott, of all people, appears to be the chief suspect.'

I was trying to take it all in. For some reason the
sentence *No one gets murdered in the morning* was
running through my mind.

I must have said it aloud, because Dolly answered
firmly, '*He* did.'

'Yes, of course, I was thinking that, but I didn't realize
I'd said it. Look, I'm still half hungover and dishevelled

and barefoot and I'm standing in a public hall. Could I possibly hear the rest of this if I drop by your office in an hour or so?'

'You shouldn't stay at such classy places. I hear there's a hotel called the Dorchester in London where they have phones right in the bedrooms. Not here, it's a madhouse. You'll need some coffee. Meet me in half an hour at the front door and we'll go to a little coffee-shop I know. No one is going to get any work done here today anyway.'

It was easier to agree than to try to think of a better arrangement. I limped back to my room, spotted the unoccupied bathroom on the landing as I went, grabbed my toilet kit and ducked in there just before a sour-looking woman in a quilted pink robe could reach it. Survival in a B & B is less a matter of strategy than quickness; the readiness is all.

'It was his birthday. I know, because Dunham's were going to present him with a specially bound set of all the books we've ever published on the sixteenth century, and I supervised the preparation. That was his hobby, did you know?'

We were seated in the back corner of an imitation New York style coffee-shop whose walls were hung with photographs of San Francisco and which did not serve bagels.

'Did I know what?'

Her eyes were jumpy and her syntax was dissociated because of her nervousness.

'That it was Gordon's birthday? Yes. That Dunham's was giving him an expensive birthday present? No. That he knows more about the sixteenth century in England than many an Associate Professor of Elizabethan Studies? Yes.'

'God, this is awful.' She poked at the sugar with the spoon. 'The speculation and paranoia in the office were bad enough before, now there'll be an epidemic. Winston is ready to disembowel himself with a rolled-up copy of our Spring List. You should be grateful to your personal and household gods that *The Lives of John Donne* is out and in the shops. There are people in there predicting that Dunham's will never publish another book. Isn't that sickening?'

'Dolly, you're going to think I'm a hard man, but you must understand that Dunham's isn't really that close to my heart. I shall be sorry to see a great old publishing house go under if it does, but I'm much sorrier that Gordon Fairly was murdered. And I'm still waiting to find out how and why.'

'You are hard. Of course, sorry. One tends to see these things in the light of one's own situation.' Her tone was brisker after the apology, colder, and she sat up straighter.

'But there are implications for the entire distribution strategy for your book, given our uncertainties about what contingency plans, if any, Fairly's heirs and successors are going to pull out of their hats.'

'OK. Now I'll say I'm sorry, and we're even. We can get back to my book and whether this means my appearance on the Willy Wisdom show is a washout or whatever, but for Pete's sake, will you tell me right now what you know about the murder?'

At which point Walter Harrison, sour morning breath and surly greeting preceding him, joined our table, coffee already in hand.

'Ah, the teetotaller's hame awa' fra' hame. Now what in hell's going on, Kelly? I heard you, you're talking about that fat bastard's murder, deal me in. Do you know anything at all? Or are we all sitting here scratching our arses like three girl gossips at the hairdresser's? Any truths, however partial, will be appreciated.' He rolled his r's at me in mock judicial solemnity.

Dolly lit a new cigarette furiously. 'Oh, Walter, why don't you go to hell? I'm telling Neil what I know. And since I got it from you, how can he tell you anything? Go away.'

It was reasonably apparent that these two liked each other a great deal. Only old friends and stably married couples can insult each other like that and always know the real meaning of it.

He turned to me. 'If all she told you is what I told her, forget it. I didn't know what the hell was going on then.'

'She hasn't told me a damn thing yet.'

'Good, because that's what she knows about it, sweet F.A. To begin with, your friend Fairly was murdered. I gather you know that much.'

'That is exactly the sum and substance of what I know.'

Dolly darted expertly into the conversation under Walter's pause to sip his coffee. 'Wrong. I told you they were questioning David Chaldecott.'

Walter shook his head emphatically. 'Wrong, wrong. We got that wrong. They found a folder with David's name on it next to the body, all blown to confetti, practically . . .'

'What do you mean — "all blown to confetti"? How?'

'He was killed by a letter-bomb. Didn't Dollybird even tell you that?'

'I thought I told you, Neil. In his car. That huge Daimler you were swanning around in yesterday. He'll go no more a-roving in that machine. Somehow someone got a letter-bomb into his case and it went off.'

'I'll bet it wasn't in his case,' I said without thinking.

Walter edged his chair closer. 'You know something, Kelly? What do you mean, it wasn't in his case?'

I told them how Gordon had his mail delivered to his car en route to work in the morning.

'How simple,' Walter said admiringly. 'How simple and how beautiful. The postman pulls up, the window rolls down—Hogarth's genius rolls down so as no longer to obstruct his majesty's view—the fellow hands in the post—the *mail* as you call it—the victim says thank you very much, the window rolls up, drive on, James . . .'

'Steve.'

He raised an eyebrow. 'Drive on, Steve, he opens the envelope, and pow, as you Yanks like to say, right in the kisser.'

Dolly shuddered. 'Walter, you really are a pig.'

He thought a second. 'His real post or a specially arranged delivery, do you think?'

I told him I didn't care for macabre guessing games. I added that, on the basis of a very limited association, I had liked Gordon Fairly as much as anyone I'd met for a long time.

'Don't be so dull, Kelly. He hoodwinked you, you poor dope. Let us have our little parlour games. Christ, how often do you think poor souls like us get a chance to have a natter about our lord and master getting snuffed? It's a serf's dream of heaven, this is. We pitiful mortals, blindly fumbling and farting our way through the darkness of our limited understanding and suddenly, there it is on the big screen in front of our eyes in glorious Technicolor. Someone has done what each of us would have loved to do had we but the means and the opportunity.'

'Speak for yourself, Walter,' Dolly said. 'Some of us don't have homicidal fantasies.'

'Sure, sure,' he agreed amiably. 'And some of us don't break wind in the bathtub, either, Dolly darlin', but very, very few.'

'If David isn't a suspect, what does that mean?' she asked suddenly. Her thinking was shifting back to the in-house implications of the murder.

Walter grinned. His teeth were an even brown.

'That's what Gerard has been learning from Chief *Superintendent* Stewart. No mere Inspector for this one.

Do you suppose our boy wonder David was working both sides of the street?'

I didn't enjoy confirming someone's most cynical suspicions, but I was under no obligation to anyone to keep quiet about what I knew of David's connection with Fairly, and there is bitter pleasure in being the messenger when your listeners are hanging on to every word.

They were shocked and impressed, as I knew everyone else at Dunham's would be within the hour.

'That little bastard,' which was Dolly's summary, was probably a fair forecast of what the general reaction would be. 'I hope they pin it on him.'

Walter Harrison applauded silently. 'For a girl with no revenge fantasies you certainly come to a boiling point fast, Doll.'

'Where?'

They both looked blank.

'Where did this happen?'

Walter raised his eyebrows twice in comic significance. 'It caused a bit of a traffic jam, first of all. They really build those Daimlers, and I understand that passenger compartment was built up like a whorehouse on wheels with bulletproof windows and all that gangster crap. How's that for irony, Kelly, you old literary scholiast, you? Man builds himself a steel safety-deposit box to hide in, then he gets in there with his morning *mail*, which contains a large surprise, and the strength of his hideout multiplies the effects of the blast. Pow.'

'Oh, Walter, stop it with your childish "pows",' Dolly snapped at him, grinding her cigarette out. 'Was anyone else injured?'

'Not a soul. Well, it did interfere something bloody awful with the steady and uninterrupted flow of morning traffic on the A501 at the junction of Cornhill and Princes Street.' He smiled triumphantly. 'Don't you get it? Don't you see the beauty and symmetry and classical, fatal

order of it? He was murdered right in front of the bloody
Bank of England!'

'My God!'

'Yours and mine both, Doll. You can imagine the
conniptions the police went through when the call came
in. Bomb out in front of the Old Lady of Threadneedle
Street. Cornhill, Princes, Moorgate — one hears it was a
merry old mess at eight-thirty in the morning. I can just
see the buggers, pouring out the troops. It's the IRA! It's
the bloody Argentines! It's Black September! It's June in
January! The sky is falling, for sweet Jesus' sake, run for
your lives! And it was only one fat, rich Englishman
ending his days sitting in a pool of elemental fire. Lovely.'

He departed abruptly to return to the scene of the
gossip and to add his new bits.

'Do you know what's the matter with Walter?' Dolly
Allen asked sadly, watching him waddle out.

'Offhand I'd say rectal cancer.'

'Jesus,' she spluttered. 'Most people say, "Walter? He's
an alcoholic." But you're right. He's got a goddam cancer
eating up his bowel. What are you, an unfrocked
urologist?'

'No, I just listen to people very carefully. People are
usually trying to tell you more than they are saying. Most
other people just don't want to hear. On the whole it
balances out. Walter just displays a lot of verbal
symptoms.'

'I can see I'd better watch more than my footnotes with
you, Kelly. '

I told her not to worry, that I only listened to what my
editors said about me, not themselves.

She changed the subject abruptly, and for a moment I
couldn't guess what she was talking about.

'Does that strike you as pathetically sycophantic?'

I reviewed our topics mentally before replying.

She looked annoyed at my slowness. The English are

the world's best at keeping three conversations going at once. At non-contact games generally.

'What we were talking about before. Dunham's presenting Gordon Fairly with this lavish set of books, all bound in green and gold — the colours of his racing stable, if you please — and all that for his damned birthday. Does that strike you as Christopher Robinish — you know, wistful? Sucking up to the Headmaster.'

'Sell them to me.'

She grimaced.

'I'm not joking. Sell them to me. It's my field and the set will be unique. Surely Dunham's will want to dispose of it. I'm ready to make an offer if I can inspect them. This house has published a long line of notable books, and my guess is that any collector will want the set. I'm just displaying my Yankee opportunism.'

She shivered and pulled her cardigan around her. 'Let's stop discussing it. It's too much like divvying up Grandmother's jewels at the graveside.'

Before we parted she made me promise to call her each morning at nine. She threatened that if I missed once, she would roust me out of my boarding-house and make me risk wounding my toe on the stair again.

I suggested that we add dinner the same night to our agenda, and after a quick, wary glance up from counting her change, she accepted.

Since she was out in S.E.15. somewhere, and I was without a car, we agreed to meet upstairs at Manzi's in Leicester Square about eight-thirty.

CHAPTER 6

One of the things which had occurred in that conversation of several hours in Gordon's office was that he had offered me a job trying to prove that his theory was wrong.

It happened after we had argued about Shakespeare for an hour or so, as gruelling an oral examination as I had ever sat at Harvard or Oxford.

The easiest thing to do when you are confronted with a good play by an unknown hand, written near the end of the sixteenth century in England, is to assign it to 'the young Shakespeare'. And that is just what lazy scholars have been doing for several hundred years. There are forty-four plays assigned to Shakespeare in one book or another which I can prove to you that he did not write, on substantial internal and external evidence. Some anyone could disprove, like the three in Volume I of The W.S. Plays found in the library of Charles II: *The Merry Devil of Edmonton, Faire Em,* and *Mucedorus.* That is the only place they are so labelled, and it is the error of whoever bound the King's books. Some, like *Sir Thomas More,* are a lot harder to get out of the official canon. But if you accept my proofs for all of them, we have only solved one problem, and we both have a new one. If not 'the young Shakespeare', who?

There are five or six playwrights waiting in the wings, all with their supporters, ready to step into the shoes vacated by Shakespeare as author of the anonymous plays—Kyd, Marlowe, Munday and that lot. But the evidence you can bring into court gets slimmer and slimmer and finally amounts to not much more than a

Kyd-like footprint here or a Marlowesque turn of phrase there.

Some good plays exist in four or five handwritings, obviously the work of committees of copiers of just groups of friends sitting around taking turns writing out speeches. We have at least one fine example of a play by someone else known, but one act in Shakespeare's hand. It was virtually unknown for a text 'approved' by the author for production to exist. Shakespeare, the most popular writer of his time, never even bothered to collect his plays, only his poems. They appeared changed, blotched, with no act or scene divisions, parts misassigned, and, yes, claimed by others.

The companies of touring actors—The Chamberlain's Men, The Queen's Men, The Earl of Pembroke's Men—lived in a state of war with each other and often stole from each other, standing in the rival's audience, scribbling down dialogue as fast as they could at popular plays, and buying up each other's scripts when one went bankrupt and had to peddle the properties to pay the bills. After several borrowings or pawnings, no one knew whose play it was.

The same title or plot might occur several times in different places. Everyone knows that old favourite, *The Taming of A Shrew*, written and acted in 1590, right? The one you have in mind, could it possibly be *The Taming of The Shrew*, really written by the young Shakespeare in 1594, same theme?

Gordon knew the period and he had done his homework on the documents. He had an encyclopædic knowledge of the acting companies and their itineraries and politics. The Shakespeare apocrypha were safely in his files, sorted and catalogued. For every objection of mine to *Arden* having been written by his remote grandmother he had a detailed and objective rebuttal.

Another thing which occurred came in the middle of

one of our most heated debates. He told me he thought he had found evidence of a murder.

He started by pointing out that the evidence in Lucy Goodman's notebooks suggested strongly that she might have been a member of one of the acting companies, The Queen's Men, passing as a boy named Wat Harris.

Some time about early 1592 The Queen's Men had gone broke, and had been forced to sell off their manuscripts and equipment and get new jobs. That same season The Earl of Pembroke's Men had got enough money together to tour the Midlands and Shropshire, including Shrewsbury and Ludlow, which means the Clee Hills.

Gordon admitted that at this point he was winging it, but I let him have one hunch free and unchallenged. His hunch was that Lucy Goodman, as Wat Harris, was always sure of a job in a company because, as her notebooks repeatedly boasted, she had the best memory in the business.

Many times have I, to the amazement of my fellows, sat at table and recited whole acts from the play I had heard that day at The Rose or The Globe.

What a script thief she must have made. Or, as Gordon liked to put it, Wat a find for any hungry company. Wat a find indeed.

That kind of memory was a gift, not something one could learn. Sheila Edwards was an example close at hand.

Then Gordon's theories got iffy. If Lucy Goodman, a.k.a. Wat Harris, was a member of The Earl of Pembroke's company when they toured Shropshire in 1592, then she was right in her own backyard when they, too, went broke and auctioned off their gear and split up. Did she then nurse her wounds at home for a while, perhaps putting the finishing touches on a play she had been fooling around with, based on a famous murder down in Kent? When she had it finished did her good theatre sense tell her it was the equal of any she had seen in London, and did she hie herself back there to sell it? Her notebooks said yes, she had been at home, caring for her dying mother in that summer, and yes, she had left suddenly after some kind of quarrel with her stepfather, one Thomas Sower.

There is, apparently in a passage she wrote in her lodgings in Southwark in the fall of that year, a curious, bitter passage referring to her experiences in 'Traytor's Field' and to 'White's gun that will win my woman's secret war for me against the Dogs of God'. 'Dogs of God' is simple enough — *Domini canes* in Latin, common slang for the Dominican Friars, or Blackfriars as they are still called today. There was a famous printer named Field whose business address was 'dwellyng in Black-friers'. He was a fellow townsman of Will Shakespeare's and printed his best selling poem, *Venus and Adonis*, for him that year. *Arden* — I almost called it Lucy's play — was published that same year, but by Edward White, whose address was 'at the signe of the Gun' in St Paul's.

Gordon got more and more passionate as he argued his case, stitching it together from a fact here and a guess there. Did she take her play to Field, and did he turn her down? But did he show the play to his good friend Will, and did that young fellow rub his chin and say, 'Hmm, I'd like to meet this young prodigy, this Wat Harris?' Make the magic machine turn faster. Did they become fast friends, these two brilliant youngsters? Did Will fall in love with Wat? Did he write scores of passionate, gallant, soaring love sonnets to this witty, gifted young man, only to be mysteriously spurned? Was he the one, who persuaded Field to reject the play in the first place, out of a frustrated lover's anger?

We know that Shakespeare did write more than a hundred singing love poems to a young man, then suddenly switch and write more to a mysterious 'dark lady' who appears as if from nowhere. For all the world as though the new 'she' and the former 'he' were one and the same? Had he uncovered Lucy's secret? What happened between them if he had? Did anything happen? Could nothing have happened, given two fiery young geniuses, each determined to dominate the narrow stage of London? And, finally, did Shakespeare at last do something to get her out of his hair, this persistent, noisy, brilliant, gifted dame?

Gordon thought he had killed her.

I had sat back and looked at him in complete astonishment. I let the whole drama he had spun out of air run past my eyes again. The notebooks, the journeys, the famous sonnets, with their puzzling dedication to 'the onlie begetter of these insuing sonnets, Mr W.H. . . .'

'Do you really think that William Shakespeare murdered Lucy Goodman?'

'I think it is possible. It seems to me at least as likely as that he wrote *Arden*, and many perfectly sane people believe that.'

'It goes rather against the grain of our received notion of Shakespeare, doesn't it?'

Gordon laughed delightedly. 'Oh yes. I'm sure that the neighbours of Will Shakespeare, Gent., in Stratford would have been aghast at the idea, especially after he moved back there and bought the biggest house in town when he retired. Contributes generously to local causes, known to be a steady churchgoer, etcetera. Impossible, etcetera.

'But it was a tumultuous time, wasn't it, and London was at least as violent then as it is now, wasn't it? Think of poor Marlowe, stabbed in a tavern brawl. And by whom? Two thugs hired by Archbishop Whitgift, eh?'

It was true.

Gordon had notebooks of his own full of hypothesis and theory, fragment of fact and logical leap of possible connection with another fact. A jigsaw puzzle less than one tenth completed in which he alone could discern the pattern.

Lucy called herself 'Syrinx' in several places in her notebook. Pan's Syrinx in myth was a girl who changed herself into a reed and became Pan's instrument. In 1592 — that same damned year! — John Lyly wrote a poem which was read all around London, hawked in the streets, *Pan's Syrinx was a girl indeed / Though now she's turned into a reed* . . .' 'Reede' is the name of the character in *Arden* whose curse finally brings Arden's tragic fate crashing down on his head. In Holinshed's *Chronicle* Reede is a woman, spelled 'Read' from whom Arden steals a field. 'Reed and Field', Gordon argued, made an awfully interesting set of points for fixing the author's intentions.

Was the play actually about Alice, that is, *Mrs* Arden? If so, it must be understood differently from usual.

Did Lucy Goodman bear a child while she was at home in the summer of 1592? Whose? Was the child registered in the parish of Corley there that summer and fifty years later registered as deceased — Walter Goodman — one she abandoned when she returned to London? Or had her own mother died in childbirth shortly after her second marriage in her forties?

I stopped the flow of his ideas only by putting up a hand and refusing to hear any more.

'Gordon, you have a whole novel in mind, but it's not a history, by any stretch of the imagination. Write it. You can call it *The Woman Killed With Genius.*'

He was not rebuffed. 'Iris Murdoch, you know, Neil, calls Shakespeare the patron saint of the modern novel, not of drama. I've always found that a provocative statement.'

'It's all provocative, but that doesn't take us one step closer to discovering who wrote *Arden*, does it?'

'That's true enough,' he said ruefully. 'But I'll probably go right on hypothesizing and theorizing about it. Probably? Hell, I will. It's too tempting not to. It is, as you see, my addiction.'

He shook his head slowly. 'If you knew for a fact that only one person who ever lived had succeeded in committing the perfect murder, mightn't you vote for Shakespeare as the guilty one?' He waited for my vote, but I wasn't offering it. 'He was, as you might recall, rather fascinated by killing and guilt; he wrote rather a lot about them.'

I shrugged. 'Well, she's your grandmother. And it's a free country.'

'But take my point, Neil. You can see how badly I need a Devil's Advocate, to do what you're doing here tonight. Keep me from going off the deep end. Sit there with a sceptical gleam in your eye when I start foaming at the mouth and say, 'Gordon, that's terrible crap, and you know it, because A, B, and C.' I'll make you historical consultant to the project with the specific responsibility for putting every scholarly obstacle you can in its way, and I'll pay you fifty thousand for two years. You'll work here, where I keep the collection. I rarely use this space, and if you take it over, I'll see that no one else uses it.'

It was a shocking large offer. And it wasn't my support which was being sought, but my learned opposition. My mind fixed it and regarded it as I looked around the palatial room at the top of this modern castle in the City of London.

'I'll think about it.'

He put his hands together in a Hindu gesture of thanks. 'Who could ask for more than that so soon? Tomorrow? Will you give me your final yes or no tomorrow?'

I laughed with him at the indulgent grant of a whole day to make up my mind.

'I think you are a good omen for me, Neil. And

everyone at Dunham's tells me your book is the last word on exactly the period and place we are talking about, the literary London of the 1590s. It is like hiring Sherlock Holmes to solve a London murder. It's your territory, your turf. Do it, do it.'

There was a great deal more talk, some of it about Dunham's. At the end of it we shook hands and parted in good humour. I asked only that he let me get myself a cab back to my place rather than riding in the Daimler.

It was a relief to ride in an ordinary London taxi from whose windows I could see rain making the lights of the city gleam like streaks of gold in the black.

CHAPTER 7

The call I was least prepared for was the one that came. Sylvia Fairly introduced herself, and it took me several seconds to realize that I must be talking to Gordon Fairly's widow. I had never even heard her Christian name.

'Do you know who I am, Professor Kelly?' she asked. She sounded less offended than exhausted.

'Yes, yes. Good morning, Lady Fairly. I'm afraid you took me by surprise. I—'

'I understand, please don't apologize. It's I who should be apologizing. This must appear unseemly, but I need very badly to talk to you, Professor Kelly. Dorothea Allen told me that you do not intend to remain for long in London. Would it be possible for you to meet me quite briefly today?'

It had taken a few minutes, listening to the edge of hysteria at the limits of her weariness, before my full sense of who this was on the phone and what a painful turmoil she must be in took hold.

'Are you quite sure that it's me you want to talk with,

Lady Fairly? I mean—'

She was a no-nonsense lady, and she was having no confused, soft-core sympathy from strangers.

'Yes, of course I'm sure. I know this must be difficult for you to grasp immediately. Let's begin again. If you will call me Sylvia, I shall call you Neil. Is that all right?'

'Of course.'

'I have been told, Neil, that you already know what happened this morning. Gordon was killed in the City, in his car. The police have been here all morning, and the damned media. The whole thing is ghastly and rapidly becoming worse. A few days of this total madhouse and I shall be on tranquillizers and quite helpless. While I have my wits about me, and regardless of how it must seem, I want to act, to do something towards satisfying myself why this happened. I am determined that Gordon's wishes shall be carried out.'

She was beginning to run on, and I didn't know if what I was hearing was quite under control.

'You realize, Lady—Sylvia, that Gordon and I only met yesterday for the first time? I'm not trying to avoid getting involved or anything like that, but I don't quite see how I can throw any light on your husband's death.'

'If you will indulge a shocked and somewhat frightened woman just long enough for me to explain over a bit of lunch, I'm sure I can make it clearer than I have. Would you be willing to do that?'

'I can scarcely refuse.'

'Good.' She took an audible, long breath. 'I'm not a neurotic woman, Neil. I understood Gordon, and I will not accept this senseless attack on him by simply weeping in the background. My husband was a man of sudden, immense enthusiasms—an intuitive personality, in the Jungian sense. I'm a rather feeling-oriented person myself, but if you know Jung, you know that doesn't mean I'm emotional. My husband trusted you immediately; he was full of praise for your quick sense of what he was saying. I shall trust you too. Oh, I'm doing exactly what I promised myself I'd not do—I'm talking to this damned instrument, not to you. Can you come here to the house in Chelsea? I'll send Freddie to pick you up.'

'Please, it will be simpler if you just give me the address and let me find my own way. I know London pretty well.'

'Are you sure? Oh, very well. You haven't had luncheon yet, have you?'

I glanced at my watch. It was just past noon. I admitted to her that I hadn't, and she promised me something decent straight away. She gave me an address in St Leonard's Terrace, one of those splendid terrace houses looking across the park towards the Wren belfry of the Royal Hospital, and I promised to be there within the hour.

Before she hung up she added an embarrassed explanation about there still being a bobby and a few reporters at the gate, but said that the policeman would have my name and admit me.

My landlord shuffled in from the corner where he had apparently been listening and told me *his* roomers didn't usually get so many personal calls, and if he was going to have to climb the stairs after me much more, there might have to be a surcharge. He grinned insincerely and brushed cigarette ash off the sideboard into his cupped hand.

I heard myself telling him that he wouldn't be bothered any more, that I was checking out within the hour. So much for nostalgia and Kensington of my youth revisited.

Something told me I'd better move into one of those newfangled places with phones in the bedrooms. I had the feeling, against all my better instincts, that I might be about to get involved in Sir Gordon Fairly's murder investigation.

I didn't mind the prospect of dealing with a semihysterical widow who wanted to give me a short course in Jung over the phone. Grief disorients different people in different ways. And since I knew that the police were eventually going to ask me about that last long conversation with Gordon Fairly, perhaps it would help me to understand what had been going on if I did talk with Sylvia Fairly first.

When she had offered to send the car for me I had imagined the variety of disguises the Rolls might be wearing, from royal coach to a float in the Rosebowl parade. It was clear that my decision to walk or take the Tube struck her as another extraordinary, if minor, event in her morning.

Chelsea lies between Kensington and the river. The Fairlys lived in that small enclave just west of Belgravia. Since that was my direction anyway, I threw my stuff into my one canvas bag and risked one more call on the house phone to book a room at an inconspicuous little hotel just off Sloane Square.

The day had turned mild and sunny, so I skipped the two-stop Tube ride and took the chance for an exercise walk.

It's a relaxed half-hour stroll, but the character of London changes between South Ken and the river. From touristland you pass through neighbourhoods where hardworking clerks and secretaries come home from work, and thence abruptly towards the Embankment, where their bosses were driven in the evening.

At one-fifteen I was outside Sylvia Fairly's house, midway in a row of unassuming brick houses behind low fences and small formal gardens. Each segment of that elegantly plain row of dwellings had a price tag of about a quarter of a million, and if it enclosed a private garden at the rear, much more.

The bobby at the gate, a freckle-faced boy of about twenty, half saluted me in. A dishevelled-looking woman in a parked car jumped out, notebook in hand, shoving a photographer towards me and growled an obscenity when they both missed me.

A black maid with a West Indian accent let me in. She had been crying. She took me to a door leading down to the rear garden and presented me to Sylvia Fairly there.

Sylvia was wearing a chiffon dress with purple flowers over some kind of purple turtleneck. She could have been forty, but was probably forty-five. Her hair was shot attractively with grey and naturally combed. She had the posture of an active athlete.

'I hope that you agree it's a nice enough day for the garden, Neil. I'm Sylvia Fairly.'

Her hand was strong and dry. Her eyes were tired and she had been crying recently, but she was under control now.

We exchanged half-blurted comments intended to convey sympathy from me and apology from her about the police presence out front, but that turned into a distracted wave of her hand and the question, 'What do you like to drink before lunch?'

I took a gin and tonic and she poured herself a Campari and soda. She made the right assumption about Americans and ice in the drink without asking.

We sat in blue and white canvas chairs under fruit trees in full blossom. The clipped grass was still damp from last night's rain, but the sun was drying everything rapidly. The scent of flowers was natural and wonderful, what funeral flowers should be and never are.

I knew that my suntans and blue blazer — my before six wardrobe — weren't going to raise any eyebrows, but I suspected that my Tredds sneakers and open-necked shirt were a tad below the usual sartorial standards in St Leonard's Terrace.

'My stepdaughter Ashley will be joining us shortly,' Sylvia said rather tentatively. 'I hope you won't mind.'

I took a sip of my drink and tried to think why I shouldn't.

'She told me that you two had a somewhat unfortunate introduction yesterday in that contretemps by the lift in Gordon's building. She does have a temper.'

'I didn't know she was your stepdaughter.'

'I am the second Lady Fairly. Ashley's mother, Gordon's first wife, died eleven years ago when Ashley—who was Carol Fairly then, you understand—was just nine. Gordon adored Gwen, Carol's mother, and he loved his daughter dearly, but I think the poor child never could understand me or being sent off to boarding-school abroad and all that. Not an unusual story, I'm afraid.'

'Did I understand from Gordon that Ashley lives in Jersey? I guess I imagined that Jersey was a sandy island full of hotels where no one stayed for more than two weeks at a time.'

'Oh, Jersey is a fascinating place,' Sylvia said lightly. 'You really should visit it sometime. It's just a dozen miles off the French coast, you know, and Gordon's family have owned property there since he was a young man. Ashley won't leave it. For one thing, there is no VAT—what you call a sales tax—there, no death duties, and a twenty per cent limit on income tax. Many people would like to :ome residents, but that's very difficult, for obvious reasons.'

'I had no idea. Isn't Jersey part of England?'

'Well, it is and it isn't. The Queen is actually their Duke, if that's not too strange for you to absorb. They have their own money and stamps and that sort of thing. I find it a dreary old place, but Ashley does seem to love it.' She paused to remove a blossom petal from her hair. 'Of course, she lives with someone there of whom she's apparently awfully fond.'

Her voice had lowered the temperature in the garden a

few degrees, and I could only gather that Ashley's fond friend did not meet with her family's approval. I wondered if it was because he wore sneakers to lunch.

'I'm not "awfully fond" of Steenie, Sylvia, I love her.'

I stood as Ashley made her entrance unexpectedly, feet first, from a window at the side of the terrace. She was barefoot and wore white jeans and a tied-up blue shirt. My wardrobe was immediately ultra-respectable by comparison.

She came over and offered her hand. 'I'm sorry I yelled at you like that yesterday. Thank you for coming over. It was me who made Sylvia invite you. I want to ask you what you know about the circumstances of my father's murder.'

The relationship between the two women determined everything else when they were together, that was plain. As soon as Ashley arrived, Sylvia seemed to withdraw to somewhere inside herself, her poise bruised.

The older woman now sat back into the violet shadow of the cherry tree and let the younger one have centre stage. It was clear that she intended to take it in any case. As she mixed herself a skilful martini, very dry, American style, Ashley continued to speak nonstop to me over her shoulder.

'I'm forever entering rooms to hear someone explaining my weird lifestyle to someone else.' She turned and lifted her glass. 'To Gordon Fairly. He was a bastard, but he didn't deserve to die that way.'

Sylvia's face was a mask. It was difficult to tell if the shock of the murder was making them both brittle, or if some older, deeper tension stretched between them.

Ashley took the chair closest to me. 'I'm a lesbian, Professor Kelly, and I live with my lover, Steenie, on Jersey. Jersey is very—' she rolled her eyes up for emphasis—'I mean veddy straight. Their idea of kinky there is sex in the nude. But it's home.' She glanced around her. 'Something London never could be.'

I had the feeling I had come to the wrong garden-party. Apparently when Ashley wasn't being a brat she felt it necessary to be her idea of a bitch. My hostess must have sensed it, because she rose and took the napkins from a plate of sandwiches and pulled a bottle of white wine from the ice-bucket. It had been pre-opened and the cork put back in loosely. Invisible servants make parties easy.

'Don't think either of us a heartless female, please, Neil, chattering away so soon after what has happened. The police have been here in droves, and the damned reporters are like ghouls, and we haven't settled yet into being a house in mourning. Ashley, I'm sure, is as close to being in shock as I am, but we have both agreed that the only thing to do for now is to go on being ourselves straight through it all. A display of feminine prostration and gushy weeping won't undo anything that's done.'

'And feminine prostration really never has been my thing,' Ashley added sweetly.

'As I said on the phone, Sylvia, I didn't really know your husband. We met, literally, only yesterday.'

Ashley crossed her ankles and looked at her dirty feet with distaste. 'The sand on my beach in Jersey keeps them much cleaner, there's that to be said for it. That's what we both thought was so extraordinary—may I call you Neil, too? There you were, riding in the Ark and the private lift, and there you were, according to Sylvia, spending the whole evening closeted privately with Gordon in his penthouse playpen in the sky, and yet you keep saying that you only just met. Would you think me frightfully rude if I just asked you how you explain that?'

'Even if it were rude, the police, I imagine, will ask me the same thing, so I'm quite ready to answer it.'

I told them as succinctly as I could how Gordon and I had met at James's house.

Sylvia only interrupted me to say with that sudden, fond amusement you hear in stories told at wakes, 'Gordon was like a schoolboy about breakfast. At home he'd dash out after a cup of coffee and a nibble of toast, then he'd be tickled pink to eat someone else out of house and home. He used to say he loved getting a free meal.' Her voice broke unmusically for the first time. 'Of all the silly things.'

I sketched the sense of the planning meeting which had taken place in Gordon's thirtieth-floor suite, and explained that he had asked me to stay afterwards. They understood without much explanation how easy it was for him to spend the next two hours arguing about Lucy Goodman and Shakespeare. His obsession was not a secret from anyone.

'Is it true, Neil,' Ashley asked me point blank, 'that Gerard Chaldecott asked you to put in a word with Gordon about saving Dunham's from becoming a schlock publisher?'

She wasn't entirely uninterested in her father's business affairs, then.

'Gerard did say that he was personally distressed about the prospects, yes, but he didn't really ask me to do any more than remind your father of what Dunham's had been, a distinguished, scholarly house of great reputation.'

I had the feeling that neither of them was especially interested in Dunham's and I decided that I might as well say so.

'That's partly true,' Ashley said, 'but Sylvia thinks that Gordon had plans to tie Dunham's to his insane Lucy Goodman project, and I've promised her that I won't interfere with that if it's true. I do have my reasonable doubts, though.' She drained her glass and went to replenish it. 'Sylvia also thinks Gerard Chaldecott is a great man, of course. Did you tell Neil that Gerard was your first husband, Sylvia?'

Sylvia took a small bite of her sandwich and looked at her stepdaughter coldly, but said nothing. I certainly didn't care who her first husband had been, but I could see better now how she might have a sentimental interest in the fate of Dunham's.

Ashley talked past the empty pause. 'I'm a painter, Neil, or I'm sort of trying to be. Steenie is a very fine painter, although she's very different from me, all vegetable forms and thick lines. I'm abstract in rather a spare, lemony way. Everybody hates it. My father has left me a great deal of money, I'm aware, as well as enough shares to be influential in FairCom, but I'm not going to accept it, if that's possible without it going to some soppy actors' fantasy fund. I have to see my own solicitor later today to see what happens if I do refuse it. All Ashley wants is what she needs, and I have that. Sylvia and even a few Lucy Goodman freaks are welcome to the rest.' She raised her eyes from looking into her sandwich. 'It's all blood money, you know.'

For the first time Sylvia spoke to her in the flat, cold, unmistakable tones of hatred.

'Don't say that again, Ashley. While you are in this house I will not hear you make accusations against your father. Not one word.'

She sat back and breathed slowly, regaining her control. 'Neil, I apologize for my stepdaughter's appalling manners. There is no need for you to be subjected to them.'

'Balls,' Ashley said bitterly. 'If he's going to be one of the beneficiaries of Gordon's sudden demise, shouldn't he know where the money comes from?'

She turned to me with a falsely sweet smile.

'Sylvia was telling you about the enchanted isle of Jersey when I came in, right? Did you know, Neil, that the Channel Islands, including Jersey, were the only part of

England occupied by the Nazis during the late, great, forgotten war against fascism?'

'I suppose I've heard that, but I certainly had forgotten it.'

She widened her eyes. 'Don't feel bad. People around here forgot it long ago. And wasn't it a cosy, chummy, little occupation, though? No muss, no fuss, no nasty underground activities. Neat little signs posted everywhere—I have one in my loo—saying that the Bailiff would fine anyone heavily and put them in gaol if they wrote the letter "V" on walls or anything else that might upset our new German friends. No looting, no shooting. And the Nazis paid for everything they used with nice, crisp new Deutschmarks.' She paused and looked at Sylvia, who seemed to have shrunk back into herself again. 'Which the British government obligingly redeemed after the war for pounds sterling. Now, guess who had a nice big construction company in Antwerp with a subsidiary on Jersey that was the main contractor for all those bunkers and coastal fortifications they built there? One guess wins a Havana cigar.' She waved airily about her.

'From the Third Reich to Chelsea, S.W. 3., and here we all are, basking in it. That, Professor, was the foundation of all the Fairly millions, the knighthood, and all that jazz.'

Sylvia stared at her stepdaughter, but spoke only to me. 'Ashley has her own obsession; this is it. We are all Hitler's heirs here. It's wicked nonsense and she's clever enough to know it, but she does like to play this scene for guests when she drops in.'

Ashley was blithe in the face of her loathing. 'I said there was no fuss, you know, like executions in the streets or jackboots against the door at midnight or any of that sort of unpleasant thing. But there was one tiny little exception, wasn't there, Sylvia?'

Sylvia turned away and poured herself another glass of wine.

'Twenty exceptions, actually,' Ashley said in a slightly louder voice. 'There were just twenty Jews living in the islands in nineteen-forty. Do you want to guess how many were still living there in nineteen-forty-one, Neil? No? Zero. Nil. They all got sent on a continental holiday. To camp, you know, by our new German friends. None came back. Steenie's parents, for example, they never came back. She survived because an aunt took her the hell out of there to Hampshire the spring before the Nazis came. She was three years old. Are you surprised now that I can't stomach Gordon and his literary pieties and all this bland crap his blood money bought?'

I did not like Ashley, but she did project a frightening sense of impassioned justice crying out at the root of her bitterness towards her family.

'You are quite wrong, referring to me as a beneficiary, Ashley,' I said. 'Gordon Fairly did ask me to undertake a limited job for the proposed Lucy Goodman Foundation. I had not accepted, and of course I cannot now. I'm afraid that's the limit of my connection with the project.'

Sylvia's voice was tight with anger, but she spoke to me, implicitly shutting Ashley out.

'In your objective judgement, Neil, was Gordon fully intending to keep Dunham's as it is, or did he intend to reorganize it out of recognition, as some sort of pulp publishing house?'

'If you are both asking me because any decision you might make should be based on real knowledge, then I must say that I don't know. He did say one rather cryptic thing, possibly about Dunham's, but that seems very little to draw any conclusions from.'

They were both listening hard. People will base their judgements on the most extraordinary casual evidence sometimes. It was clear to me as I was speaking that whatever I said might very well tip the balance for or against Dunham's continuing as a scholarly publishing house.

I was reminded suddenly of a similar moment when I stood in the state dining-room of the White House on a spring afternoon in 1971, in a small group chatting with the President's wife. A roomful of scholars involved with the National Endowment for the Humanities had been invited for tea, and although the President wisely absented himself from a cageful of liberal lions, his wife presided uncomplainingly. She seemed the tiredest, saddest woman I had ever met, being bright-eyed and attentive when she must have felt very much at sea among fifty notable scholars, almost all of us on her husband's political enemies' list.

At one point she said absent-mindedly, 'Oh dear. I've got to go over to the Corcoran Gallery later and vote on that Navaho acquisition. I'm on their Board. Tell me which way I should vote, someone.'

I hadn't the least idea what the Navaho acquisition was or how she should vote, but I didn't doubt that hundreds of people had worked thousands of hours filling out forms and bringing their applications to the attention of their congressmen so that this meeting could vote their proposals up or down. Perhaps five thousand dollars was involved, perhaps five hundred thousand. Fifty people or five hundred. It would have been easy to say 'vote for the Navahos', but I had no idea what that meant, so I didn't. I told her that if she really didn't know, she should abstain.

She looked at me squarely for the first time that day and said, shocked, 'Oh, Professor, they expect me to vote, not abstain. I'm sure John will tell me what to do.'

That was the end of it. I suppose John did. I wonder which of the Johns later to go to prison for malfeasance, misfeasance, or nonfeasance in the service of her husband it was. Would my prejudiced and ignorant advice have been any worse than his?

'You haven't told us yet what it was,' Sylvia said, appearing slightly puzzled.

'I'm sorry. I was reminded of something else. Before Gordon and I parted last evening, he did say that he was going to have to tell David Chaldecott in the morning that all bets were off.'

I looked from one to the other, tacitly inquiring if that remark had for them the meaning it implied to me.

Sylvia seemed quite sure what interpretation to give it. 'Did you infer from that, Neil, that Gordon was going to abandon his whole scheme to computerize Dunham's and make it more efficient? Or that he intended to cut his losses there and simply let Dunham's become some sort of meretricious distribution service? Dear me, I think he might very well have meant either.'

Ashley hooted sarcastically. 'You're both wrong, no matter which you think.'

I added quickly that I was aware of David's having worked with Gordon on the planning of the Lucy Goodman project, pointing out that he had been the recorder at our meeting. From what I had heard him say on the subject, I had to say that David Chaldecott was very much in favour of letting Dunham's become something cheap and profitable.

Ashley cut across my remarks with contempt. 'David is a shit-kicker. He actually had the cheek to show up here this morning, po-faced and mouthing platitudes about dear Sir Gordon.'

Sylvia defended David. 'Ashley, must you always put the worst possible interpretation on things? David did not strike me as any different from the rest in his expressions of sympathy.'

'But then, Sylvia, he didn't call on you last night, even as dear Sir Gordon and Neil were playing literary detectives with Lucy Goodman's notebooks, did he? It was Ashley he called on. And guess why, all panicked and sweaty and full of self-pity?'

Sylvia said sharply, 'David Chaldecott was here last night?'

'Oh yes. He and I had a little gay lib support group meeting.'

'What on earth do you mean?'

'David is as queer as I am. His lifestyle, as we say, may look as straight as his goddam brolly, all wrapped in respectability, but Gordon found out just yesterday that David and Mark Darrow at Dunham's are boyfriends.'

She looked over at me with an exaggerated pull of her mouth. 'We're supposed to stand with each other against the oppressors, right? A little bird had just told David he was about to be dropped from the FairCom bandwagon right on his tender *tuchus*, and there was dear David, his bridges back to Dunham's burned and his free ride in the Ark a bust. He wanted me—*me*—to intercede with Gordon for him. I laughed in his face.'

She went for another drink, still talking.

'In case you don't know our entire family code, Neil, Gordon Fairly was absolute death on sexual variety of all sorts except straight old-boy heterosexual screwing. He considered his only daughter a Very. Sick. Girl.' She intoned the words with mock solemnity and shook her head. 'David was right about one thing. If Gordon had proof he was gay, that was it for his future with FairCom.'

I asked her, 'Did David say who told Gordon that?'

Ashley smiled and put her hands over her eyes, her ears, and her mouth, spilling her drink on herself as she did.

Sylvia seemed to be off in a cloud of reverie, and I suspected that my usefulness to them was at an end, so I stood up and made my goodbyes.

Ashley waggled her fingers without getting up or

speaking. I reminded myself that she was twenty-one, a little drunk, and trying to act much more experienced in suffering than she was.

Sylvia accompanied me to the terrace. 'The question of the Lucy Goodman project is bound to come up immediately with our solicitors, Neil. Gordon has already committed large sums to it on paper, and was redrawing his will. God knows where that stands. Can you tell me in twenty-five words or fewer what your honest opinion of it is?'

'I know it's worth further study. I'm entirely unsure if it's worth pursuing beyond that. And since I have some fifteen words left, let me add, I'm not the person to do the study. I might be able to recommend a young scholar if you request it, but that's as far as I could go.'

She thanked me and the maid showed me out. As she had been when I entered, she was weeping. I wondered for whom.

The reporters had left, but the young policeman watched me out of the front gate. Two cars driving by slowly showed faces peering from the windows, the staring faces of the curious who peer at tragedy and are thrilled.

CHAPTER 8

Scotland Yard was somewhat unhappy with me when they finally tracked me down.

A detective-inspector named Bowie finally made the collar while Dolly Allen and I were having dinner at Manzi's.

'Are you some sort of master criminal disguised as a mild-mannered Professor of Literature, Kelly?'

He had brought his own chair across the room with him and joined us without any introduction. The captain at the reservations desk was looking unhappy.

'I'm Inspector Bowie.'

'Do join us, Inspector. May I introduce Miss Allen?'

'Her I don't care about, unless she's your accessory.' He lifted the wine from the cooler, studied it and signalled a passing waiter in broad pantomime that he wanted a glass. He got it and filled it for himself as he continued to talk. He was a lanky, black-browed man of about thirty with a shock of dark hair and a crooked smile.

'You probably think I'm a rude bastard barging in here on your dinner like this, but will you tell me, in the name of God — ah, that's a lovely wine, so that's what Verdicchio tastes like — is that how you pronounce it?'

'No.'

'Oh well. Will you, in the name of God and the British love of order tell me why you left that place over in South Kensington —' he consulted his notebook hurriedly — ' "hastily and in a suspicious manner, after receiving a number of mysterious phone calls at all hours of the day and night"? Your ex-landlord provided the dramatic narrative there.'

'I decided to move. And, of course, I wanted to elude the police. Would you mind getting to the reason you think it necessary to interrupt our dinner and drink our wine?'

'You probably thought the police weren't supposed to accept drinks on duty. True. But since you didn't offer, I couldn't be said to accept, could I? What am I doing? I'm trying to keep my Chief Superintendent happy by getting your answers to his questions into our books. My Chief Superintendent is a large figure of a man named Alexander St John-Stewart, but known and loved for yards on either side of him as Sinjin. He cracks walnuts with his eyelids, does Sinjin, and when he tells a poor DI to get Professor Kelly's answers to his questions, the poor bugger had better do it. That is why I have been chasing your ever-vanishing figure in the fog all day, sir.'

He broke a roll from my plate in half and buttered it with my butter.

'This a fish place?' He peered at our neighbours' plates unabashedly.

'You're a remarkable detective, being able to deduce that from the mere fact that everyone in the room is eating fish,' Dolly remarked through clenched teeth.

He waved her praise away amiably. 'Ah, that's nothing. I followed a pickpocket into the Albert Hall once. There was this great band playing on stage—violins, the lot. I knew within five minutes I was in a concert hall. It's a skill you develop after intensive training and years of street experience.'

Dolly and I had been discussing the possibilities for marketing my book outside England, the translation problems, and so on, but her heart hadn't been in it. I poured her what was left of the wine and silently encouraged her to enjoy the comedian Scotland Yard had sent to lighten our cares.

She looked immensely bored and angry, but drank it up.

Bowie signaled the waiter and gave him the empty bottle. 'Fill that up again, will you? We're running dry here.'

With his jaw crammed with bread he laid his notebook on the table and jotted in it. 'Well, we've established that you haven't left the country, haven't we? Now, if you'll be good enough to invite me to join you, I'll put Sinjin's other questions to you. That all right with you, Miss, ah—?'

'I'd ask to see your identification,' Dolly said to him, 'but it's obvious that no one but a cop could be quite so boorish.'

'Good, good. Now then. First—' he thumbed his ballpoint pen and indicated proudly that it had extended its point — 'tell me the right way to pronounce this wine.'

I said it slowly for him.

'Ah, that's like a "k" there in the middle, is that it? Got it. Now, what else, let me see.' He scratched his ear, put down his pen, drank some water from my glass, and thought very hard. 'I think I'd better have a bit of fish to go with it. What's good?'

'It's all good,' I said. 'This is the best fish restaurant in London.'

'Do eat some of mine,' Dolly hissed at him. 'God!'

'I wouldn't do that, Miss, ah —'

He got the waiter back and ordered quickly and efficiently in fluent Italian.

'Now, where were we? Ah — which is proper, Professor Kelly or just Mister Kelly?'

'Please, you've eaten my bread. Call me Neil.'

'Neil, then. My Chief Superintendent, the redoubtable Sinjin, over at the famous New Scotland Yard, Broadway, S.W. 1., tells me that you were the last person except for family with whom Sir Gordon Fairly spent any time before he was — ah — blown up in the City.'

'Just a point of curiosity, Inspector . . .'

'Please, Thomas or just Tom. Think of this as a social occasion.'

'Didn't the killing of Sir Gordon Fairly take place in the City of London, and doesn't that part of metropolitan London have its own police force?'

'Yes. Fancy you, an American, knowing that. Why, most Londoners don't know that. It's true. But it's a very limited thing, you see, very limited indeed. Now, for example, we have seven Commanders down at Metropolitan, which is what we are properly called, just in "C" division alone. "C" for Crimes, you know. The City now, they have just the one Commander for all divisions, don't they? So when something as big as this blows up in their face, so to speak, no offence, ma'am, in rush the brave and numerous men of "C" division, Metropolitan police, ready for action.'

His dinner arrived, his place was set and he berated the waiter in what sounded like a comic dialect in Italian and sent him away in stitches.

'They're all my countrymen. My mother was a Wop,' he explained cheerfully. 'Eat, eat. Your dinner is getting cold sitting there. Drink some of this good Verdicchio.'

He tasted his fish and kissed his fingertips to the captain, who was now looking at him benevolently.

I reviewed again what I had told Sylvia and Ashley at lunch about my last meeting with Gordon Fairly. He listened without any more buffoonery and took it all down.

'One funny thing, though.' He was talking with his hands now. 'I mean, it's a marvellous story. Yank writes bestseller about famous English poet, comes to England, meets the richest man in the UK who isn't an Arab, they become fast friends, spend a lot of time together — breakfast, supper, so forth — the Yank author even gets to ride in the soon-to-be death car, something people queue up for years for without ever getting invited — all that, and then suddenly the richest man in the UK gets a bomb in his morning post and dies in a way that would spoil all our dinners if I went into detail about it.'

Dolly put down her fork and just drank.

Bowie ploughed on. 'Is it true that you were actually with Sir Gordon in the car the previous morning — that would still be yesterday, am I right?' He checked his watch. 'Right. When he received his post, Neil?'

'Yes, I was. Would you like to know how that went?'

'I'd be fascinated, quite apart from any relevance it might have. Think of it — no, never mind my boyish pleasure in the games the rich play, just tell me about it.'

I described the entire sequence as well as I could recall it. Bowie pinched his lip and looked thoughtful. I asked him the question that had been bugging me since Walter had raised it that morning. 'Was it his actual mail, Inspector, or a specially sent packet?'

'As far as we can tell, his regular British Royal Mail. Chap came to his house in Chelsea from the usual agency (we checked him out), picked it up, called his office, they phoned the car—whew, eh?—and the chauffeur told them when and where they were going, and the fellow intercepted them right in front of the Bank of England.'

He used his fish knife skilfully on his turbot.

'Terrible place for a traffic jam at eight-thirty. Of course, if you show me a good place for one in London at that hour, I'll prove to you that we're both in Highgate Cemetery.'

'Have the police any further leads?'

He looked up from his fish guilelessly. 'Leads? Do you mean is Alexander St John-Stewart making progress in his inquiries? Christ, I don't know. I'm just a foot soldier. If I worked for the Mafia like my brother Dominic instead of the Met, I'd be going about collecting money from strip clubs. An inspector is not an exalted rank in the British police chain of command, did you think it was? I was a chief inspector once,' he said wistfully, 'on the Flying Squad. Doesn't that sound great and hairy? It was, too. I never got so frightened in my life as I did running about with the old Flying Squad, bashing people right and left. Made an awful muck of it. Couldn't bash properly or something. They led me back here to this sort of thing and offered me a guide dog to get about London if I felt the need. I report to them, you see, but they're not required by law or custom to tell me anything.'

I tried a different form of the same question. Obviously it made a difference in the answer you got just what you asked Thomas Bowie.

'Do you know anything more?'

'Hell, yes.' He grinned enthusiastically. His plate was

now clean, Dolly's and mine still half full.

I knew that the meal was, to all intents and purposes, over. I signalled the waiter for a pot of coffee.

'For example,' Bowie said when the plates were gone, 'the postman remembers that one of the envelopes might have had a Jersey stamp on it. He knows that one did either that day or the preceding day. There were either two or three thick envelopes that day and maybe three or four thin ones. We are having a jigsaw and confetti party down at the lab, trying to fit it all back together.'

'That's not much.'

'There's more, but you don't want to hear it, even with only coffee. Forensic stuff. Blast effects on the victim, etcetera. Interesting if you're a cop or a psycho, but not otherwise.'

The coffee arrived and Bowie immediately rose to his feet.

'Hey, I couldn't possibly intrude on your coffee. What would Miss, ah—think of me?' He put a ten-pound note on the table. 'I reckon I owe you about this much. Now, don't be recklessly hospitable, take it.'

No one had made any move to refuse it.

He left, embracing the waiter as he went, talking volubly to all the help as he headed for the stairs.

Dolly puffed out her cheeks. 'It's been nice having dinner with you.'

'Well, it wasn't much of a meal before he arrived, and at least it didn't get much worse afterwards. I could tell, you know, with my enormous sensitivity to human misery, that you weren't having much of an evening.'

She really hadn't been. I had experienced one heady moment of male pride when she had first appeared and walked to the table. She looked chic, with her hair drawn back into an elegant pleat. Her dress was soft and green, and it caused me to realize that she had misty green eyes.

Now she poured coffee for us both and looked at me.

'Would you like to know why?'

'Well, naturally, I assume that Gordon's death, with the fate of Dunham's hanging in the balance . . .'

'Wrong. All that ghastly business aside for a moment, I was genuinely pleased when you invited me out for dinner. I love seafood. I love your book. It was a God-given chance to talk about that and to know you better, and you seemed a really nice, decent, attractive man.'

'You hate my tie. Sorry, it's the only one I have with me.'

'I think your tie is super. Coat, shirt, trews, boots—all super.'

'Then why?'

'What haven't I done since I sat down?'

'Smoked.'

'You're damned right. I'm dying. And I've been dying since six o'clock, when it struck me suddenly, in the shower, that I badly wanted a smoke. And then it struck me you didn't smoke. And furthermore, you have that monstrous hobby of watching people and figuring out how they're going to die.'

She stared at me with undisguised venom.

'You think I'm going to die horribly of lung cancer, don't you?'

'Oh no. Not if you've given up smoking.'

'I can't possibly give up smoking. I'm a pathetic cigarette junkie. I am prepared now to abase myself in the Ladies' Room, to chat up the bus boy, or if necessary to rent my body out in Leicester Square for a smoke. Reason with me.'

'Reason has nothing to do with it.'

'Pray with me then, goddammit. Do a fast diagnosis of my body language and tell me that on the basis of my extravagant use of my hands when I talk I'm obviously going to die of torn cuticles. Then I can start smoking again in peace.'

I drank my coffee and she drank hers, still glaring balefully.

'If it's any help, I think you might kill yourself by falling out of your chair if you lean any further over towards that woman smoking behind you, trying to breathe her fumes.'

'Is it that obvious? Let's get out of here. These people who ruin everyone else's dinner by smoking really give me a pain.'

She left for the Ladies' while I took care of the bill.

'Don't abase yourself,' I said.

The waiter said, '*Scusi?*'

'Not you, her,' I told him. I used Bowie's ten to pay one-third of the check.

CHAPTER 9

Dolly was still bitching and moaning, but hanging on to her vow of self-denial when we finally located her little green Mini all the way down by the National Gallery. Before driving off she handed out to me, through the driver's window, two packs of cigarettes, muttered 'Thanks for a lovely evening, you sadistic bastard,' and made a weak try at grabbing them back, but caught her own hand in time.

I watched her swing out into the circle of wrong-way traffic and tossed the two packs to a man my own age bedding down for the night in front of the National Gallery on two unfolded cardboard boxes. His grab was surer than Dolly's, and he blessed me profusely in a torn, whiskery voice. His bed was directly under a huge poster of Monet's *Pond With Water-Lilies*. I admired his taste. His smell was another matter.

'Trying to corrupt our proletariat with bourgeois

pleasures, are you?' Bowie said from his car. 'Hop in, I'll
give you a ride back to your hideout.'

I got into the low-slung wire-wheel MG. I felt as if I was
sitting one inch above the road.

'Why do cigarettes cost so much over here?'

'It's part of the subtle schemes of the Tories to
undermine evil by making it so expensive. The price of
stamps is another example. Of course it doesn't always
work.'

'I take it that while you are shadowing tourists you are
still turning over in your mind the means by which
Gordon Fairly was murdered.'

'Which way?'

'Sloane Square.'

'He had a postage stamp blown into his forehead, just
above the left eye. True as I sit here. Made a sort of
purple tattoo, the royal profile as plain as a photo.'

'Murder by appointment to the Queen.'

'That sort of thing. Bizarre note for them to pass on to
recruits later. Sinjin grilling them about what it might
mean if they found a corpse with the Queen and fifteen
and a half p. etched on his brow. Autopsy tomorrow, if
they get the go-ahead. Would you like to see it?'

His voice was that of a friend asking if you had any
interest in the Impressionists show at the National
Gallery.

'I'll skip it if it's optional.'

'Suit yourself, Yank. Tell me again how Fairly behaved
when he accepted his post in the car.'

I had suspected he wasn't through with me when he
had left so abruptly after dinner. He had clearly just been
getting his car positioned to follow me.

I told my story again, wondering how many more
times, to Bowie's immediate Chief Inspector superior
and to that man's Superintendent, on up to and including
the great Sinjin I was going to have to repeat it.

He stopped me at the part about Gordon tossing the unwanted portion of his mail into the wastebasket.

'He threw away the stuff he didn't want before he opened the good stuff, is that it?'

'When I was with him, yes. That's no guarantee he always did, is it?'

'Habit, Kelly. Habit is what clever detectives look for. Don't you always deal with your post in the same way?'

'Over here I get almost none. The odd letter from my publisher. Once in a great while a letter from one of my daughters asking if I'm all right. They think I'm mired in an interminable mid-life crisis.'

I told him of the flow of unstoppable junk mail I used to get at home, in Old Hampton, Massachusetts. 'I used to keep an ashcan next to the porch. I'd sort the mail with my foot and kick the crap into the basket. Then, if I invested the energy to stoop down and pick up the rest, I had some assurance it was worth it.'

'Really? You read some of yours, do you? I never touch any of it. Germs, demands for money, threats — I wouldn't be able to sleep at night if I read that lot. They'll never get me with a letter-bomb. Now, if they hide it under a pile of fettucini Alfredo . . .' he took both hands off the wheel to speak Italian.

'Speak English. Lives are at stake.'

'Where? Here?' He cruised to a stop in Sloane Square. 'When you got your ashcan full of junk mail, what happened to it?'

'I took it out to the rubbishmen the first available Tuesday.'

'Ah, but you're poor. I mean, in comparison with Fairly, you and I and that bloke sleeping on the pavement outside the National Gallery are all in the same boat. Do you imagine Sir Gordon Fairly emptied his own wastebasket?'

'But shouldn't it be easy to sort out which letters were in

the wastebasket on the floor from which ones were in his lap when the explosion took place?'

'Oh sure. I meant yesterday's wastebasket. And the day before that. Who dumped them into which dustbin? I wish we called them ashcans, that's a very dirty word. What would you like to bet his housekeeper or someone goes through it first to take out the free coupons and the prize-drawing offers and all that lot?'

'So?'

'So? How do I know so? It just seemed to me like a very clever bit of detecting to ask that.' He put a hand on my arm to restrain me from getting out of the car. 'Let me ask you just one more thing, Neil. Are those people at Dunham's upset enough about Fairly planning to use them to publish *Peekaboo* Magazine or whatever that a couple of them might do something drastic to prevent that happening?'

'My experiences of editors and publishers, Thomas, is that their idea of concerted, forceful action when they are exercised about something is to call a committee meeting and appoint a sub-committee to draft a memo for the file.'

'They're not bomb-throwers, eh?' He pursed his lips and pinched them. 'Still. A priest tried to stab the Pope in Portugal, yesterday, how about that?'

'When a Carmelite nun makes a run at the Miss Universe title, let me know.'

'That unlikely, eh? Think of that. Good night, Neil. Keep us posted on your changes of domicile, will you, there's a good chap.'

I climbed up to the sidewalk.

He roared away, calling, 'I'll be in touch.' His car needed a new muffler.

The first thing I did in the morning after coming back from a walk, eating breakfast and getting shaved and dressed was call Dolly on my own private room phone.

While I dialled Dunham's I looked over the front page of the paper I had picked up. Gordon Fairly's murder was a big enough event to share the front page with the Falkland Islands and the attack on the Pope.

'Sir Gordy', to my mild surprise, was apparently something of a folk hero with a lot of Englishmen. He came in for rapturous praise from men in the street for making holidays in the Canary Islands cheaper, bouquets from Labour leaders for enlightened work practices, and Conservatives for his enlightened bank account. His notable contributions to the charities of all faiths were well attested.

In among the pæans there was one small dark cloud of disagreeable speculation by the paper's business writer that FairCom might be about to come under official investigation because of allegations of under-the-table deals to gain the new African outlets and over-extension of their borrowing limits.

FairCom stocks had closed one pound thirty down the previous day. The men in the street might be tossing flowers, but the men in the City were reaching for their hard hats.

Dolly was still abstaining from nicotine.

'It's all I can do to let go of the desk with one hand to hold the phone. Everyone I see is smoking. *Helfen mir!*'

I ignored her cry for praise or pity, whatever it was.

'Tell me what I need to know about today's agenda. Am I or am I not to go on the Wisdom Tonight Show this week? Are these things still on, or off? Will we all dance at the Savoy? Shall I wear black patent leather pumps? I want to discharge my obligations to Dunham's and go away.'

'God knows what's still on and what's not. Gerard isn't speaking to anyone, and Winston sits in his office eating antacid tablets and rubbing his duodenum. David is either in the doghouse or fired, depending on whom you listen to, and Mark Darrow's definitely fired. "Staff cutbacks" complete with instant justification from the Accountants are not unknown in such cases. Walter calls it a legal screen for masking Sir Gordon's absolute horror of homophiles. George Adamson is rushing about biting the end of his pipe off and telling anyone who'll listen that it's unlawful to discriminate against gays, as if we didn't know, but he's really simply pissed because he must now do the work of two men. Walter says he knew that Mark and David were having it off, but he would say that, the cynical bastard. In other words, it's rather the usual thing around here, but with a few novel features.'

I told her what I had omitted at dinner about Ashley's account of David. She groaned audibly; I could picture her shaking her head.

'Given Gordon's widely advertised obsessive concern for Victorian gender fidelity, poor David's status truly is untenable. Well, Walter proves right again. He says that if you believe the worst of people, you'll usually be right.'

I listened to five minutes more of office gossip, considered my duty to Dunham's finished for the day, and called James.

He was still in bed, but Sheila was doing the laundry. The score from *Guys and Dolls* was playing in the background.

They were both due at Sid Dawkins's office by eleven, so I agreed to meet them there. I thought we might as well get *Arden of Faversham* and my resignation from any part of it settled once and for all.

Sid's office was in the Strand, in an anonymously neat low-rise building almost across from the Charing Cross Hotel.

Not surprisingly, I got there before my friends. Sid asked me to take a chair and read his current copy of *Private Eye* while he finished dealing with someone in the

next office. I discovered that *Private Eye* was neither a
girlie magazine nor a detective weekly, but a
compendium of pallid topical jokes and cartoons.
Auberon Waugh seemed to be arguing that Heathrow
would be a better airport if the unions were all banished
so that passengers could carry their own luggage. I
wondered vaguely if this is what the whole fiery tradition
of British satire had smouldered down to. *Pacet* Gulliver
in the land of Gilbert Pinfold and Cecily Centrefold.

'Now James is determined to do the play, but Charles
wants out. That was Stan Giftos, his agent.'

Sid Dawkins had his feet up on his desk, American
style. His shoes were handmade, very British style. I had
priced such a pair in a moment of giddy affluent fantasy.
About what I paid for thirty-five pairs of Tredds. His
socks did not permit a glimpse of his shins; gartered, I
suppose.

'Out of *Arden*, or out of the whole Lucy Goodman
schlemozzle?'

He looked alarmed. I had imagined all theatrical
agents spattered their talk with Yiddish patois;
apparently not Sid.

'Out of everything. He did make one condition for
remaining in, but I rather think James and Sheila won't
agree.'

Whatever it was, I wasn't going to find out
immediately, because the secretary buzzed him to
announce that James and Sheila were on their way in.

James arrived first, in full oratorical flight. 'Have you
fixed it yet? Does that cretin grasp the fact yet that Sheila
is not going to do his bloody new farce, the blackmailing
bastard?'

'Good morning, Neil,' Sheila said, waving from behind
her husband's bulk in the doorway.

Sid was unruffled. 'You've made your entrance, James.
Now be a good fellow and cross left to sofa and sit. Good

morning, Sheila, darling. Neil and I have just been reviewing the bidding in your little contretemps with Charles.'

'You're my mouthpiece,' James barked at him. 'What's the legal status of the planning grant for doing *Arden?* Can we do it without Charles Splendid or not?'

'Don't rush me, James, especially in that half-baked Damon Runyonese. I haven't the faintest idea what the legal status is of anything connected with Sir Gordon and neither has Stan. FairCom has battalions of mouthpieces, as you call them, regiments of them, and they are all determined to draw matters and therefore their fees out as long as possible. It will be weeks or months before we know. That's one reason I'd like to talk to Sheila—' he emphasized her name in an ominous tone as a hint to James to shut up—'about the feasibility of doing Charles's show anyway, simply to fill the gap in time.'

James picked up *Private Eye* and held it in front of his face. 'Wild horses couldn't get me to speak.'

Sid turned to Sheila, who was sitting calmly to the side waiting for her cue. 'Did Charles call you about his new play, *Penance?*'

'He called, but our conversation was interrupted.' She jerked her head towards *Private Eye*.

'Have you seen the script?'

'No. All I know is what Charles told me. He makes it sound rather wonderful.'

'Jaysus, the ignorance. Did she expect him to pan it?' came from behind the magazine.

'Stuff a sock in it,' she called over to him. 'Have you?' she asked her agent.

'Yes, I have. It's absolutely his best thing since *Both the Ladies and Gentlemen.*'

' "In a brothel, both the ladies and gentlemen have nicknames only" W.H. Auden,' Sheila quoted helpfully for me.

Sid added a bit of history. 'That ran for three years here and is still running everywhere else. Charles would like to write a comedy of ideas, but his real forte is farce.'

'His real fart is farts,' came in a falsetto from the corner.

'Sheila, it's brilliant. You know what my advice is going to be.'

'Of course she does, you treacherous ponce,' James said evenly without lowering his reading. 'Go ahead, lure her into a commitment with that bargain-basement Ayckbourn. Forget me. Who am I? What do I matter? Never mind that every bite you eat—' the magazine hit the ceiling—'every pair of bespoke bloody shoes you shuffle about in are paid for out of my earnings.'

Sheila put in another word of explanation for me. 'Charles is a wonderful playwright, within limits. He is also a fine director, and a pretty good actor in the right part. What Fatso the Whale here cannot abide is that he was also once my sweetie. We lived together before I married his nibs.'

James stormed at her. 'Have you no shame at all, woman? Do you want to take down your drawers and show us all the three-leaf clover on your left buttock?'

'I don't have to now, do I, luv,' she crooned at him.

'I want to do *Arden*, dammit,' James thundered, slamming the sofa arm. 'I don't care if Lucy Whatshername wrote it or Shakespeare's Aunt Tilly or Charles, for that matter. I spent four hours last night realizing that I know exactly how to do it, what it's about. It might not be *by* a woman, but by Christ, it's about one. Alice Arden—Sheila—is the whole focus of the play. It's her story, not his. *She* is Arden of Faversham. The idea that the victim was the central character in a murder mystery was just the half-arse mistake every writer had been making till this got written. Shakespeare learned something from this play, whoever wrote it, and so did every other writer up to P.D. Whatshername.'

'James,' Sheila said.

'And I'll tell you another thing, Gordon was right about Charles to play Mosby. It's just the sneaking, treacherous, bounding part for him. I'll give the bloody West End an *Arden* they'll be talking about for years after Charles's *Confession* or *Extreme Unction* or whatever the hell it is has been forgot. You get that for me, Sidney, you hear? I want the means to do that play from those bloody solicitors.'

Sid was right after him. 'Why not develop your idea of *Arden* slowly while I prise the rights loose for you, James? Let it grow together for a year. Meanwhile, Sheila can play the ex-nun in *Penance* — I'll get a guarantee of a year's limit on her contract; Charles will buy that, he really wants her for the initial production. And listen, both of you.' His voice slowed, as if he were explaining Christmas to children. 'Hollywood are dangling megabucks. If Sheila is a smash, I'll get her a contract to play the film, I swear it.'

'If!' James howled. 'If? Of course she'd be a smash, you bloody twit.'

'Shut up, James,' Sheila said, sitting forward, all attention to Sid. 'Can you give me that? A guarantee that I get the film if I do the play?'

'Stan Giftos says he'll guarantee not to sell the film rights without that.'

Sheila said, almost plaintively to me, 'I had a part as a child in a Swiss Family Robinson type movie when I was seventeen. Then, at twenty-three I stood in a crowd at a train station and waved at Ingrid Bergman and Peter Ustinov boarding the Orient Express. They cut the close-up of my face. That after two great build-ups and special tickets to California and all that. I'm dying, I'm hungry, and thirsty and lustful to get a lead in a film. That's why this sounds so juicy to me.'

Much as I liked them both, and much as I admired the negotiating and persuading skills of their agent, I had to let them know that I couldn't stay for their conclusions.

'I only wanted to be sure that, however we left it the day before yesterday, now I can't possibly continue to have any interest in the Lucy Goodman project.'

Sheila, at least, expressed keen disappointment. 'Oh, really, Neil? I'm so sorry. I rather thought that Gordon had you convinced his literary mystery was worth your efforts as a sleuth.'

'Gordon did. Well, nearly. But now . . . ? I'm not a theatre man, as your great-voiced spouse has remarked on so many occasions, I'm a book man. And all I want now is to get my book launched here and go off to the country again. Perhaps to Ireland; they tell me writers pay no taxes at all in Ireland.'

'Go ahead, swim off now the boat's stove in,' James chimed in from the sofa. 'Herself didn't bother to tell you that I'm apparently their prime suspect for blowing Gordon to smithereens, did she?'

'You? Is he dramatizing himself again, Sheila?'

'Well, the rozzers have been on him, that much is true. Three different ones yesterday. The first one said they had a tip.'

'A tip!' James gave a long raspberry. 'I'll tip the one that played that cute trick, as if I didn't know.'

'Don't blame Charles, because you don't know,' she spat at him. 'He's got better things to do than that.'

'The turd, I'll blame him. I'll squash him if I ever find out he did. As for that Alexander Sinjin MacDougall or whatever the hell that big fooker's name is down at the Yaird, he'd just as soon put me down as look at me, I'll tell you that.' He turned on Sid. 'It took you long enough to get your arse in gear and get down there and bail me out or whatever the hell you finally did.'

Sid spread his hands in a gesture of patience. 'I have

explained to you more than once, James, that I am not a criminal lawyer. I'm a contracts man. Before I could haul you out of the clutches of Scotland Yard yesterday I had to confer with a solicitor who specializes in these matters and instruct him. You'll get the bill, by the way. He assured me it was nothing but an attempt to shake the case down. The police apparently think that most murders are solved in the first seventy-two hours or not at all.'

Sheila sniffed. 'I should send a bill too. I'm the one who got him out. I told that Scotsman that James hadn't written a letter or posted one since I'd known him. He wouldn't know where to stick the stamp. I told him if my husband wanted to kill someone, he'd talk them to death.'

'I'll tell you one thing,' James said gleefully. 'Sinjin MacDonald was asking after you, my American chum.'

'I'm convinced that I'm very small potatoes in this case, James.'

He chuckled evilly. 'Well, that big devil down there might just have you in for a bit of mashing, Yank, so watch it.'

I left them still arguing about whether Sheila should take the part in Charles's play or Charles should be persuaded to play Mosby first, with the promise that he could have Sheila in six months' time.

As I feared he might be, my friendly personal police inspector was parked in the Strand, waiting.

'I thought you'd appreciate a ride to my shop. Hop in.'

'Hop down, you mean. I hadn't really planned a visit to your shop today, thanks anyway. Perhaps I'll come through with the Grayline tour next Thursday. Watch you all harass aliens, take each other's fingerprints and so on. It must be fascinating.'

'Sinjin wants to show you his muscle.'

I dropped into the bucket seat next to him and watched

London traffic stream by at kneecap level for the next ten minutes.

Thomas passed the journey telling me outrageous lies about his master's cruelty.

Sinjin-Stewart was the size of a house, with a flat combed head of blond hair and a red Guards moustache to make him look manly. His office had half panelling, with a massive black leather swivel chair for him and a stiff green plastic one for me.

He told Bowie to shut the bloody door with himself on the other side and turned his attention to intimidating me.

Thomas gave me a parting wink as advice.

'You are Neil Kelly?'

'I am.'

'Hmph.' He appraised me without appearing to approve. 'Where do you fit into all this?'

'I've no idea.'

'That so? I find it odd. Do you know why I find it odd?'

'I've no idea.'

'I hope you're not trying to be a smartarse, Professor.'

I sat attentively. His expression of hope seemed purely rhetorical, requiring no response from me.

'It's odd because everyone I talk to in this case sooner or later mentions you. Don't you find that odd?'

'I am surprised.'

'Sir Gordon Fairly was seeing you for half the night before he died. Yet you met him only that morning, according to you. You have some sort of tie with this actor and actress couple. Gerard Chaldecott had you in a private meeting the day before the murder. His son David says you were his father's lever for influencing Sir Gordon in favour of his publishing house. The son also says you slandered him to Sir Gordon by telling the old man he was a homosexual, an allegation he denies. Lady Fairly, the widow of the deceased, had you in for drinks the day her late husband was killed.' He paused to look astonished at me. 'I don't find that odd, I find that extraordinary. The daughter, Carol Fairly, otherwise Ashley, says that her late father had you picked up and driven around in his private car—this, mind you, the day he met you—and given the use of his private lift.

He sat back in the oversize chair he needed to swivel his bulk around and put his fingertips togther in a flexible steeple in front of his face. I have never been able to figure out what that means, but many men I've known do it, and no women. It's like the residual gesture of an infant cramming a very large breast into his mouth.

'And that's not the half of it.'

I fervently wished that I could think of some response to make to his ejaculations of pious horror. One didn't want to say anything which might be interpreted as smartarse, and I didn't think he'd care for my breast theory, so I merely raised my eyebrows.

'You're surprised, eh? Well, I called back to your home territory today about you, Professor Neil Kelly. My, my, you've been about a bit for a schoolmaster, haven't you?'

Another rhetorical question. My eyebrows were still up, so I widened my eyes.

'The Chief of Police in your home town tells me that you have a bit of a reputation as a—what is it now he called you— He checked his notes. I could hear the illiterate precis provided by Chief Scalli in my head.

'Here it is: "a goddam super-sleuth." And what more do I find as I pursue this enigmatic figure of the sleuthing schoolmaster through the police chiefs of two continents? Do we not discover that the Devon Constabulary and the London Metropolitan Police—my own force, mind you—and our own intelligence people all know you well enough to have a file on you, giving a very mixed picture of your involvement in a matter of multiple murder and the death of a Chinese diplomat.'

He took from his desk what appeared to be a kit of small torture instruments, but proceeded to apply them with maximum cruelty to his pipe, which he then packed with shaggy compost and set afire.

Through the resulting billows of filth more words came.

'You might be as innocent as the Queen of the May, a complete virgin. Or you might not. I admit I don't know. Yet.'

He waved his way through the cloud and pointed the business end of his briar at me and stabbed the air with it several times. 'Get this straight. I only intend to give you one warning. Don't try to play policeman on my patch or I'll skin you alive. You'll be watched every minute, and you can go right over and file a complaint with the American Embassy if you like. I'll have Inspector Bowie drive you there to make sure you don't get lost. But if you so much as begin appearing on my radar, if you bend over to pick up a scrap of paper in the city of London, I'll assume you are interfering in police business and obstructing our inquiries. Consider yourself under suspicion, and if that gets your civil rights in an uproar, so be it. Now that's what I call fair warning. Heed it. Out.'

He hit a button on his desk, a door behind me opened, and a policewoman led me away.

Instead of to the American Embassy, Thomas Bowie drove me to a pub half way to Islington.

'I told you you'd love him, didn't I? We all do on the force. Die for that man, I would,' he pledged, one hand over his heart.

'He thinks I'm involved in Gordon's murder.'

'We all do. Are you surprised?'

'Although I used that word facetiously to your leader, no. I am amazed, or offended, or astonished, but not surprised.'

We entered a nondescript pub, edging politely past six louts trying to make back the price of their pints on the slot machine. Thomas bought the first round and we took our glasses to a seat against the back wall.

It was easy to loathe Chief Superintendent St John-Stewart.

'Ben Franklin once asked the important question,' I said to Thomas after he had said the obligatory 'Cheers', 'if they are going to hang you for stealing a little tiny lamb, why indeed not grab a full size sheep while you're at it?'

'He did, did he? Fancy.'

'I'll make a deal with you, Inspector,' I said, after I had sunk my first swallow.

'No deals, Kelly. If I find you done it, into Scrubs you go for life or four to six years, whichever comes first, I forget.'

'How about if I help you find out who did it? As your chief, the redoubtable Sinjin pointed out—'

He was drinking and watching me warily with one eye.

'— I appear to have established contact with each and every person close to this case.'

He belched. 'Suppose some Arab terrorist sent the bomb.'

'Does the refillable Sinjin think one did?'

'He allows for it as the likeliest possibility, although so far none of them has claimed responsibility. I don't quite grasp, with my feeble knowledge of macro-economics which sounds like it might be the economics of macaroni, so you'd think an Eyetie would be right at home in it, exactly why the Arabs don't want him distributing Israeli products in Africa, but I think I see enough to believe they'd try it, yes.'

'Have there been any gentlemen with burnooses seen in the City this week, special delivery letters in hand, riding bikes on Threadneedle Street?'

'If you mean was any of his post from overseas, carefully labelled Handle With Care Terrorist Packet, no. That doesn't mean they didn't send it from Queen's Gate.'

'Or the IRA, I suppose.'

'Right. Or the IRA.'

'Or the reversible Sinjin, for that matter, Thomas. Obviously, it is logically possible that anyone sent it, but we are looking for the probable, aren't we, and not the merely possible?'

'Golly, Yank, is this how it's done back in Dodge City?' he asked me in awed tones when I brought him a second pint. 'We sit here boozing and figuring out who done it, using Socratic method, then we go shoot the bastard at high noon in front of the old corral?'

'Nobody, Thomas, to quote the regurgitant Sinjin, loves a smartarse.'

'Will you explain something to me, just one small thing?'

A lout hit his combination and the slot machine vomited ten coins to cheers.

'Not if it's macro-economics. Anything else.'

'How does it happen that you and you alone *were* in bloody touch with every single person around Gordon just before he died—and just afterwards, too?'

'One thing is becoming blearily clear and even blearily clearer, and if I drink another one of these before I eat something I'll float through the window, so no, thank you, but let me try to answer your acute Socratic question. If someone close to Gordon sent him that bomb, and if that person concludes that I might know something implicating him or her, then two more things are possible.'

'I wondered when your wonderful brain would finally see that. And do you want me to tell you what they are, oh, Socrates?' Bowie was cold sober and very grim now that we had arrived at the place where he had been trying to lead me. 'It means that you should be hearing from one or more persons around Gordon immediately again, and that one or more persons just might decide they'd better kill you, too. Hold that thought.'

Having delivered the lesson for today, my mentor told me he'd drop me anywhere I wanted, but that he had to go back to honest work.

He drove me back to Sloane Square and my hotel.

'Come on, out. You've been fair warned, as the re-useable Sinjin-Stewart might say, now watch it, smartarse.'

I ascended to the sidewalk. It was clouding up to rain. I felt vulnerable without hat or umbrella.

CHAPTER 10

I didn't hurry through the mist, it felt good. For one thing, over many months tramping around the Hebrides, wearing only Harris tweed against the constant chill mist in the air, I had developed a fondness for damp walking, and I realized now that I missed it. For another, I had been trying to decide whether to try lunch in the little Italian place I had spotted around the corner, next to the building with the sign saying Lillie Langtry had lived there.

Within two minutes another nostalgia bit the dust, if that doesn't mix the metaphor and the weather too badly. I found that fine English drizzle goes through a hopsack blazer much faster than Hebrides mist penetrates tweed. And when the handwritten menu outside the restaurant proved to feature steak and kidney pie and fried plaice, I decided I didn't really want any Italian food.

I cut through Cadogan Gardens back to my hotel,

wondering whose telephone message would be waiting for me.

It wasn't a message. He was just pulling up in a white Porsche outside my hotel. From the way he leaped out and ran to my side, hand outstretched, you'd have thought David Chaldecott and I were old friends reunited at long last.

And from the way he then importuned me to let him buy me lunch, you'd have thought he had something to sell me. I realized that he probably did.

He agreed to wait for me in the bar while I changed out of wet clothes into dry ones, which meant dressing up in my other, after-dark, outfit, or wearing a navy cardigan with a hole in the elbow. I wore the cardigan. I wondered if he had come to explain why he had told Stewart I was the one who told Gordon he was gay.

If I couldn't have Scotch tweeds, at least I could have scotch. Two ounces of Glenfiddich healed everything except the hole in my sweater, and made David's somewhat hysterical gabbling easier to tune in on.

'You've probably heard that I accused you — I use the strongest possible word, Neil, because I want to emphasize that I'm not trying to worm out of it — I accused you of turning Gordon against me. Let me explain that and get it out of the way.'

I stretched my legs out and let the malt do its smoky interior work in the warmth. 'There's really no need, David. I had nothing to do with whatever was done, and it doesn't concern me.'

'Well, I'll feel a lot better if I go to confession, as the Irish say, so please, for my sake, hear my little *mea culpa* and it will be over with.' He sipped continuously from a sherry pale as water.

'When I heard from Mark the other evening that he had heard from that bitch Swindon, who is secretary to Gordon's PPS, that she had heard from Marker's assistant

in the loo that Marker had been told to get my entire
dossier together, and that you were in there with him for
hours, and then that Mark and I were both getting the
sack forthwith, well—you can imagine. Panic city. I
called George, who said yes, he had got a call at home at
ten o'clock telling him Mark was *persona non grata* for all
Dunham projects, especially any further PR for your
book. Well, it seemed pretty clear at the time that you
had put the seal on it.'

It was fascinating, in a sick kind of way, to see that
there were people who really did balance their careers on
the knife-edge of office politics, as though the corporation were the court of James I. One knows that many do,
heteros and gays, but I have never spent much time at
court myself and the glimpse of that world in David's
frantic eyes was enough to convince me that one
shouldn't.

'Now of course I know the truth. It was Ashley who got
at Gordon about me and Mark. Oh, it's true, by the by.
Mark is my lover, and, God, I've decided—we've both
decided—to come out of the damned closet and live with
pride. That's another story. God, the agony. The point is,
Ashley, of all people I trusted, was the one who screwed
me. What made me think a woman could be trusted?'

He made the right sign to the bar-tender, who brought
him another manzanilla. I took a second scotch to nurse,
but I knew that what I really needed was some food. I
didn't think that I could endure David all through a
lunch, though, so I sipped and let him finish.

He was saying something I was missing by thinking
about my stomach.

'. . . apologize. It's the least I can do.'

'My conscience is clear.'

'God, that must be wonderful,' he said bitterly. 'I'd be
the last one to stand up in court and swear to it, Neil, but
does it strike you that Ashley is just the tiniest bit suspect

in her alleged lifestyle?'

'No, that hadn't struck me.'

'I mean. She lives in luxury over on Jersey, right? Somewhere out in St Ouen's, for Christ's sake, where no one in their right mind ever goes. If it were St Helier now, I could understand. But there they are, supposedly, her and her kosher friend Steenie, out in the back of beyond. No one sees them, mind you. Chris Locke swears he saw Ashley over there at the Royal Ark with some lithe blonde boy he said he'd like to get his own teeth into, I know that. Do you suppose for a moment there really is no Steenie, and that, far from being gay, Ashley has been playing her own derisive game with Gordon, just to drive him wild? She hates his guts, you know. Hated.'

He was enjoying his scenario, selling it like mad to me.

'Mark said the day he met Ashley that if she was gay, he was as straight as the Queen Mother. Mark's awfully sensitive. He actually discovered me before I knew myself.'

'So you are convinced Ashley made the whole thing up?'

'Why not? I made my story up. The one I told Father, I mean. About planning to marry the Shaw girl eventually, all that garbage. People do, you know. Live lies. Don't tell me.'

'I'm afraid I could see your motive, but not hers.'

'Oh, Neil, the strongest motive of all, hatred. To drive her father right round the bend. Making him suffer more than anything else she could do, sitting there with all his power, no son, and his only daughter a lesbian with a Jewish lover who went around telling everyone his money had Jewish blood on it. He must have opened every letter from her praying for a miracle, waiting to read that she was giving it all up and coming home to Poppa.'

'Dangerous games. What if Gordon had cut her off without a cent?'

He lifted a finger dipped in sherry and sucked it daintily. 'Aha, but she knew he never would. Because he had told her years ago that he would always provide her with a regular allowance, whether she chose to take it or not, and also leave her a share of his estate. He wanted her to be forced to refuse it. Gordon knew better than anyone the seductive power of all those millions.'

He set a bowl of peanuts opposite an ashtray in front of him.

'Look, we have two artful, wilful persons playing a game with each other. Ashley wants that money. Of that I'm sure. But she lets some twenty thousand a year pile up in a deposit account—' he almost swooned with disgust—'drawing eleven per cent interest, without laying a claw on it. Meanwhile, what's so hard about living in a beach house on Jersey, with her stepmother also slipping her a few thousand each year—oh yes—while she paints or bangs about on her boat or whatever? She's only twenty, Neil. This only started three years ago when she did a bunk out of that Swiss school they had her in and allegedly found her true love on Jersey.'

'Well, if you're right, she's not the first person to put on other people's legitimate sorrows as a disguise.'

'It's a romantic, bitchy, trashy movie she's made up and is starring in. And I think Gordon finally found out and told her he had found out. I know he was furious with her last Tuesday.'

I remembered Gordon striding white-mouthed into the meeting in his suite last Tuesday evening, late and angry. Had he just come from a clash with his daughter, and had his habitual control slipped enough to tell her that the charade was over, and that his support was, too?

David was deeply into directing his own film fantasy now, gossiping and spinning it out happily.

'Gordon Fairly knew one thing very well. No one—and please don't tell me you're an exception or Mother Teresa or anyone else—no one can actually resist large sums of money when they are suddenly right there. He knew that sooner or later, straight or gay, little Carol Anne would sigh and pick up the lolly and say, "Daddy, you are so right. It's lovely to be rich and I'm going to stop this childish phase of rebellion and settle down and marry some brawny goon in Buckinghamshire." Money corrupts, Neil; absolute money corrupts absolutely.'

All I could think of was my temptation to buy handsewn shoes for £350, but perhaps that would have been just the thin edge of larger self-indulgences to follow.

David began another train of chatter, and again I missed his transition. I realized I'd better eat something before Bowie's two beers and David's two scotches got together and started convincing me I needed another suit.

'. . . and I agree. If they are going to set up their damned Lucy Goodman Foundation or whatever it's to be called, Mark would be perfect to direct the fund-raising and development aspect of it. He's a brilliant public relations person, whether you think he's rather brutishly stupid or not. Perhaps that's why he's so good at an essentially mindless task,' he said to himself aloud thoughtfully. 'Would you do it? Speak to that appalling actor about it?'

'You want me to ask James to appoint Mark Darrow PR and development man for the project? What an extraordinary idea. I'll tell him that Mark is interested in the position, yes. I'm afraid the rest will be up to him.'

He was quietly jubilant. 'Who could ask for anything more, as the song says. I knew it would clear the air, Neil, if we had this talk. Listen, I'd love to join you for lunch, but I've got a million things to do.' He stood and shook my hand. 'Did you see what FairCom's shares are doing on the FT index?' He made a nosedive swoop with his free hand. 'One is better off out of that disaster, it seems. You know, I'd have done anything—I suppose, in the circumstances, I'd better say anything short of murder—to prevent my being discarded by Gordon Fairly like a piece of trash, but here we are, and I've never been happier, actually. It's rather dreadful, isn't it, how the death of one gross little tyrant can change people's lives?'

It always had been. Acton says something about that, too, somewhere. I made a mental note to ask Sheila where. If she ever read it, she'd remember.

My battered instincts told me that my next call would probably come from Ashley, if she was still calling herself that, but they were wrong. Never bet on your instincts under the influence of too much scotch and too little lunch.

My next call came from Sylvia.

'You'll probably think I'm mad, Neil, but I should like to talk to you about Ashley. It's impossible. She has decided to move back here, to St Leonard's Terrace. And she says she is going to claim a place on the FairCom board.'

I had just taken my socks off and lain on the bed to read my paper at leisure. I propped myself up on my elbow.

'Sylvia, what can I say? I certainly have no advice to give you about a girl I don't really know at all.'

'But you do. Or at least you know girls. Please, Neil, this is all quite unfathomable to me. I've never had a daughter of my own, nor a sister. Children this age all seem like monsters to me. But you're a teacher, you've lived around twenty-year-olds for half your life . . .'

More. Much more than half.

'. . . and you understand them. Gordon was so right about you, Neil. He said you were *simpatico*, sensitive and responsive, that you had the gift of listening and understanding, that you had genuine wit, in the old-fashioned sense he appreciated so much. Would you indulge a very lost-feeling woman to the extent of meeting me to give me your advice just once more before you leave London completely?'

Her pathetic question hung between us. I had been told ever since I was twenty myself that I was a great listener. College drunks—once a revered professor emeritus who wanted to tell me that I reminded him of his son lost in the war and who had cried in my arms—and later any number of colleagues had made their confessions to me. I discovered over the years of my teaching that I often knew far more of my students' lives—especially the girls—then I did about their knowledge of literature.

Show time, folks.

We made an appointment to meet away from St Leonard's Terrace. She suggested Claridge's. We compromised on the coffee-shop of the National Gallery. I was going to see the Impressionists show one way or another, and if Sinjin still had Bowie keeping an eye on me, now he'd get an educational eyeful of Monet at the same time.

CHAPTER 11

Simpatico Kelly, a.k.a. Nice Neil, having ogled the Manets and swum in the Monets for a dreamy hour, was sitting in the barren lunchroom having tea when Sylvia arrived wearing a tweed skirt and cardigan and glancing around her incredulously. There was probably a gilt and ivory Members room upstairs somewhere in which she usually took her tea with people like Prince Charles, while Monet and Manet performed on the harpsichord.

She accepted my offer of a pot of tea and a buttered teacake with her hand on her pearls, a portrait of uncertainty.

'It's difficult to know where to begin all this, Neil. The one thing I do wish to make clear is that I'm not going to have widow's hysterics on your shoulder, but I am as close to being distraught about this whole thing with Ashley as I have ever been, and I imagine it shows.'

'What has Ashley done, specifically?'

She touched her pearls again. 'Where does one begin? She has, first of all, announced that she will move back into the house forthwith. Did I tell you that much over the phone?'

'Just that.'

'Yes, well. And, because she will now apparently control thirteen per cent of the voting stock in FairCom—the largest single block of shares, mind you—she says she will sit on the Board and eventually take her place as an officer of the company.'

'Can she?'

'Oh yes. Oh my, yes. For a girl who has allegedly spent the last three years beachcoming over on that island she demonstrates an amazing grasp of the company's affairs. I'd guess that she has studied the quarterly reports very closely and reads the *Financial Times* daily. She has a mind strikingly like her father's, you know.'

'Blood will tell.'

She shuddered imperceptibly and hugged herself, pulling her violet cardigan closer around her. Her eyelids matched her sweater and for that matter, accented the indigo of her eyes sharply. I realized that she must have been quite a sensational-looking girl once.

'Genes, that is,' I amended my *faux pas*, as one never should attempt to do.

'If I tell you what she said next you'll think I'm making this up. It's really too incredible.'

'She's not gay at all.'

'My God, she's talked to you already, hasn't she? I knew she would, she said she would.'

'No, she hasn't.'

She looked at me aslant. 'Then you do understand young women, I was right. And you are right. All her filthy bragging and swearing and all that poisonous — ' she leaned across the table again and spelled the word softly — 's.h.i.t. about her friend Steenie was some sort of fantasy she concocted to hurt her father. She even said she had hoped when she started it to give him a heart attack, but she was getting bored with it and was glad another of his enemies had found a way to make him pay for his sins.'

'There is far too much I don't know, Sylvia, for me to make much sense of all this. I am sorry if I seem deficient in sympathy or wit or whatever, but how can I possibly advise you about Ashley? She's a fully competent, legally aged woman who has decided to go straight. Leaving aside her callous attitude towards Gordon's death, you do see the irony of your sense of shock.'

'Oh I see, all right. Most parents would be offering hymns of thanksgiving. But her whole purpose on the Board or in the family will simply be to wreck everything Gordon's done, to smash it. Once she grasped the fact that *I* intended to continue that work to the best of my limited ability, she dug in her heels and made up that vicious mind of hers to stay and prevent me.'

'Can you be sure of that? If she really has inherited her father's business instincts, she might well be the ideal replacement for him on the Board. Like Elizabeth I coming after Henry VIII.'

'This is bound to sound selfish, I know, but let me say it in any case. She will move heaven and earth to see me out, Neil. Out of St Leonard's Terrace, out of the house in Hampshire, out of any role in FairCom. Gordon left me, personally, very little except five per cent of FairCom and a bit of property and a tiny flat I keep in Mayfair.'

I was trying to guess what those odds and ends might add up to. One hundred thousand a year after taxes?

She sipped her tea and even broke off and ate a piece of teacake before putting the rest back on her plate and dusting her fingertips against each other.

'Let me tell you a little history, please.' She extended a richly ringed hand. 'If I bore you just say stop.'

I thought I'd better hear it now or expect to be called in the middle of the night with the untold historical footnote.

Encouraged by my tacit assent, she went on. 'Gordon's first wife died when Carol was a child of nine. He remarried—to me—just one year later. I had been divorced from Gerard Chaldecott for just over a year. His first wife, Laura Merritt, was David's mother. They had divorced over some religious quibble after she converted to Theosophy.

'While Gwen Fairly had been in hospital with a terminal illness, Gordon and I had begun an affair, and Gerard, who was and is a very strict high churchman with the most extraordinary scruples, found out. He is not a forgiving man, Gerard, nor a resilient one. He's never married again, unless you could say he's married to Dunham's. It was a humiliating divorce for everyone, awful publicity.'

I was thinking of Carol Fairly, aged nine.

'I will confess that one finds the religious view consoling in all this, and to be fair, Gerard has not been the least uncharitable. Rather the opposite, quite comforting. Perhaps he does now forgive this ancient sin of mine.'

If Gerard Chaldecott could find it in his heart right now to mourn Gordon Fairly sincerely, I admired his breadth of charity. It was difficult to believe that Sylvia would fabricate such a testimonial to Gerard.

'Gordon and I genuinely loved one another, but of course there were those who took a more cynical view. Gordon wanted a son. I knew that, and I promised to give him one. More than one if he wished it.'

She swept the room with a nervous glance. 'God, what an appropriately dreary place for soap opera. I failed. At the one thing I had ever really attempted with all my strength. I miscarried six months after we were married, and it was necessary to have ovarian surgery.

'Gordon was a saint. You may smile, if you have ever seen him being master of all he surveys and ordering idiots around as if they were idiots, but he was angelic to me. He came home from the office one evening and informed me that he had been to his doctor that afternoon and had a vasectomy. It was his way of letting me know that if one part of our contract had been cancelled, everything else was still operative.'

The lovely eyes had tears in them.

The very rich are more different than I had thought. Operative indeed! I marvelled to think that at that very moment, in terrace houses in Belgravia, lovers wearing nothing but cashmere bedsocks and diamonds were discussing contracts and reaching orgasm.

Sylvia was not through with her intimate history. 'Oh, Gordon had occasional episodes of sexual indulgence with a girl or two, I was perfectly aware of that. That diet girl for one. I knew and I understood. Men need outlets like that for their erotic energies, and girls like that provide them. It means nothing and Gordon and I both knew that it had nothing to do with our marriage.'

'All his hopes depended upon his daughter, didn't they?'

'Yes, and she gradually came to realize that. It made her the heir to the throne, so to speak, and I think she discovered in herself something like the power of life and death over her father. It became the basis of their war.

What Gordon wanted, she opposed. If he gave in, she changed her mind.'

She stopped, as if weighing the propriety of what she was saying, then continued. 'I really tried to be a mother to her. Does that sound horribly trite? I took an interest in her school studies. I went, even when Gordon could not, to visit her headmaster on Parents' Day so that she should not be moping about feeling sorry for herself. I think I made it worse. You're a parent, I'm sure you know that feeling of awkward helplessness.'

She touched my hand, then withdrew and pinched the bridge of her nose painfully.

'Now she is doing exactly what he wanted, yet, paradoxically, still opposing him.'

'Because she is now opposing you.'

'Precisely.'

'I'm bound to keep saying that I see nothing I can do. I promise you, she doesn't strike me as very much like the undergraduates I've had to deal with. Or like any of my own daughters. She *is* sui generis, the clearest case of a self-invented, self-made woman I know.'

'You can talk to her. Believe me, if she hasn't tried already to get you to listen to her tales, she will. Perhaps if she tries her imaginings on you and you tell her plainly that you see right through them, it will have a salutary effect on her.'

She drew herself up in her chair and became regal again. I felt I was about to be knighted.

'You're extraordinarily skilful, Neil Kelly, in touching people. I sensed that immediately, and here I have spent an hour telling you my most intimate secrets. I think anyone would trust you.'

'Some do.'

'Many do, I think. And that makes them tell you things. Gordon told me the morning he died, while we were having coffee together, that he had found himself

revealing his deepest dreams for the Lucy Goodman
project to you almost immediately after meeting you. Did
I tell you that he was a powerfully intuitive man?'

'Yes, you did.'

'There, you see? That's the second time I've become
aware that I said something quite personal to you when
we had only just met.' She fiddled with her pearls and
looked past my ear. 'Did Gordon tell you much about all
this—about his family—that last evening?'

'Nothing. About Lucy Goodman a great deal, most of
it speculation. But about you, or Ashley not a word, I
promise you.'

'Oh, my dear, I take your word for it. After all, you're
not a David Chaldecott, you're rather more like one of us,
if I may say so.'

'Thanks.' If she was being ironic I reserved the right to
be laconic.

'What I should like you to promise me, Neil, is that if
Ashley, or Carol, or whatever she is going to be calling
herself now does phone you, you will talk to her. I rather
suspect you might just be the proper sort of father figure
she feels lacking in her life, and if that should have a
moderating effect on her conduct, all to the good. Will
you do that for a totally exhausted widow, my friend?'

She touched the back of my hand again and let me look
deeply into her once spectacular indigo eyes.

I wondered if I wanted to be a father figure to a girl
who had tried so hard to kill her last father, but I didn't
really expect that the call would ever come, so I agreed.
After all, if I am, at bottom, one of them . . .

CHAPTER 12

No one had suspected that there were two letter-bombs in Gordon's lap that morning rather than one.

'Could have been three actually,' Bowie grunted morosely. He was chewing a toothpick and reading the football results as he drank and talked.

Since he had indicated that everyone at Scotland Yard, up to and including the recessive Sinjin, had been dumbfounded when Forensics had brought in the analysis of more than one letter-bomb, I didn't mind appearing astonished.

'But that doesn't make any sense.'

'Hmm?' He took a sip of bitter and winced at something Liverpool had done to Arsenal. 'Why not?'

'I don't know, it just doesn't. You're the cop, does it make any sense to you?'

'No. I just thought your keen American scholar's mind might respond creatively if I challenged you. Trick they teach us in cop school. It never works.'

'Are letter-bombs particularly unreliable?'

'Hmm? How am I supposed to read my damned paper if you keep mumbling questions at me?'

'Are they unreliable? If I wanted to kill you with a letter-bomb, and I wanted to be absolutely sure I got it done right in one, would that be a reason for sending two?'

'Might do. But have you thought about coincidence, Professor Kelly? Have you considered the fell hand of coincidence? And what does "fell" mean, used like that?'

'Fierce or terrible. It's considered obsolete.'

'Well, so is Sir Gordon, so to speak, may God rest his rich, roasted old soul.'

'Do you think he was a good man, on balance, Thomas, or a bad one?'

He folded his paper into a pocket and considered the question. We were back in my pub this time, the St James's in Soho. He looked around admiringly.

'I must say you have a nice local here, Neil. It's a hard thing, as the archactress said to the archbishop, isn't it, to tell that about any man. But if I had to come down on one side or t'other, I'd say he was a right first division bastard.'

'That's not what the papers say. Tributes from high and low, actresses and archbishops alike. Cheap flights to Spain, all that. Make him sound like the greatest thing since Robin Hood.'

'Our old friend the man in the bloody street, is it? That chap is a figment of the bloody impoverished imaginations of the drunken slobs who put together these tit and bum papers for people like me to read. Cheap holidays, is it?' He lifted one buttock and farted savagely.

'I'll be banned here for bringing you in. I don't think much of your coincidence theory, anyway.'

He smiled beatifically. 'Neither did the retractable Sinjin when I suggested it in our staff meeting this morning. He suggested I hire my own computer and try to compute the odds of two murderers having exactly the same m.o. at exactly the same moment. Fair disgusted he was. It was a fine sight to see. Cheered me up right through lunch-time.'

'Then it has to be the work of a somewhat compulsive personality, doesn't it?'

'Well, Professor Young, ja, ja, dat might be zo. Did Sylvia Fairly get on to you, too, about Professor Carl Young and Sir Gordon's intuitions and all that bumf? She's a riot when she gets going, our Sylvie. She told Sinjin that from a Youngian point of view he was approaching the whole thing sensationally. He didn't know whether to shit or sing alto. The rest of us were all falling about while he tried to decide whether to arrest her for slander or take a short swim in those purple pools.'

'Jung. With a "J", but pronounced like "Y". You may smile inwardly at my naïveté if you already knew that. The adjective is "Jungian".'

'No, I didn't know that. Italian I know; that's my party trick. German or Swiss or whatever I don't know from ancient Greek. I'm grateful. I won't fart in your pub any more, just to show you.'

He raised his hand as if taking an oath. I didn't know if this was a new level of kidding he had moved to, but I liked him and I didn't really care. I suspected that Thomas Bowie had been born with an intelligence which had not quite fitted within the confines of the eleven-plus and O-levels and A-levels system of education, and he had been shunted out of the chance of an education before he knew what was going on.

He explained to me what the forensic tests had shown: that when the explosive in Gordon's hand had detonated, or just a millisecond later, too fast for there to have been a discernible second blast, something in his lap had also blown up.

'The chauffeur said it sounded like one big wallop to him. He said he thought a bomb had hit them, or something like an aeroplane had crashed and a piece of it had hit them. The Daimler lifted about three feet in the air, he says it felt like, then it was like he was being pushed in the back of the head.'

'Two is fantastic enough. Three is crazy.'

'Tell Sinjin. He'll be thrilled to have your point of view. He's always telling us soldiers not be afraid to present our point of view. Anyway, the lab thinks they have enough pieces to add up to three, maybe.'

'Has your computer told you yet what the odds are on that? Three villains all with the same m.o. at the same point in time?'

'Better than three to one was the closest I could get. More like five or six to one, I don't doubt. Very long odds, anyway.'

After half an hour he left the table to make a phone call. 'Be back. Mate at the office said he'd let me know the final score.'

When he returned he was holding up three fingers.

'Three. I'll be damned.'

'Makes you larf, dunnit? I can see the lab sharks down there, sticking their bloody heads under the ultra-violent hoods and screwing microscopes into their good eye, bobbing up and down like those Chinese dolls on a stick. I see one. Blimey, I see two. Anyone for three? I think I see three, no, no, wait a bloody minute, there's thousands of the buggers . . .'

'Curiouser and curiouser.'

'One in the wastebasket on the floor, they think. That's the one I like.'

'Why that one?'

'Must be the one he threw away, mustn't it?'

'If I wanted to kill someone with a letter-bomb, why would I send him one I knew or suspected he'd toss in the wastebasket unopened?'

'Insurance by mail scheme?'

I looked at him uncomprehending.

'Look, suppose you wanted the bugger to throw it away, and you knew he'd throw it into the wastebasket at his feet, and you knew that the one — or two — he didn't throw away would detonate it anyway. It gives you a little insurance, dunnit? Spreads the blast about a bit, in case number one only blows off his ear and number two only blows off his left nut, there's good old number three, making sure by blowing off his left great toe. Always fatal that, the loss of the left great toe. Learned about that in cop school.'

As he talked he was watching with close interest the progress of a chesty young woman wearing a St James's Tavern T-shirt as she carried two dripping glasses at arm's length to her girlfriend.

'I think I'll get myself one of those,' he murmured appreciatively. 'Do you think it will look as good on me as it does on her?'

'Is it very hard for an ordinary person to get his hands on one?'

He glanced at me coyly. 'A T-shirt or what's wearing it?'

'A letter-bomb.'

'Ah, those! Christ, it used to be impossible. Now you can buy a magazine up the street that will show you how to do it in your basement workshop or mail in the bloody coupon and they'll send you the kit to assemble. It's like handguns. When I started on this job, you never expected to meet a bloke with one. Now half the yobs out there probably have one stuck up their armpit. We call it the American influence. Dead easy, I'd say, if you know where to shop and have the price.'

'What do you think?'

'I'm letting the repellent Sinjin do the thinking for both of us. My job is to keep you and that lass with the enormous lungs over there under surveillance.'

'Do you tell them back at Scotland Yard everything I do?'

'Every jot and every tittle. Scratch your arse and in my report it goes. And I have my own network of agents helping me night and day. Actually that bird there with the tremendous jugs is one of mine. You probably saw her give me the secret sign when she went by. I'll get her full report later on. I'll sweat it out of her if I have to.'

'Well, save yourself some effort. I'll tell you now that I'm off to see my editor. You can stay here and debrief your mate.'

'Good show, old chap. Do watch for any suspicious bulky letters in your post, won't you?'

'Who knows where I live at the moment? It's not likely.'

'Always a first time, as the starlet said to the seminarian.'

When I left him he was brooding over Arsenal's mistakes again, with an occasional glance at the two birds across the room.

There was a special delivery letter waiting for me at the desk when I returned to my hotel. The clerk, a young Asian in a tight, powder blue suit, called after me as I headed for the stairs. He pulled a fat brown envelope from the shelf behind him and tossed it on the counter.

'This came for you just an hour ago, Mr Kelly, sir.'

He seemed a bit puzzled by my frozen inability to walk across to him and pick it up.

'Are you sure it's for me? Neil Kelly?' I asked him a little breathlessly. I felt suddenly as I recall having felt once when I was very young, awaiting a letter to tell me if I had won a scholarship or not. 'Only my whole life depends on it,' I had said to myself as I picked it off my mother's front hall table.

'Who brought it?' I called over to him.

'Sorry, Mr Kelly, sir, I don't know. Erica was on the desk then. She told me to be sure you got it. I read in the *Mail* that you're going to be on the Wisdom Tonight show.' He smiled brilliantly. He was clearly thrilled to be so close to glamour. I wondered how thrilled he'd be if I told him how close he might be to a bomb.

I felt like a complete horse's ass, but that didn't make me move any faster. Here was a piece of mail in the familiar brown British envelope. It had my name clearly typed on it, and the name of the hotel. The words *Private and Confidential* were doubly underlined in the lower left corner.

I could hardly ask the clerk to open it for me. Nor could I ask him to put it back on the shelf until I called Thomas Bowie and asked for his advice. A woman with a young boy in tow came to the desk to ask about the hours of meal service. I stepped forward and put myself between them and the letter, although it meant giving her little boy a tough nudge with my hip.

She frowned at me and grabbed his hand. 'Come with mother, Robert,' she hissed, and they hurried off.

I am normally one of those diffident souls who would rather suffer personal catastrophe than cause public commotion. Now I felt suddenly in a position to do both at once.

I reviewed sweatily what I knew about letter-bombs. Why hadn't I paid attention to those paragraphs in the papers with the cutaway drawings showing how they worked? I had thought them ghoulish and resented the comic-strip journalism at the time. I glanced around to see if anyone had left a paper in the lobby. Confront an academic with a problem and he'll start looking for the research angle.

They didn't explode until ripped open, of that I was reasonably sure. Unless detonated by another explosion nearby. Or perhaps if jarred suddenly. It seemed to me that I had read of mailmen being injured just handling them.

I swallowed, or tried to, and picked up the envelope very carefully. My fingers seemed much thicker than I remembered them being, and I dropped it. I closed my eyes for one long moment and picked it up again, trying to hold it hard enough to retain a grip without squeezing it.

The only decent thing to do was to get the damned thing to my room as quickly and silkily as possible and call Scotland Yard. I wondered in a rag-end of panic if dialling a telephone could set off a bomb, or was that the use of a walkie-talkie? I had read that somewhere, too.

The clerk was watching me with complete absorption now. 'It's a very big thing,' he said.

I nodded insanely, staring at it. Once he said that, it actually seemed to be getting slightly larger as I looked at it. I must move.

'I wish I could go on the William Wisdom show, yes.'

Apparently I didn't answer him, so he thought I might be deaf. He shouted, 'I am hoping to be a writer, too, sir!'

I dropped the letter.

He pounded on it with his forefinger, right in the centre of the *WW* monogram, encircled in blue, in the centre of the back flap. 'I see that even you, a famous writer, are excited. I can see that,' he bellowed in my ear.

I took a slow breath. It was from my old chum Wisdom, of course. I picked it up and fanned myself with it casually.

'Yes, he said he'd be sending this by. Thanks so much.'

I walked with great steadiness up the one flight to my room, where I sat down on the bed feeling like a great fool.

I looked at the offending packet which had brought out some of my worst traits so easily and was quietly glad that the sarcastic Bowie hadn't been there to witness my panic. Or worse, hadn't been actually called, bomb squad mates all in asbestos suits, to remove the threatening envelope from the hotel to be opened under water or riddled with machine-gun bullets or whatever they do to suspected terrorist mail.

I held it in my hand and permitted the last of my self-disgust to ebb away. Fear is nothing, it's the shame that follows it that's hard to live with.

If I was ever going to know what the Wisdom wanted to tell me, I was going to have to open the thing. Probably his own PR releases for my scheduled appearance and times for getting to Make-up, etc.

Unless, of course, someone in a position to know that I was expecting an agenda from Wisdom had simply picked up one of his office envelopes and popped my gift bomb into it.

Back to square one, suddenly just as scared. I had a thick envelope in my hand which might contain a bomb. Shame fled before a fresh bout of fear. I put it down on the bed and put a pillow on top of it, realizing as I did so that it was the hopeless gesture of a bankrupt intelligence. I said a fast silent prayer and repeated it. I repeated it again. I went into the bathroom and shut the door.

I suddenly had to urinate urgently. As I did so, I had a foolish glimpse of myself in the mirror and saw what an undignified way it would be to die, pants open, penis in hand. I flushed, wondering if a flush could set it off.

If these indignities were filmed and I were made to watch them over and over later, it would be definition enough of purgatory. If I had felt like a fool before, now I felt like a moron, cowering in the john, afraid of my mail.

There is a time to assert one's sense of proportion and priority, and it was certainly such a moment. Either that or spend the rest of the day hiding behind the washbasin until the maid came and saved me. It isn't heroism, it's ordinary common sense taking over from ingenuity and imagination when their resources are sunk.

I opened the bathroom door, walked to the bed, took the damned envelope by the corner from beneath the pillow, walked back into the bathroom, and put it gently but firmly into the toilet and closed the lid.

I left the room immediately, hanging the Do Not Disturb sign on the outer knob so that no maid eager for a tip should go in to freshen my towels.

From the lobby I called the St James's Tavern and asked them if a gentleman answering Thomas's description was sitting at one of the back tables.

They told me he had just left in the company of a girl

wearing a St James's T-shirt. Apparently she really was one of his undercover operatives.

I called Scotland Yard and left a message for him to call me soonest. Then I went to keep my date with my editor.

'That's certainly the first place I'd think of putting anything from him,' was her first remark after I had confessed most of my pusillanimity.

'But I must either decide to take it out of there and open it or I can never use my john again.'

'Does this Bowie character actually think that whoever killed Gordon is going to try it on you?' She seemed to think it a dubious thesis at best.

'Don't you?'

'It's the silliest thing I ever heard.'

She wasn't leaving me much pride.

She reached into her In-tray and tossed a handful of unopened mail into the air lightly. 'I'm not afraid to open this lot, just a typical two days behind with it. Dora has been ill for a week with some mysterious viral ailment, and the temporary help who arrive periodically all seem unable to read or write English.'

'Why don't the English teach their children, etcetera.'

'Bloody schools are no good is why. You should hear me on that line sometime when you have a good long holida to spend listening.'

'Everyone needs a hobby. If you don't bore me with yours, I won't bore you with mine.'

She bristled. 'Political and social reform is not a hobby, Yank. It's a commitment. You either care about the quality of life and education and housing and childcare and work conditions in the society you're responsible for or you deserve what you get. Garbage.'

I looked around her battered, cluttered, two-hundred-year-old office. Her view was a brick wall two feet away.

The window obviously wouldn't open and hadn't been opened for a century. There was a water stain the shape and almost the size of Australia on her ceiling, and the plaster sagged perceptibly.

'Then why do you put up with working in this rotting cell, using a twenty-five-year-old typewriter, two flights of stairs up from your own department? I should think your first priority for improving anyone's work conditions would be right here.'

'Are you mad?' She looked around her office proudly. 'It took me twelve years to work my way up to this. What you see as rotting, I see as hallowed. Would you call a mediæval church rotting, just because it's mildewed and falling down? Besides, I'm a professional class person, and it's the working-class person who needs help.' She grinned delightedly. 'You're right about the way they think of it, though. One of the temps was here just half a day before she told Winston, "Oi'd rather sell home perm kits in Woolworths than stick in this dump. This plice is fallen dahn, innit?" '

'I didn't know you had sold home perm kits in Woolworth's before coming here, Dolly. I knew you didn't know much about editing, but this explains everything.'

Walter Harrison had come through the closed door unannounced by any knock. An unlit cigarette was pasted ostentatiously to his lower lip.

'Go back to your own rotting room, Walter. I am conferring with this very classy American writer who is pretending not to be impressed by sitting in the same chair once graced by the bottom of Fielding.'

I looked at my chair. It was standard bentwood drugstore type, circa 1930.

'Not Joseph, you fool,' she said airily. 'Gabriel.'

'Gerard is on his way up,' Walter announced. 'Do you persist in your infamous pretence of having given up tobacco? Where am I to get matches? You —' he rounded on me. 'I blame you for this unseasonable reformation of this woman's habits. What entitles you to come barging into our country preaching the gospel according to H.M.G. Health Departments and upsetting the lives of perfectly happy, slovenly people with filthy, disgusting, self-destructive habits, eh?'

'Nonsense, I don't believe you,' Dolly snapped at him. 'The last time Gerard was up here was in nineteen-seventy-six, to tell me that he had been selected by lot to tell me that I had been selected by lot to run the office Christmas party.'

Walter found a single wooden match in his jacket after much conspicuous rummaging, lit it on his thumbnail and applied it to his cigarette.

'Ahhh.' He crooned the word, making the act of inhaling poison gas seem an ecstatic joy.

Dolly ignored him, speaking to me.

'You are going to think we do nothing around here but have drunken parties and play childish games in our rotten rooms. Please understand that we are all somewhat at sea in recent days.'

A polite, almost inaudible knock on the outer door preceeded Gerard Chaldecott's upper body leaning in.

'May I? I'm not interrupting anything, am I?'

Walter blew smoke at the ceiling in exasperation. 'Gerard, for Christ's sake, come in. You own the place, remember? If you want to interrupt a serious editorial conference with our currently bestselling author, do it, do it, but don't pussyfoot.'

Everyone apparently was expected to tolerate Walter.

'Good afternoon, Dolly. Good afternoon, Neil.' He was bowing left and right in the best mandarin fashion, dressed immaculately in a navy chalkstripe suit so muted that it almost looked ready made. 'I'm glad you're here, Walter, actually.'

Walter Harris stopped in mid-stride towards his own office door to do a music hall double take.

'May I sit here?' Gerard gingerly lifted a pile of page proofs off the only other chair in the office and set them atop another pile on the filing cabinet. It was, I was sure, an act of heroic self-denial that he did not dust the chair with his handkerchief before he sat on its edge. Gerard Chaldecott remained an exceptionally tidy, well-groomed man, however rumpled the look his face wore these days.

'If you came up to talk with Neil privately, Gerard, Walter and I can go somewhere else,' Dolly assured him.

'Sure,' Walter said to the brick wall outside the window, 'we can go to *your* office and throw your papers around and smoke your Havana cigars.'

Gerard approved of Walter's studied rudeness with a cheerful nod. 'Dolly, my dear, if I had wanted to send Marilyn up here to fetch Neil for me, I could have done it quite simply. No, I *want* you and Walter here, I really do.'

He looked around him like a stranger visiting rather than the proprietor of the store.

'This is where Dunham's lives, where it has its soul, Neil, in rooms like this. This is where the work gets done. Not down in the boardroom or in my office. Here. Permit me to indulge in a moment of foolish reminiscence, but that office next door, your office, Walter, was mine once for five years. Before the war. I don't mind telling you that when I retire from Dunham's, it will be those five years I shall look back on as the best, not these of my seniority.'

'If you want it back, go right ahead,' Walter rasped. 'Then you can have a mile run to the bog every morning.'

I was beginning to feel like the intruder. Dolly and Walter settled back, as though they knew Gerard in this garrulous old boy strain and accepted the necessity of hearing him out.

'Whatever happens to Dunham's now, I shall be stepping down as President and Chairman forthwith, and I want all my senior staff, to know that. I have said this to Winston, and I shall continue my sad pilgrimage from room to room in this remarkable rabbit warren of a place until I have personally said it to all of you.'

'It's the wrong move, Gerard. There's no one in the shop who can do your job,' Walter said with characteristic bluntness.

'It's the right move, Walter,' he answered sharply. 'Whatever the job of my successor will be — and as you all know, I had fondly and foolishly expected my son David to be the fifth Chaldecott to occupy that chair — it will not be the one I have done.'

Some of the tension went out of him and he seemed drawn fine, down to some last level of resources.

'Sylvia Fairly has told me personally — I am not sharing this with everyone, but you, Dolly, are my own dear favourite among the editors, and if I have never said that before, so much the better to say it now. And as for you, Walter, we all know that you were the best editor Dunham's ever had when you chose to be, and I still cherish your honesty. When I can't be sure if anyone else is telling me the truth, Walter, I know that you are.'

He brushed his tiny moustache abstractedly, unbuttoned and buttoned his jacket.

'Dear, dear, this is beginning to sound like a Papal visit.'

'Spit it out, Gerard,' Walter growled at him, as he knew he was expected to. 'If you're going to totter about the building handing out plenary indulgences on your lachrymose way, do at least try to be coherent.'

'Sylvia told me that she would bend every effort to save Dunham's. As it is now; a serious, scholarly and proud publishing house.'

Dolly clapped her hands. 'Hallelujah for that.'

Gerard's response was drier. 'Yes. But it is clear that, whatever the fallout from Sir Gordon's untimely death, she very well might not have the final say in whatever is done.' He gestured helplessly. 'Neil, has Sylvia told you about all this already?'

The two editors both looked at me amazed. I had to admit, in the face of their obvious puzzlement about why the hell I had been consulted by the widow Fairly, that she had indeed taken the trouble to tell me about all this.

'The problem,' I said to them, 'seems to be the mercurial Ashley, née Carol Fairly.'

'Precisely,' Gerard said, looking ashen and helpless again. 'And I shall not stay at Dunham's to preside over the savaging of this house by a person like that.'

'I wonder if that isn't exactly what Dunham's needs now, Gerard, your guiding hand. Who else has your knowledge of the company, your savvy, to use an Americanism for the moment? What hope is there for Dunham's ever surviving her influence without that?'

Dolly and Walter added their passionate and sarcastic votes against Gerard's decision, but he heard them out unruffled and unmoved.

'I have said what I came to say to you two. Now, if I may, I shall take Neil away from you and impose a bit further on our friendship downstairs.'

He rose, and I saw no course open to me but to rise with him and accompany him back downstairs. I realized that I had never got any final assurance from my conversation with Dolly that there was not a bomb in my toilet, and I could picture Walter's profane amusement when she told him of my dilemma.

The Chairman's office was on the ground floor, two handsome rooms furnished rather like the Daimler. I had never, on any previous visits to Dunham's, been invited into this particular sanctum.

Gerard ushered me in with grave courtesy and asked if either cigars or brandy had any attraction for me at the moment. They did not, so with a mild apology for his unusually disordered state, he took a tiny snifter of armagnac.

I watched his deliberate movements, and the fussy touches at the end of each. He seemed to have changed since the publication party, as though he had passed through to a final place he had resisted entering before.

'There are other considerations, of course,' he began, after appreciating the aroma of his brandy. 'I must take these into account, and my editors cannot possibly help me weigh them. All their thoughts, naturally, are for what my departure might mean to Dunham's.'

He again gave me the rather shy look I had glimpsed upstairs. 'You've been a Dunham author for how long, Neil? Twenty years?'

'Just. Ever since you published my *Jacobean Religious Writers.*'

'I've always admired you, Neil. As a scholar and as a man. Balliol, weren't you? Thought so. I was Trinity, but of course we're a broad-minded lot there.'

I smiled politely at the donnish, well-worn humour. It was clearly the precedent to something else.

'As most of my colleagues know, but kindly forbear from mentioning at my request, my two older brothers both died as a result of an accident to their motor-car. In Sussex, eight months ago.'

He sipped his armagnac and pursed his lips before going on.

'My eldest brother, Richard, was something of a drinker, and was almost certainly drunk while driving. He died immediately, as did the other driver, a greengrocer in a delivery van. My second brother, Raymond, lived on in a coma for over four months before succumbing. He had a broken neck in any case. As a result, there then devolved upon me an obligation which was as unforeseen as it was unwelcome.'

He paused mistily, but set his jaw and continued. 'My grandfather, Godfrey Chaldecott, was made a peer of the realm by Victoria. My father was his eldest son. Therefore, by the deaths of my two brothers I became Lord Marchmill. Marchmill is our home in Hampshire.'

He took an immense cigar from its wrapper, rolled it between his palms, smelled it gratefully, sighed, and put it on his desk.

'It gradually became my intention, as matters here at Dunham's have deteriorated, to withdraw with as much grace as possible from this desk and go to Hampshire and take up my family's historic responsibilities in the House of Lords. It's ironic that I, the youngest son, and farthest from ever being eligible for the title, should have been the one brother who was proud of it. Richard was at best remiss in meeting his responsibilities—oh, dash it all, he was a disgrace. He drank and he rode and he fornicated as though this were the eighteenth century. Little else. Raymond was under his influence and as good as his twin. It seemed to me that I might undo some of the harm already done, play a decent part in the affairs of our time in the House of Lords, and pass on a somewhat restored title to my own son, David.'

He picked up the cigar again, put it down again, and refilled his brandy glass.

'Now that my son has indicated by his conduct of his personal affairs—'

I wondered how much British starch it took to reduce his agony about David to that stiff precis.

'—that his future lies neither with Dunham's nor with family responsibilities as I understand them, neither all this nor the Lords seems worth the candle. I know that you are a literary man, Neil. Are you also a religious one?'

'Yes, I am. I'm a Catholic. That's the best definition of

my hopes as well as my faith.'

'Good, good. Roman, eh? Well, it's all coming back together now, isn't it, Rome and Canterbury? Then what about Hamlet's question and Camus'?'

'Good Lord, Gerard, you can't let yourself think of suicide.'

'Why not?' he asked mildly. 'For me the sole remaining question is whether God will forgive me, not does the world need me any longer. It's obvious that it doesn't. I'm going to resign my title—you can do that, you know, Douglas Home did it, for one—so that it can never pass on after my death to a son who will bring more disgrace on it. Then I should like to see my affairs reasonably in order and go quietly off to Marchmill and help myself to a hunting accident. Is that so great a crime?'

'Yes, by God, it is.' I would battle him for his life if that's what he wanted, gladly. 'You know it is, or you wouldn't be trying to have me confirm it for you. It's wicked, Gerard. None of us has the right to decide when we've accomplished our created purpose, none of us.'

'I could have asked a Unitarian, I suppose.' He sighed. 'There is just one blessing at the heart of this whole trying time, and I have asked myself in a more optimistic moment what it means. Sylvia and I have been brought closer by all this, and that is something I should never have expected. I was very bitter towards Sylvia in the past, and she . . . well, let us say it was not entirely unreciprocated.'

A soft summary of what must have been a protracted and ugly enmity.

'Now she and I have both been gentled by tragedy, I suppose. Is it entirely unimaginable to you, Neil, as a man of the world and a Christian gentleman, that she and I should become reunited as well as reconciled? I have never stopped loving Sylvia, that's the truth of it. Is that the distorted looking-glass of self-delusion I'm looking in?'

I encouraged him now as much as I had opposed him moments before.

'Compared with what we were just talking about, it's the fresh wind of sanity and sweet charity blowing away the cold fog. Pursue it. It's a marvellous idea. It's a hold on life, and that's what you're wanting. Listen to me, Gerard. You'd think for all the world that I'm qualified to talk to you like this . . .'

He jumped up, full of sudden new energy. 'You're a life-saver, Neil—almost literally. I feel as though I've received a shot of adrenalin. I have few friends left, you know, and there are times when a man needs them. No, it's I who have imposed myself dreadfully on you. A thousand thanks for hearing me out. Marvellous, marvellous. I can't thank you enough.'

Since we never can know when we really help someone, not with the same certainty we can be sure when we hurt them, I accepted his gratitude at face value and left him with a promise that I would indeed accept dinner at his club if I stayed in London.

'If someone doesn't decide to send me a letter-bomb in my post,' I added.

'You writers, eh?' he chuckled. 'Never know when you're going to pull the other one.'

The phone was ringing when I unlocked the door of my hotel room. Could a ringing phone detonate a bomb after it had soaked in the toilet for three hours? Apparently not.

It was someone named Mandy from the Wisdom Tonight show.

'Did you get a special from us today?'

'Yes. It's in my toilet.'

'Well, gee, you don't have to be like that. I'm supposed

to call you and tell you that it's all been cancelled.'

'What is?'

'What's cancelled? You know, called off.'

'I know what cancelled means, Mandy. What has been cancelled?'

'All that schedule. You were pencilled in for the Friday show. We had to move Gloria Monday out just to do that, and was she tearing. But Mr Wisdom has just scrubbed the whole thing. I mean, he's wicked upset, and Charles Leonard is going to take over as host for the whole next week, Marianne Kiss turned him down I guess after all he did for her rotten film, and well, I mean, OK?'

'It's off. Is that the message, Mandy?'

'Yeah. Right. 'Bye, luv.'

I lifted the sodden envelope from my john and dropped it into the receptacle reserved under all hotel washbasins for the disposal of sanitary napkins. So close had the wing of fame brushed my shoulder. Mine and Gloria Monday's. What idiots we all are.

The next time my phone rang it was Thomas demanding to know what the hell was so urgent.

I told him that my toilet had been plugged up, but a girl named Mandy had fixed it for me.

'You're crazier than I am, you Yank bastard,' he hollered, and slammed down the phone. They must have buzzed him while he was debriefing his underling.

CHAPTER 13

The inquest into Gordon's death, as required by English law, was held and quickly adjourned, since there were criminal charges pending. I was not called, and I saw no reason for submitting myself to the ordeal voluntarily.

Thomas, who had been the officer leading the first

team to arrive on the scene after the initial call to Scotland Yard, testified concerning the state of the body and the car when the police got there. He was then permitted to leave the hearing to attend to his other police duties.

Gordon's family and employees had to endure the entire hearing in the cold little courtroom, where the proceedings were unsoftened and undramatized even by the gowns, wigs and finery of British trial justice.

'The coroner was Dalrymple,' Thomas told me, 'the old fart. You have to say everything twice to him, he's thick as mud.'

'Why aren't you out pursuing your duties, then, instead of hanging around with a lot of dissolute French painters?'

We were sitting on a backless brown leather bench in front of Renoir's *Portrait of Two Girls*. I was determined that I'd spend at least ten hours studying this garden of light sitting in the middle of London while it was briefly here.

'You're why. Sinjin still wants me to keep on your back. He liked them husky, didn't he?'

'The Lord God made them all, Thomas.'

He breathed an admiring sigh. 'It's almost enough to make a man religious, that thought. We found a postmark.'

'Hooray for Scotland Yard. Londonderry? Libya?'

'London.'

'Not much help. There are those who dismiss Renoir as a painter of valentines, but they are the kind of people who think Cummings was a verbal cartoonist.'

'Six days old. May the fifth.'

'Complain to the post office.'

'We couldn't be happier. See, we've got ten thousand bits of charred paper. Bits of bits, half bits, burned bits, blank bits, letters, and groups of letters. First they had to sort them all out by paper, the machine they were typed on, and so on. Then they had to make them make sense. One was easy, handwritten. A letter from some lady named Mary Goodman up in Shropshire about a baptismal record in her family bible that Gordon had asked her about. The rest looks like the bloody sweepings from a Chinese fire drill. And then we make out this bit of a postmark on an envelope like they sent out these samples in. Suit swatches by mail, this one was. Can't you just see Sir Gordy getting his suits by mail from some Paki tailor in Highgate? Six lovely days old.'

I found I could listen to Thomas and still study the women of Renoir. My eyes simply had to be told to ignore my ears.

'So what?'

'So what, you ignorant foreigner? Do you remember my theory? My own personal theory that we'd better look in on Sir Gordy's help and ask who dumped his wastebasket for him? Look, are you listening to me, I'm blowing my own horn here.'

'I'm listening, but don't tell me to look, too. I'm listening to you, but I'm looking at Renoir.'

'You're looking at tits, same as I do. You professors give us yobs a larf. You like a little tit and bum too, but instead of paying fourteen p. for the *Sun*, you go to museums and get off on these French paintings.'

'As long as the admission's free I'm ahead by fourteen p. That's what education will do for you, Thomas.'

'Well, it made sense, dinnit?'

'How did it make sense?'

'The West Indian maid is supposed to dump the contents of the garage swing bin into the dustbin behind the kitchen every evening. Steve takes it out of the car and puts it into a plastic liner, along with the contents of the ashtrays, whatever he vacuums off the upholstery, and so on, and then he puts the liner, with a nice tidy twist on it, into the garage bin. She takes it from there. Every Thursday the dustbin gets collected.'

I looked away from Renoir and at him for the first time. 'So every Thursday there are seven bags of discarded mail, etcetera, in the dustbin.'

'Six. Never on Sunday.'

'Six then. And you went through the dustbin.'

He polished his nails on his coat and blew on them. 'Yes, guvnor, 'appen I did. I almost didn't. The collection truck came while I was sorting through it. We had a fair old jurisdictional dispute. They get paid by the binful or some such. I almost had to arrest the bastards before they'd leave without the bin.'

'And you found that something was missing, didn't you?'

'This Socratic method really is something, isn't it? I scramble on my bloody hands and knees all over Chelsea and half of Belgravia sorting through last week's garbage, and you sit here staring at yon actress thinking great thoughts, and between us we solve crime after crime. Yes, you ancient Greek foolosopher, there was one day for which no post had been put in the bin. All right, you say, so there was one day when Sir Gordy got no throwaway post, happens to us all some days in this vale of tears.'

'What did the postman say?'

'By God, Yank, you've done it again. You're good at these parlour games, aren't you? Would you care to guess the postman's name?'

'Timothy Clegg.'

'Wrong, you twit. What made me think you were good at this? Moorcomb Pettensby.'

'And what did the euphoniously named Pettensby tell you?'

'That to the best of his recollection—you see the pun there—collection, recollection?—he had handed over to Sir Gordon, in his car, every day last week, a regular mixture of personal and business post, with some adverts and so on added in.'

'Don't those companies who sent out suits by mail offers and so on usually send them out in batches?'

'Ah, you sly dog, Professor, you're back in the game with that. And did Moorcomb P. not tell us that on the previous Thursday he had delivered such a packet to Sir Gordy? You will love this, now listen to this, because police work is a thousand tiny details like this. A packet which he recognized, mind you, because, as the proud holder of a Barclaycard himself, he is on a number of posh mailing lists, and he, Pettensby, got his suit swatches just Wednesday week over in Camden Town and thought they were first rate. Ordered a suit, he did. He said it tickled him to think that Sir Gordy and himself might some day meet at the racecourse or somewhere wearing the same forty-three-pound suit.'

'Complete the lesson for me, o clever policeman.'

'That envelope arrived in Chelsea on Thursday and was handed to Sir Gordon on Thursday. Since it was postmarked London Wednesday, we thought it must have been. So someone went to the trouble, didn't they, of taking that bit of junk post out of the bin and using the envelope again to hold something else, and probably not samples of suiting.'

'Thus we have the bomb in the wastebasket.'

He pretended to punch my arm gleefully. I flinched. Thomas is wiry, but hard as nails. 'Yes, you æsthetic pervert. That's what we have done. And now would you like to hear something else equally fascinating?'

'Not if it's going to cause you to haul off and slug me with joy at your own cleverness. Let's face the other way and look at Cezanne for a while.'

We changed direction and regarded the Cezanne landscape.

'Brown hills?'

'Just look. What's equally fascinating?'

'Well, apart from Sinjin commending my initiative, hem hem, they have been interviewing every damned body who was within two hundred and fifty yards of the murder site at eight-thirty that morning. Would you care to guess how many people, afoot, in cars, in buses, and looking out of office windows that might be?'

'No.'

'Me neither. But they've taken over fifteen hundred statements so far, and they're still coming in. One of them is the fascinating one. The statement, to be exact, of Mr Philip Boney of Finsbury, who was proceeding in a northerly direction from Bank tube station towards Gresham Street and his place of employment when he looked admiringly at the Daimler motor-car of Sir Gordon Fairly.'

'He saw it blow up?'

'He saw it before it blew up, which is better. Just one or two seconds better.'

'And?'

'And he saw the chauffeur, who is not hidden from the vulgar mob by smoked glass for reasons of safety, perform an instinctive, but telltale action.'

'He flinched.'

'He bloody ducked. Same as you just did when you thought I was going to hit you. Now why would a man do that, crouch down in the middle of traffic in one of the busiest intersections in the City, except out of an atavistic inclination to self-preservation?'

'He knew the blast was coming.'

'He bloody must have known it. And even if his head told him that the back of the Daimler would contain the force, his bowels told him to duck. He was shit scared was why he ducked.'

'Nice going.'

'It was. Not mine, of course, but nice. A young cop

named Delahanty got his statement and pulled it right out for the analysis team. He'll go far, that lad.'

'Have they taken Steve into custody?'

'By now they have. He didn't know it when he testified this morning, but he was scheduled for a long session with Sinjin and his heavy mob right afterwards. I almost felt sorry for the poor bastard sitting there pressing his hair back into place, making his sorrowful statement. He'll think the bloody Tower of London fell on him when Sinjin gets going.'

'Do you think a man like that did this on his own? Made up the bombs, mailed them, slipped the extra one into the post before leaving that morning, and so on?'

'It's first of all a question of motive, innit? Motive aside, though, I don't think that dumb Wop was anything but someone else's errand boy.'

'Will Sinjin be able to persuade him to say whose?'

'Remains to be seen if the bugger will stand up to it or wilt, as the artist's model said to the monsignor, eh?'

He stood up. 'If all you're going to be looking at is brown hills, I'm going to talk to my people.'

'The one in the St James's T-shirt?'

'She's a student of comparative literature at London University, that gel. Very impressed when I told her I was hanging about with a professor. I told her that in a Jungian sense I was a very sensational person, and I suspected she was, too. She was, too. Lovely. No, my brother Dominic.'

'Does your brother really work for — you know?'

'The British Branch of Godfather's? Who knows? Let's say his friends are not my friends. I spend most of my time with known criminals and he spends his going to the opera with peers. Keep in touch.'

He paused once more before the Renoir before leaving.

The afternoon paper had no doubts about the significance of Steve's arrest.

CHAUFFEUR ACCUSED IN SIR GORDY BOMB KILLING ran the scrawled poster on the front of news stands.

Thomas's favourite paper, as usual, minced no words.

Steven Francis Nocera, filmstar handsome driver of Sir Gordy's custom-fitted Daimler, was being held in custody this morning at West Central police station.

The muscular, dark-eyed Nocera, 'Steve' to his democratic millionaire boss, is suspected of being part of a conspiracy with unnamed others in Sir Gordy's murder.

The morning paper from the same stable had had a half-page picture of Steve and Ashley, both younger, dancing together in evening dress, the story headed: *Valentino Driver and Playgirl Heiress—Their Last Tango??* It had been on the streets before Steve had been taken into custody, so the implications were entirely coincidental. The editor who had decided to run the picture for lack of anything juicier must have been patting himself on the back all afternoon.

It was Ashley, a good deal less sure of herself than usual, who told me when the picture had been taken.

'I was sixteen, for Christ's sake. My father gave a birthday party for me at the Dorchester, and Steve and I danced a few times. That makes me a co-conspirator or bloody something.'

She hurled the paper against the wall.

'Ashley, if you are going to confess your sins with your father's chauffeur to me, don't. And if you're going to spin out some great web of self-pity, don't do that either. You came here to me, not I to you. What precisely is it you want?'

She had come to my hotel room unannounced and

asked for fifteen minutes of my time. My hotel room had apparently become the best-known address in London. I was expecting a busload of German tourists any minute at this rate, and I had decided that Ashley should not be given an inch.

I had been laundering my underwear and socks, so there was little I could do but sit in my terry robe barefoot, maintain my lukewarm *sang-froid* and listen.

'You were there when he blocked me from getting into that damned lift, you saw how he treated me. Did we look like conspirators to you?'

'Frankly, you looked like two idiots who had probably done something idiotic together once and remembered it with different emotions.'

'Sylvia says you're the great psychological expert on the emotions of young women. That moron and I actually went to bed together, twice. The night of that stupid, appalling party at the Dorchester, and the next day, in mid-afternoon, in his quarters over the garage. I must have thought I was Lady Goddam Chatterly. He certainly thought he was giving me the treat of a lifetime. He was crushed that he hadn't got me first. I told him one of my teachers had taken care of that in the fourth form. God, when I think of that hairy bastard now. He's got a pelt on him from neck to knees, like an ape.'

She sucked in her cheeks and watched herself in my mirror, speaking with a Swedish accent.

'Octually I prefair smooze men.' She puffed out her cheeks. 'And yes, I am quite normal in that respect. My long charade to annoy Gordon is over, *fini*. Actually—' she twirled herself into the other chair—'I had rather a nice boyfriend in Jersey, nothing mad, just a sweet poet who used to sit at my feet while I painted and read Ted Hughes aloud. Sometimes we'd make love, and mostly we'd swim together and lie in the sun talking.'

'I'm very sorry for you, Ashley, but I don't really want

to hear any of this, there's no point to it.'

'Do you think I should keep my name?'

'I think you should do what makes you happy.'

'I've grown rather fond of it. I'm going to have it made my legal name and add it to Fairly. Do you think Ashley Fairly sounds too—you know, alliterative?'

'Why don't you take your story about Steve to Chief Inspector St John-Stewart and ask him about the name, too?'

'And have it splashed all over the *Mirror* the next morning? Garage Orgy For Heiress and Hairy Wop?'

'It will come out, you can be sure of that now, and far better that it should come from you, in your version. The police will obviously follow every lead they can find connecting Steve with anyone else in Gordon's life.'

'Shall I tell you who I think paid that cretin to put those bombs in Gordon's post?'

'No. I forbid it. Again, I tell you this—tell it to the police, not me.'

'Well, I understood from Sylvia that he's your old friend,' she said. Her smile, head tipped to one side, was as thin as a razor blade.

'Who is?'

'Gerard Chaldecott, that pious old bag of pudding.'

'Whatever you think of Gerard Chaldecott's personal style, I can assure you he's no murderer.'

'And don't you think he might be if dear old Sylvia got into bed with him and planted the idea in his poor old head?'

'You're saying wild, improbable, and offensive things, Ashley. Stop it right now and leave.'

'OK, I'm imagining it, right? Sylvia would give her bloody eye teeth to be Lady Mushmill or whatever his fucking title is now. I know her, you don't. When Gordon only got a K, she was ready to poison the Queen; life peer was what she was after.

'Now Gordon's companies have been under investigation for months, the whole travel and airlines scheme is on the edge of perishing bankruptcy right now. I know. A receiver will be appointed tomorrow to investigate the deals with the banks over the Israeli contracts.'

She stamped her foot in frustration. 'I ought to bloody know, the value of my shares has dropped three and a half million quid since Tuesday. The estate faces a call of two million more against personal guarantees Gordon gave on company holdings. At this rate they'll be worth sweet F.A. by the time I've actually got them in hand, won't they? That bloody man Pease keeps pulling fresh disasters out of his fucking briefcase.'

With pure money the subject, she was a tigress, truly and unmistakably her father's daughter. She strode back and forth, kicking anything that got in her way.

'And do you think Lady Sylvia didn't know the sky was falling? And do you really think it's beyond her to sweet talk your chum Gerard about saving his damned old wreck of a publishing house from becoming the Sex Aids Shopping News? You tell me if you think he wouldn't move heaven and earth to save Dunham's, and then tell me if he ever stopped hating Gordon for taking Sylvia away from him.'

I had reached the end of my patience. I stood. 'Ashley, I won't hear any more of your poisonous ravings. Tell Stewart or forget it. I'm sorry, but you must leave right now.'

She stood at the door, but made no move to open it. She knew she could have the last word if she chose to, I wasn't going to throw her out bodily.

'I just wanted you to know and to tell that cop amigo of yours that it was not Charles Leonard and I who put Steve up to whatever he did. Your friend James has probably already put that bee in your bonnet, and I want you to know that it's categorically, stupidly untrue.'

'Ashley, I didn't even know that you and Charles Leonard knew each other.'

'Now tell me another one. Charles told me about Hugh James — their ancient rivalry over that skinny actress and all that incredible trivia. And now that Charles is taking over the Wisdom Tonight show for FairCom — God, would you ever imagine any show could run for seven years and account for nine per cent of network advertising revenue with a name like that? — a lot of people are sharpening their knives for him. But Gordon was right about his smarmy appeal, just as I'll admit he was about William. Now that leaves James and his lost plays of Lucy Goodman and Sheila and her Hollywood film contract rather with their bums out in the cold, doesn't it?'

Matters were obviously complicating themselves too fast for me to keep them sorted out. I had the sense that all these events were passing in front of me on a screen. The faces were talking, but I was like a man with the sound off, completely at a loss to know who was actually saying what to whom and with what reason.

She let herself out while I was still trying to absorb her exit lines. She had saved the best till last.

'It's true,' Sheila said over the phone. 'Let me put down my vacuum cleaner and sit for a minute and I'll tell you.'

She fussed at the other end of the line and I heard her settle and sigh. 'Whew. James is our drinking with some cronies from his show. I'm here with a scarf about my head from seven this morning. He has his therapy, I have mine.'

'When did all this happen?'

'Ashley let them know at FairCom that she intended to take her position on the Board immediately. The whole business of the investigation into their funds and all that is beyond me, but I do know that didn't have anything to do with it. James says that she wanted to get in there and manage the vote on renewing their sponsorship of the FairCom TV show that's been the Wisdom show. Anyway, the Lucy Goodman thing is bust. Charles is like the fat cat with the canary inside him.'

'Have she and Charles actually known each other for long?'

'Oh yes. He told me all about that more than once. He was her drama teacher in that fancy Swiss arts school she went to. She hates his guts, but she's smart enough to see he's the bloody idol of the West End and capitalize on it. God knows when they cooked up him taking over the TV show. Probably while they were paying off Steve for putting the bombs in the Daimler.'

'And I used to think the Court of James I was a hotbed of intrigue. If I can get permission from Chief Superintendent Stewart to leave London, I'll be off to Ireland on the first flight.'

'I thought he was the one who wanted you out of it.'

'I'm caught in Scotland Yard's version of Catch-22. I've been warned to stay out of the investigation, but I've also been warned not to try to leave the city without police permission, and, of course, everyone I know in London is involved. I really am going to try to get it. Look, I'm sorry that all the plans I heard you discussing with Sid are up the spout.'

'Save it for them that needs it, guvnor. I've got three scripts to pick from and himself will never hurt for work. He did have his poor heart set on doing the *Arden*, though.'

'There's no royalty payment on a three-hundred-year-old play. Can't he do it anyway?'

'Sure, he could, but in a loft somewhere in Hoxton for an audience of fifty or a hundred? He'll never do it without the money to do it right. And by the time he gets that we'll both be in a home for wacky old actors.'

Her voice had that tough, practical twang in it that I had heard before when she was coming to terms with reality. Bermondsey is a better school than Balliol for some things.

I hung up wondering if anyone now would ever finish piecing out scraps of information about Lucy Goodman into a coherent account. If Gordon's questions about his remote ancestor ever would be answered.

Had Lucy Goodman written *Arden?* It was possible. Had she been Wat Harris, the actor. That sort of thing had probably happened more than once. Had she been murdered by a fellow artist and rival named Shakespeare? Improbable, but conceivable. Perhaps I could give the whole puzzle to Thomas to solve. After all, it was a police problem, wasn't it?

CHAPTER 14

Steve was released the next day before noon. Despite what the cheap press had blared, he never had been arrested for murder or conspiracy, merely taken in for questioning.

Lies usually run to elaborate lengths; his explanation to the police was simple and uncomplicated enough to be true. He had told them that while he was parked for the postman to make his delivery, he had noticed the petrol gauge acting up, so he had leaned forward to tap it.

Thomas told me grudgingly that when they started the engine on the Daimler down at the police garage, feeding petrol into it with an attached line, the gauge had acted up exactly as Steve had described it doing.

'Of course it could have been doing that for weeks before the event.'

'True. That doesn't help, though. He said he was bending over to tap the gauge just a second before the blast came and that's his fucking story.' He bit a potato crisp savagely. 'I thought we had a lock on the bastard.'

'What did you learn from your brother?'

'What did you ever learn from your brothers? What does anyone ever learn from their brothers? Nada.'

'If you knew that ahead of time, why did you go and ask him?'

'Aha.' He smiled an evil smile. 'Not from him. It's a sad, dirty world, Neil, my old teacher. I only went to ask Dominic what he might have heard about Steverino so that his close business associate Franco Farinetti would get the message.'

'I don't get it.'

'As I said, it's a dirty old world. Franco is my brother Dominic's driver. He is also my source of information about what the Little Brothers of The Poor are doing for the community this month. Franco got caught with his big greasy finger in a safe over in Holborn a year or two back, but we made a mutually useful arrangement with him. Franco is one of that tremendous breed of good citizens known and loved by the press as a Supergrass.'

'You planted an informer on your own brother?'

'Why not?' he asked reasonably. 'His people have several down at my shop. Fair's fair, right? Franco is special. He's *my* grass, nobody else's. Sinjin gave him to me. He beats up on me for show, old Sinjin, but I'm his only line to the Brotherhood and he knows it.'

He smiled expansively and stuffed three potato crisps into his mouth and took a drink of his Campari and soda.

'The crisps are OK, but do people really like drinking this guinea piss? he asked for the third time. We were in a pub in Drury Lane and I was introducing him to what he called the wonderful world of coloured drinks.

'I'm only a civilian, but I can't believe you could

actually get one of them to inform on the Mafia. Won't he be automatically killed if they find out?'

We were both talking with our heads down, like two characters planning a crime.

'Killed will be the last thing he'll be, sure, but not the first, second, or third. You don't know Franco. He is as dippy as Donald Duck. The safe we caught him opening belonged to them. It was in the back of a confectioner's where he was supposed to make a pick-up the next day, but Franco needed some sudden funds to cover his horses, so he figured why not go down there and get the lolly before the morning rush. He not only would have done hard time — after all, he'd had thirty-seven arrests and eleven convictions, and this would have been his third big one. When he got into the Scrubs, you see, he would have had to explain to the mob inside why he had been stealing from the mob outside. He offered me everything in the safe that time to let him scarper. Forty-one thousand quid. We had his ugly nuts right in the nutcracker and we squeezed him.'

'I'm glad I'm not in your line of work. How do you make contact with him? Obviously you can't meet him at the National Gallery in the Impressionists room.'

'Hell of an idea, that.'

'Really?'

'Really. Lots of ways. You ever read Le Carré, those spy novels of his?'

'Sorry, I don't have time for mystery fiction.'

'Pardon me. I get lots of ideas from this Le Carré. Drops, the spies call them. I should've been a spy. If my friend Franco has something for me, he prints it into the crossword puzzle in the *Sun*. Then he throws the paper in the basket in front of Frosty's juice stand on Wardour Street. Frosty gets it for me, and I give Frosty fifty p. for it.'

'What if Frosty reads what Franco has written?'

'What makes you think Frosty can read?'

'He could identify Franco, couldn't he? I mean, if anyone leaned exceptionally hard on him?'

'What makes you think Frosty can see? He's blind. Franco just says, "How they hanging, Frosty?" and he knows there's a paper for me. Pick your voice out of a thousand if he's heard it once, Frosty can.'

'He just fills the message in the crossword puzzle squares?'

'Isn't that lovely? My brother has contempt for people who handicap horses or pick the pools or waste their time reading horoscopes or filling in crossword puzzles when they could be out stealing money from people or hurting them. What's he going to do, challenge Franco's solution to the crossword? He's sitting in the back seat reading the *Financial Times*.'

'I find it hard to believe.'

'You might find it hard to believe that there are people standing around in Leicester Square who will let you urinate on them for twenty p. Would you like to meet one?'

'No, thanks.'

He finished off the potato crisps by wetting his fingers and scooping up the last salty crumbs.

'Come on, I'll show you.'

I stayed where I was. 'I really meant it. I'll take your word there are such people. I've no desire to meet one.'

'I mean my John Le Carré super-secret spy drop at Frosty's. Would you like to see slam-bang police work in action or not?'

'Have you had a call from him, from Frosty?'

'Stickler for procedure, aren't you? No, I haven't received the agreed signal of three puffs of smoke over the spire of St Martin-in-the-Fields, but I need some orange juice to get the flavour of that ponce's cocktail out of my mouth. Coming?'

I went. I was getting tired of talking without moving my lips, and a character who looked as if he might be one of the urolagniacs from Leicester Square was sidling over into Thomas's vacated place.

The MG was parked illegally right outside the Drury Lane Theatre. Thomas indicated the theatre with a jerk of his head as we got down into the car.

'You go in for theatre much?'

'I thought I'd better see Charles's long-running hit, see what all the fuss was about.'

I started to tell him about the time in my life when theatre was my ruling passion. Well, theatre and Sonia.

Sonia had been a Freshman at Old Hampton when I had been a serious, library-dwelling sophomore, intent upon scholastic honours. Intent as well upon making up the awful gaps between me with my ludicrously inadequate early education plus three Navy years and the swarm of my classmates all of whom seemed to have missed the war and spent six years at Exeter.

Sonia Porshin had starred in the winter play of OH Drama. It was postwar, avante garde, and adapted from a French existential philosopher by Sheldon Starr, our theatre genius in the making, who later went to work for New England telephone. Sonia played Therese, who was actually Lust or Accidia, if I grasped the theme correctly. I'm not sure Sheldon did, so I felt little obligation to. Whichever she was, lust or sloth, Sonia became my sin for a month. Two months, actually.

I switched my major to drama and began wearing no necktie and hanging around The Black Box, OH's coffee shop for thespians. I also began feverishly writing a witty, unfashionable Catholic comedy full of brittle sophistication, somewhat in the manner of Wycherley, but leaning towards Waugh and Clifford Odets.

Sonia, to my incredulous delight, agreed to read the part of Marguerite, who was also the Virgin Mary, in the

scene from Act I of *Work In Progress* which I entered in
the new plays reading competition. When you are twenty-
two, the idea of Lust reading your Virgin Mary in a play
set in a Boston housing project has both the power to
intoxicate and a potent aphrodisiac effect. I felt godlike.

We did not do well. Sonia blamed me, pointing out
that my lines lacked an honest relationship with
disillusion. That hadn't struck me as the main problem,
but her inability to realize that, as the mother-to-be of the
Messiah of her people, she should be less rabid and more
radiant.

'For Christ's sake, Neil,' she whined at our final coffee
date, 'it's not the goddam Messiah who's important, it's
the fucking audience.'

In those days girls, even actresses, didn't talk like that.
I stayed a theatre major for a half year, but the early
promise of *Work In Progress* was never realized. I drifted
back to Literature through Philosophy. The godlike sense
was gone, but discovering Chaucer that spring made up
for the loss.

Sonia waxed fat and married a supermarket chain. I
never looked back.

Thomas had a good laugh at the expense of me and my
play before gunning his car into an illegal turn. 'How was
Charles's? Better than yours?'

'Well, the rest of the audience seemed to be getting
their money's worth. Screams of laughter in the dark in
there.'

'That's what matters, innit? Isn't that what your bird
Sonia said?'

The reviewer I had read wrote that 'Charles Leonard
had evolved a production combining the elements of
pantomime, cabaret, and a heightened theatrical
naturalism.' I thought it had been a little Tom Stoppard,
a little Neil Simon and a lot of performance by a long-
faced, perpetual motion comic who had stolen much

from Ray Bolger.

'Hardy's worth seeing.'

'What, the TV comic? Bloody riot, but why pay a fortune when I can see him at home for free?'

'Perhaps TV is the real legitimate theatre now.'

'Of course it is, you wet.'

'Perhaps the loss of Sonia Porshin, Sheldon Starr and me all at the same time was too much for the old theatre to survive.'

He grunted. 'You three and me. I never told anyone this, but I tried out for a part in a community theatre once under the name Curt Douglas. Eighteen I was. Bellhop in a Tennessee Williams play. Tried to talk with an American southern accent after reading *Tobacco Road*. Sounded like bloody Idi Amin.'

'I don't think I want to hear it.' He was letting me laugh at him now, and I was. There is some projection of ourselves in all our friendships. Each friend sees in the other something of himself as it might have been. Thomas Bowie was me without an education, and I suspect that to him I was Thomas with one.

'I tried it on a Welshman in Blackpool once and he thought I was speaking German. He called me a bloody krauthead and took a swing at me.'

Wardour Street bisects Soho from Oxford Street to Shaftesbury Avenue, exactly half way between Soho Square and Golden Square.

Frosty's juice stand was one storefront enterprise jammed in among the hundreds scraping a living out of the traffic through Soho of those thousands who thought either the sex shops or the few good restaurants worth finding in the maze of streets.

The stand opened in two directions, facing on to both Wardour and Old Compton Streets. Thomas parked on the sidewalk and took me to the closed side on the delivery alley and spoke through the hatch to Frosty.

'Harya, Frosty.'

'You one o' them psychics er wotever, Thomas?'

'Yes?'

'Ten minutes since. 'ere.' A folded *Sun* came through the hatch. The hand stayed. Thomas took the paper and put fifty p. in the hand, which then withdrew.'

'Much obliged, Frost.'

We were back in the car and gone in ten seconds.

Thomas tossed the paper in my lap. 'No big mystery. Franco eats his supper at Como's in Dean Street every night at six. That means he has to come by here. Simple. Try the crossword, same page as the comics.'

That didn't help me much, I didn't know my *Sun* the way he did. The front page was all war news and racing crashes, with a banner across the bottom about Sir Gordy Suspect Seen? I thumbed my way past a naked girl who said she wanted to be a nursing sister, three rape stories, a page of pictures of the royal family looking at each other in a collective stupor, and finally found the crossword. It was under the astrology column, filled in with soft pencil, and it all looked like gibberish.

'First tell me my horoscope for today. I missed it. I'm an Aries, strong and virile. Go on, how am I supposed to get through the evening without that?'

I read him his forecast from the paper. Aries had mustard on it, but it looked like, ' "Others are relaxing, but you must stay busy. You could interfere with someone's privacy and not be thanked for it. Plan something special this weekend." '

'See now? That's true. I am going to interfere with someone's bloody privacy. Now read the crossword and find out whose.'

I studied the jumble of letters again.

'See that?' Thomas said, pointing to the top left-hand corner, and not bothering to look where he was driving. 'If you looked at that over some bloke's shoulder, it would look like any messy old crossword.'

He pulled into a No Parking space behind the British Museum and took the paper from me. With a ballpoint pen he made lozenges around the words he found in the puzzle.

'Anything with a Z in it is out, so is anything with a Q or a double Y. He writes the words in any direction at all. I just put them in the logical order. Simple?'

He continued to circle words until he couldn't find any more, then he read them to me.

'S.N. trying to buy a piece of Jacky's Loretta. Claims he can front one huge property.'

He looked at me in a superior way and tore the puzzle out of the paper, shredded it and threw it out the window.

'What does it mean?'

'Friend Steve has been nosing about the casino lads for a long time. We knew that. Fancies himself a gambler, our Steve. Likes to put on a dinner-jacket weekends and lark about Jackie Wallace's Loretta Club. His hobby, you might say. Now it appears that he has been making noises about one hundred thousand quid—'one huge' to Franco—in real property which I suppose he is anxious to shift to Jackie for a share in the Loretta.'

'Is he an idiot? He's under suspicion of conspiracy to murder and he's flashing that kind of wealth around?'

He backed out of the illegal parking space slowly and explained as we tooled through the evening traffic of Bloomsbury.

'First off, Neil, they're all idiots. But second of all, he probably got his hands on whatever it is he's bragging about six months ago, maybe more. My guess would be that someone, with not much cash to spare but owning a nice piece of country estate off somewhere, quietly had it transferred to a blind owner—a straw man, not Frosty, with Steve Nocera as the actual new owner. All he would have to do is have the deed transferred again to Jackie Wallace the same way he got it, and his next job would be a floor boss at the Loretta or some such lark, and he'd be a member of the club. My brother's solicitors handle arrangements like that all the time.'

'So he was paid off.'

'It does appear so. Sinjin will achieve orgasm when I tell him.' He hammered the steering-wheel joyfully. 'He bent down to tap the petrol gauge, did he? The next time he bends down Sinjin will have it up his arse with spurs on, the brutal bugger.'

He swung the car into a gap in front of Russell Square tube station. 'Out. Find your own way home. We real men of C Division have better things to do than play taxi for you civilians who like the taste of danger and intrigue real police work affords.'

I struggled free of his car. He leaned out of the window and sang to me in an atrocious southern accent as he drove off, 'Watch for de mail, I'll never fail. If you don't get dat letter den you'll know he's in jail . . .'

CHAPTER 15

Steve and Freddie, the Fairlys' other driver, were both arrested and charged the next day. Confronted by police knowledge of his pending deal with Jackie Wallace, Steve made a deal with the police and promptly implicated Freddie as the one who had come to him with the idea originally and as the bomb-maker.

Thomas said that it wasn't Steve's idea at all, but the solicitor and barrister team the Brotherhood had sent round to help him with his legal problems had decided to keep the heat off the Loretta Club by applying it squarely to Steve.

Freddie steadfastly denied everything for twenty-four hours, then made his own deal and agreed to turn Queen's Evidence for the Crown and testify against others if he got immunity.

Justice, everywhere in the free world, is the same. Some negotiation underlies every prosecution and every eventual sentence. One understands that there is none of this in Russia, for example, and those who think that a better system are encouraged to commit their crimes east of the Urals.

Freddie, to the delight of the dailies, was an electronics and CB hobbyist, and had, moreover, taken out half the books in two separate branch libraries about arms and explosives in the previous two years.

Eunuch he might have been, but beneath his off-duty black leather jacket and shining black helmet when he cruised around Somers Town there lurked a figure to be reckoned with, who read comic books religiously and owned a collection of plastic guns.

He had resented, he confessed to the *Mirror*, the fact that Sir Gordon had treated him like dirt because he was a homosexual. I COULD DRIVE RINGS ROUND ROMEO BOASTS FAST FREDDIE was one summary. GAY ROLLS RACER WON'T TAKE THE RAP was another. The burden of Freddie's contention was that if his late employer had given him the Daimler to drive, none of this would have happened.

'Sir Gordy's Tart Wagon' was the memorable phrase he gave the interviewer as a description of the Rolls he drove the women in. I ruefully reflected that my own summary of the service had been not much more of an epigram.

When Freddie's deal, which apparently included a furnished cell at a North London police station, complete with comic books, was consummated, he finally named Sylvia Fairly as the one who had paid him to make three letter-bombs to kill Sir Gordon Fairly.

That, as Thomas was to say later, was where we left the hired men having tea in the kitchen and went up to the withdrawing-room to sup champagne with the quality.

I saw Dolly the next day, to sign contracts for portions of my book to be used as the basis for a condensed edition for younger readers. Since the condenser was to be Dolly, in exchange for a very small stipend and her name on the title page, I was doubly willing. It would be done as well as such things can be done, and it would mean a steady, continuing market among schoolchildren needing a Literary Great for their book reports.

We were going over the seven pages of small print which constitute the typical book contract of this sort, when almost predictably, Walter Harris came in, sat down, and lit a cigarette.

'Go away, Walter,' Dolly said, without looking up. 'There are no ashtrays in this office, and I don't want your droppings on my rug.'

'I've told you before, Doll,' he growled in his Scots Bogart side-of-the-mouth voice, 'rugs don't cover floors. Carpet covers floors, and is distinctly non-U. You have non-U carpet.'

'It's been non-U for years to say U and non-U, so clear out.'

'You might want to light up when I tell you.' She looked up from page five, section 18A, Reversion of Rights, which was giving us some trouble. The tone of Walter's voice contained some note of menace beyond the usual.

But she wasn't showing her eagerness to hear the latest gossip that quickly. 'What did we do with Fuller's book on John Wesley about 18A? Did we stick with the nine months or allow a full year?'

'We cut the chiselling bastard back on his percentage in exchange for the allowance. Do you remember Winston raised hell about it, but Gerard calmed him down and said it was a good idea? Gerard's killed himself.'

Dolly was in the midst of an expression of relief at his first answer when her expression froze.

Her voice was suddenly weak. 'Gerard?'

'He drove down to Marchmill yesterday and shot himself with his army pistol.'

Suddenly section 18A and all that seemed not to matter at all. Tomorrow or the next day we would pick it up again, or someone else would for us, because the one thing sure is that workaday life goes on. But at that moment I was as shocked and lost for words as Dolly Allen.

Each of us looked at the others. Each of us probably had heard a slightly different version of the gossip. The one I had heard from Ashley swam back into my mind from behind the dam I had built to hold it in.

'Did he care that much about David letting him down?' Dolly whispered incredulously.

'He cared. But no one thinks it was just that,' Walter said quietly.

They both looked at me. They knew that Gerard had taken me into his confidence not long since, had walked the two flights to Dolly's office to fetch me for it. Now they expected an explanation.

'He was bitterly disappointed by David, I do know that,' I said slowly. It is always difficult to measure one's obligations to the dead. 'That and the deaths of his two brothers seem to have taken the last of the will out of him.'

'But he told Winston . . .' Dolly began abruptly, then stopped just as quickly.

'Give it,' Walter croaked harshly. 'What did he tell bloody Winston?'

Dolly temporized, shuffling papers together. 'Winston confided to me last week that Gerard was beginning to look forward to having the title now — did you know about the title in the family, Neil?'

I nodded.

'Well, he thought it was just what Gerard needed to snap him out of his funk about all this.' She gestured vaguely at her office and Dunham's. 'House of Lords, etcetera. I rather thought that was to be his lifeline.'

Walter knew about that, too, and the aftermath.

'George says Gerard left a formal resignation from the peerage. Gave the bloody title back, just the way Beaverbrook or somebody did. George says he knew Gerard was damned if he was going to pass it on to a homosexual son after his brothers made a farce of it.'

I saw no point in dissembling what I knew further, so I added what I knew of Gerard's decision to surrender the title.

Dolly looked at me sharply. 'Are you saying that Gerard was on about all this when you spoke with him here?'

I met her eyes. 'To go down to Marchmill and shoot himself with his army pistol? No. He did say he would resign the title. He was depressed at first, but when I left him, after he had got some of his woes off his chest, just talked them out and so on, he was positively buoyant.'

'Then why the hell does a good man kill himself? A religious man, too. There had to be something else.'

Walter was speaking out of some deeply enraged conviction that a good man never let go, never gave it up, hung on until fate broke his grip by main force. As a starving man might be furious with a man he saw throwing away food, Walter was angry with anyone who threw away precious days and years of life.

I thought of the sad, terrible things Ashley had said, accusing Gerard and Sylvia of having conspired together to kill Gordon. I allowed myself to consider that possibility now, as I had refused to do then. Had that, then, been the real root of Gerard's agony of spirit when I talked with him — guilt and shame about Gordon's death?

Since the working conference over contract details was shipwrecked anyway, we all sat back and contemplated the sad news.

'God, I never felt more like a cigarette in my life,' Dolly moaned, combing the tangles from her hair tiredly with her fingers. 'I feel a fright. Didn't you bring anything to drink, Walter?'

He lifted a finger and placed it beside his nose, slipped from his place against the wall back through the connecting door, and was back again in ten seconds with half a bottle of Cutty Sark.

He held it up. 'Appropriately, stolen from Neil's party.'

Dolly dug out two unclean coffee cups and a rather suspicious styrofoam mug with a bite out of it.

'Neil gets the plastic. Americans think that's what all drinking vessels are made of anyway, right? If you insist on a clean cup, Walter, wash yours. You know where the sink is.'

He peered into the stained and layered cup sourly. 'Aye. Only ten minutes' walk from here. I'll chance this.'

He poured a dram into each vessel and lifted his own.

'To Gerard, the poor bastard.'

We all drank. I suppose we all wonder at some time what unofficial epitaph our friends will speak after us. It's a poor bastard indeed whose life and work get that for a tag-line.

Dolly's phone rang. She indicated by her answers that someone else was handing around the news we were already waking. Then her slackness vanished and she was paying closer attention to what she was being told.

'Yes, thanks, Gillian . . . Yes, later . . . Yes, Walter . . . God, isn't it?'

She hung up with slow preciseness, took the rest of her drink and held out her cup to Walter for more.

'I need another. Gerard and Sylvia Fairly were planning to remarry. No, that's not exactly it. Gerard was planning to remarry Sylvia. I'm numb.'

Whatever she thought now, or her telephoning friend had suggested, indeed, regardless what the police might be thinking, I at least knew Gerard's original intentions in that regard.

'That doesn't mean he was her co-conspirator,' I said too loudly, hearing myself pronounce the words dully, unconvincingly.

'Jesus, she hasn't been proved guilty of anything yet, you two,' Dolly blurted with sudden tears in her eyes. 'Let's give someone the benefit of the doubt at least. She has denied everything those two goons have said.'

Walter wasn't having any of that innocent until proved guilty line. 'Not all they said she hasn't, Doll,' he said acidly. 'She did sign over the property in Margate that she inherited from her father's brother, the one who was also her godfather. That's admitted and in the record. Now she's made a statement through her solicitor that she was being blackmailed by them for sexual indiscretions — the phrase is hers — involving whips and masks and narcotics. You'll be able to read all about it in your favourite slime sheet on your way home tonight.'

'Jesus.' Dolly held out her cup again.

So did I. We finished the Cutty Sark in miserable silence.

My second letter since arriving in London was from a dead man. Gerard had posted it before he took his own life. I found it waiting for me that evening, when, after a supper I could not taste in a small restaurant on Victoria Grove, followed by an endless wandering walk through Kensington Gardens and into the puzzle of Bayswater, I finally flagged a cab and went back to my hotel.

I had been sorely tempted to lose myself in the fake gaiety of Raymond's Revue Bar or even pick up an obliging girl outside the Hilton. There are times like that.

The scotch I had drunk in Dolly's office had only deepened my depression, and I suspected that the sordid eroticism of hired sex would have sunk me.

Sylvia's sordid confession was still in my mind. It was the sort of thing so base that one almost hopes that it is a mask for something worse, but cleaner.

I took the buff envelope to my room and lay on my bed, prising my shoes off with my toes, and opened it.

My dear Neil:

Because you are so much on my mind at this time, I am writing to you and not to my solicitor or to my only remaining family, the son I disown.

When I told you so recently that I had contemplated suicide, you spoke splendidly and honestly, like a Christian rightly wrathful at my pagan despair.

But I did have one hope left on earth then, and you helped me see it for a hope. Now I no longer have that. So I have chosen to return to my former purpose and end my now pointless life.

Please know, dear old friend, that it was no failure of yours, but my whole life which brought me here. Whatever is said of me after this, I want you to be curator of these few facts and make what use of them you will.

First, it came to me as the most profound shock that Sylvia had been charged in Gordon's death. If I believed for one moment that my standing by her in this could make the difference between her happiness and unhappiness, please accept as truth my utter willingness to do so. I have always loved Sylvia. If I have been uncharitable and unforgiving in the past, I have tried to be less so as I have grown older and a bit wiser about our common frailties.

I had placed a good deal of hope in some future value in my work as the sad heir to my family's title.

The absolutely final sense I expressed to you of my intention to resign that title would, I thought, be understood by Sylvia as no mere gesture of angry denial to my son of what he did not deserve to have. I can forgive him, but I cannot condone or reward his choice.

Sylvia, when I proposed to her that she and I, after a decent interval, in order to separate the event from her recent tragedy, remarry quietly, seemed at first warmly receptive to the idea. Then, when I explained to her my resolve to resign the title, she was at first incredulous and finally, I'm sad to say, abusive. It became clear that she had little or no interest in me, rather solely in that abominable title.

Now, poor woman, she has become implicated in some unspeakable way with those two men who murdered Gordon. I pity her and I pray for her even as I say my last prayers for myself.

Do not say God cannot forgive me this final act of reparation for all the sins of the Chaldecotts. My father and his father were decent men, but something seems to have died in us since then, and we are hollow men. I have always been pointed to, I know to my shame, as the pillar of rectitude in the family, but like any man I suppose who faces up to his flaws, I feel utterly worthless.

If I have done little that is wrong, and no great wrongs, nevertheless, I have done nothing at all which seems to stand the test of lasting right. Only God's grace can redeem this final wretched action.

Pray for me.

Affectionately,
GC

I lay there a long time holding the letter. I read it again. It was unmistakable Gerard, down to the elegant scrawl of initials I had seen on a dozen Dunham memos.

Gerard had not, then, been complicit with Sylvia in any plot against Gordon. That at least could be written off, in the light of this final humiliating confession, as a figment of Ashley's septic imagination.

Was Sylvia, too, wholly innocent of murder? Whatever the baseness of her conduct had been, against Gordon or Gerard or against herself, she did not deserve to suffer for something she had not done.

Why would Steve and Freddie have agreed to their story pointing to her as the source of their payoff for killing Gordon Fairly? Clearly, if they could make the police believe their contention, then their guilt as hired men would seem somewhat mitigated as compared with a proven charge that they had acted on their own initiative. But if they had acted on their own, why had they? Freddie swore he hated Gordon Fairly and had often fantasized doing him harm, watching him suffer, or having him beg for mercy.

Those fantasies of Freddie's were featured by one of the daily newspapers as a sort of continuing comic strip. 'Fast Freddie' had become 'Fantastic Freddie', whose dream of driving a turbocharged Ferrari to the Grand Prix championship was his confessed reason for wanting a lot of money immediately. Steve had wanted to buy his own piece of a cheap casino. His boasts in the press of the many occasions he had 'conquered the boss's luscious daughter' in the back seat of her Rolls-Royce were run page for page with Freddie's lurid imaginings.

Were they both simply borderline psychos who had conspired to kill the man who represented what they both wished to be — rich men with the power of life and death? They were certainly capable of blackmailing his wife, and of involving her in some macabre sexual circus if she would let herself be drawn into it.

I fell asleep with the light still on, fully clothed, and Gerard's letter still in my hand.

When I awoke at three in the morning I forced myself awake enough to undress properly, put the crumpled letter on the night table, and went to bed with the light out.

When I awoke again, my telephone was ringing and it was after nine.

CHAPTER 16

Sheila's call had got me out to Hampstead in time for a disorganized lunch of cold smoked mackerel, which she loved but James would not touch, and ham sandwiches on pumpernickel with large thick slices of red onion. These Sheila turned away from when her husband set them, a tottering pile on a plate, in front of me at the table.

'He doesn't want that mountain stuck in front of him, James, don't be obtuse.'

'Who wants kippered fish when he can have fresh Russian rye from the bakery this morning? Try that gammon, man, try it.'

'Neil might like to start with the mackerel. Why don't you take that ridiculous pile of food from in front of him and let him choose for himself what he will eat?'

'I know the man. He's too polite for his own good. Eat a sandwich, Yank. Beer?' He was wrenching cans of beer from his side pockets.

'There's a pot of Twining's fresh made,' Sheila said sprightlily, ignoring him drinking his own beer from the can after popping the ring and tossing it inaccurately at the wastebasket.

I let them act out their fussing over me. It was, in some awkward way, intended to jolly me out of my mood, I knew. We negotiated a serving of mackerel with chutney for my first course and a sandwich to follow. I passed on the beer. Yesterday's small wake at Dolly's, followed by a drink or two here and there between Kensington and Bayswater had left me with no urgent wish to drink again.

We could not have avoided getting down to the enormous swim of events going on around us, and as soon as our banter and jockeying about lunch was settled down, the murder and Sylvia Fairly's arrest surfaced.

What could be known from our several shamed but thorough readings of the papers we all knew.

James blasphemed and cursed through his mouthfuls, but even his noises were muted by the complexity of swift events storming around our exchanges.

Sheila cross-examined me with the ruthless efficiency of a prosecutor to get the inside story I knew of what was happening down at Dunham's.

I had not yet fulfilled my three a.m. vow to myself to take Gerard's last letter to Thomas for the police records. I planned to do so with an eye to precluding any possibility that they might feel it necessary to probe his death further if Ashley went to them with her wild story. I was not concerned for David's being discomposed, but simply for Gerard's own decent final repose. He had died in another place, alone. He had done an irremediable thing. Enough. There must not be a week of horrible, dredged-up headlines and photos of him and Sylvia at some inane New Year's party from 1962 with captions like: LOVER LORD LINKED TO SEX BOMB SCANDAL.

I read Gerard's letter to them because they were decent friends who would understand what his desperate words about sin and grace meant.

Sheila wept.

James lifted his beer can and said, 'God rest his soul, the poor, poor bastard.'

The front doorbell rang and Sheila wiped her nose and eyes and went to answer it.

James and I were parceling out the final ham sandwich between us when she returned with Ashley.

'She says she needs to talk to you, James. Urgently.'

Ashley looked half-frozen with indecision. There was no warmth in Sheila's voice. Her appraisal of the visitor was unrelenting and ironic without disguise. Those tremendous eyes seemed to unnerve the girl.

'Why the hell does everyone in London who wants to talk to me think the way to do it is to land in my home at the bloody crack of dawn?' James inquired of the ceiling in his crudest Southwark accent.

Ashley was pale and breathless. 'I thought at noon you might be . . . I'm sorry. I really do need . . .'

James, I could see, was as suspicious as Sheila of this Dresden doll version of Gordon Fairly facing him.

Finally he waved off her apology. 'Sit,' he barked at her. 'Beer or tea?'

She glanced to Sheila for approval and got no more than a continuation of that stare, but she edged into the chair across the table from James and half way round from me.

'Hello, Neil. I didn't . . .' Again her words trailed off in an entirely uncharacteristic, uncertain way.

Sheila brought her a cup from the kitchen and poured tea and put it in front of her. Certain decencies get maintained.

'Oh, thanks. No, no sugar. Really, this is . . .' She faced James squarely and pulled her chair up hard so that she sat erect against the table. That seemed to give her more assurance. 'I need advice and help.'

'I'm an actor. What makes you think I give advice?'

'Look.' She drew a breath, expelled it, and took a sip of her tea. 'God, that's really good. Thank you. I forgot to eat yet this morning. I thought I could . . . manage all this.' Suddenly her face crumpled and she looked like a miserable child.

Sheila's instincts were satisfied and aroused enough to go back to the kitchen for a plate of hot mackerel and some toast.

Ashley's loss of control was only momentary. A single tear escaped, but she scrubbed it off and took another hard breath.

'A lot of this . . . what has happened just floored me. I thought . . . I thought it was great larks at first, when I decided to wade right in. It was like Tevya's song in *Fiddler on the Roof*—"when you're rich they think you really know"—they do, they actually do. I knew some, but . . .'

'Eat while you talk.' The practical voice of Sheila was at her shoulder and the plate of food in front of her.

'Thank you.' She seemed bewildered by uncomplicated common kindness.

'I should think you'd have squads of solicitors standing about just aching to explain all the ins and outs of it to you.' James was not being impressed by her bewildered rich girl role.

'Them. Oh yes. Harper Pease and that mob. God, I should be grateful to Harper, I suppose. Without him the red tape would have me buried by now instead of only up to my arse in it.'

She glanced swiftly towards Sheila to see if the lapse had cost her any sympathy.

'It's not that, though. It's not the FairCom part I'm worried about. A thing that big has a kind of life of its own, and no matter what you do, it just grinds along going the way it goes. Engineering and distribution contracts and the goddam FT index are just there, I can see that.' She was gaining momentum as she ate and talked.

She looked directly at James and waited for him to look back. When he did she said, 'It's Charles Leonard. I need you and your man Dawkins to help me hang on to Charles.'

James was disgusted and let her know it. 'Hang on to him? Hang on to him? His voice was rising through the range of an octave as he mocked her in falsetto. 'Now that he's got that bloody TV talk show everyone thinks is the holy grail, I'd be surprised if you could get rid of him with an axe. That's what he's wanted all along, our Charles. To be a TV Personality. I knew the theatre would eat him alive if he stayed in it, and so did he.'

Sheila brought the conversation back to fundamentals. 'What do you mean, "hang on to him"?'

Ashley turned to her. 'Charles has resigned from the show. After signing the goddam contracts. No explanation, and no justification except a letter from his goddammed solicitor saying that for reasons of health Mr Leonard would be unable, etcetera.'

She was raging as volubly as James now. 'The bastard never even began. I'm putting ads in every trade paper and every daily featuring his stupid mug. We've been shooting footage like mad to run. This is the one goddam thing the Board gave me, handed to me to manage, the biggest single part of our advertising budget, but the bastards think it will keep me busy enough to get me out of their hair. I won't let that bastard do this to me or to FairCom. Take risks for him and then let him walk out on us?'

'What am I supposed to do, find him and hold his hand and tell him you're upset? Is that supposed to bring him trotting back?'

'I want your man Dawkins. I need one solicitor who really knows the theatre and knows Charles, not some City dummy in a bowler hat who doesn't know the West End from his own arse. Pease hasn't been to the theatre since nineteen-twenty-nine. He thinks Gilbert and Sullivan are the hottest act in show business.'

'You want Sid? Call him. He's in the bloody book. People hire him all the time, I don't have him on a string.'

'I called him three times this morning. I placed two calls through my secretary and finally picked up the goddam phone myself and tried personally. Mr Dawkins is not available to me.'

'Sid's stock in trade is to know before anyone else does what's going on. If he's going to deal with you he'll do his homework first. That's why he's so good.'

'Is there some conflict of interest or something? He isn't Charles's agent or solicitor, is he?'

James hooted. 'No, luv, he's not Charles's agent. He might like to be, but there's no connection. Stan Giftos represents Charles, and they deserve each other. You'll have to talk to Stan, but wear your chastity belt.'

'Is he that odious man Harper Pease told me about who was on about special dressing-rooms and a driver in the contract?'

'Probably. And read that contract. The driver might be for himself. Stan is what we call a legend in show biz.'

'I need your man Dawkins. I don't know all these people as he will. Will you make him see that? Tell him?'

I could see Gordon ever more clearly in her style, her instinct for using one person as a lever to move another. She was her father's daughter and she was fighting with his instincts, since they were very much all she had to go on in the sudden swamp of intrigue and calamity into which she'd stumbled.

'Forget Charles. Get someone else. The world is full of flashy talents one inch deep.'

'We've banked on Charles Leonard. Literally. They handed me that show when I walked in there and ranted at them pretending like mad I knew what I was talking about. Trendy this and audience impact that.'

'In theatre that's a technique called "the assumption of expertise". If they cast you as an Eskimo, you've got to walk out there and *be* a bloody Eskimo, never mind how absurd you feel under the parka,' Sheila said.

Ashley looked at her gratefully for the image. 'I suppose that's what I was doing, isn't it, acting? But now the damn igloos are melting, aren't they? We can't change the programme format again now, the adverts, everything. It would be impossible. People would start thinking FairCom was falling about over its own feet like a drunken sailor.'

She mugged comically, ruefully. She really was a bit of an actor, too.

'It was bad enough riding out the storm of criticism from the Wisdom fanatics when I got the Board to dump him. Do you know they picketed the building?' She was pumping an imaginary sign to show her astonishment.

'William was dim, but that was the most popular sponsored show on the telly,' Sheila reminded her gently.

Ashley rounded on her furiously, in a reflex half relief, I suspected, to have an adversary rather than a mother in this woman. 'He was fading. Anyone could read the damn charts and see it. His audience share hardened two years since, and it's been slipping ever since.'

Even Sheila was taken back by the combativeness of her reply.

'FairCom products are going to have enough problems on High Street, which is where it bloody counts, without being tied to a failing, middle-aged throwback to the nineteen-seventies.'

Here was the mentality in action of those who held nostalgia festivals for the last decade, then. The kind of market place which found more than anything else that timeliness counted. Six weeks old was out of style, and ten years old was classic. Whatever happened to her in her current struggles within FairCom, Ashley was obviously destined to go far in business. Unless, of course, someone tougher and shallower came along in six weeks and made her obsolete.

She stared around at us as though she would like to drive right through us. 'Doesn't anyone understand what the problem is? My problem? That fading superstar of yesteryear is right back on my doorstep demanding— demanding, mind you, to be reinstated as host of the show. He'll accept a new format, do you like that? He'll allow—that sleazy little prick will allow—FairCom to revise the logo. He says it will double our popularity if he's brought back now, as a result of public acclaim, that it will show the housewives on High Street that they make the decisions, not heartless business types or computers.'

James was yawning, not bothering to let her imagine he might be remotely sympathetic. He popped another beer and sank half the can, watching her, but saying nothing, unless a melodious belch counts as comment.

'Will you talk to Sid Dawkins for me?'

'I will not.'

'Will you, Sheila?' She was quick enough to turn back to Sheila when there was something she really wanted.

'Sid would laugh at the idea that I was trying to tell him who to take on as a client,' that honest woman admitted.

Ashley sagged perceptibly, her face a mask of fatigue and disgust. 'Great, just great. I'll tell you both one thing. I'll see him in hell before I put that toothy little shit back on the show. I'll scrap the whole Charles Leonard show if I have to, but I'll invent something else to go in its place until we can enforce his damned contract, then I'll nail his balls to that damn chair.'

Sheila kept getting back to the facts. 'If he has an out for reasons of health and he has reasons of health, you aren't going to be able to do much enforcing. That happened in the *Hedda Gabler* I was in, Phillip Arnold had that clause.'

'He'll have reasons of health enough when I get through, but if the bastard can work, he'll work.' She turned from vicious to clever in one change of expression and leaned across the table to James.

'Suppose we use a format of monthly replacements to mark time? Theatre personalities stepping in to pinch hit as they say, for their old, ill friend Charles. Would you take a month on Britain's top-rated TV show as host?'

James snorted beer and wiped the table with his hand. 'Like hell I would.'

'Eh? Like hell you wouldn't, do you mean? You don't know how much money it would mean yet, for one thing. And you, or any other actor, once your agent got on to you about spin-off benefits, the exposure — God, the films aren't in it with TV — would be slavering to do it. I'll put it to you right now.' She was bright-eyed, winging it and loving the challenge, playing jazz and watching James watching her.

'Take one month of the show. We'll call it anything you like under the general title *West End Tonight. West End Tonight Starring Hugh James?* You'd walk away from a month of that for twenty-five thousand quid? It's an acting job, man, no more, no less. You've got to act the part of a TV host, would that be too much for you? Outside your range, is it?'

She was a bloody marvel, was our Ashley. She was badgering James, taunting him, challenging him, and it was all something she was pulling out of her head as she said it. Her reality was just that — anything she could think of, whatever was spurring her. The past was anything older than this morning and the future was whatever she could make it be. Perhaps we were all in the presence of the final evolutionary product of our times, the first thoroughly existential woman.

'Would you reinstate the Lucy Goodman project?'

Sheila, with an actress's impeccable timing, thrust her question into the tension between Ashley and James and riveted both their attention suddenly on her.

'Forget it,' James shouted at them. I think that I knew when he had to shout that it was what he wanted.

'Yes, I will,' Ashley's triumphant 'yes' almost over-rode his refusal, and she knew Sheila had given her a pressure point. 'I'll draw up a guarantee, in lieu of salary, that for one month of your services as host of *West End Tonight* FairCom will underwrite a full production of that play—' she glanced at me for help—

'*Arden*.'

'Of *Arden*, with you as producer and director.'

James looked at her speculatively. 'London production?'

'London production.'

'West End theatre?'

'West End theatre.'

'Preferably the Savoy.'

'The Savoy if we can get it.'

'Within the calendar year.'

'Deal.' She smacked the table with the flat of her hand and sat back glowing. She had a contract with James now as binding as any writ and she knew it. His whole reputation in his profession was based on his unswervable dependability. If he had said it, he was bound by it. I had known that for thirty years: Ashley somehow knew it immediately.

Her father was dead less than a week. She had been linked in the cheap press with one of his murderers in a sordid sex exposé. Her stepmother was charged in a conspiracy with the killers, and her stepmother's former husband was a tragic suicide. But she sat there with a line of sweat edging her blonde hair grinning and lifting her fists in ecstasy.

I thought of David Chaldecott, his schemes for himself and his boyfriend taking every precedence in his mind over murder and betrayal. She was very like him. My God, I wondered silently, sitting there watching this enactment of the triumph of will over decency, have we produced a whole generation of spiritual Nazis?

Ashley had gained a major tactical advantage, and like the young Napoleon at her age, who had been similarly gifted and inclined, she pressed it to gain a larger strategic one.

'And will you work on Sid Dawkins for me? I'll really need him now, all this together, with you tied into it.'

James was still blinking, looking at her. I think he looked like a sleepy cat who has suddenly been bitten by a cornered canary.

Sheila inserted herself into it again drily. 'We'll have to talk it all through with Sid. The arrangements. We'll see what he says about it, if it's even legal.'

Ashley looked annoyed at the implication of Sheila's answer. 'Christ, tell him I don't want his soul, all I want is a good theatre law man who can screw Charles for me.'

I asked her if she wasn't afraid that there might be a conflict of interest for Sid in having these people for clients, profiting from the TV show, and FairCom for a client too, trying to replace them with Charles.

She waved away my question as if it were an impertinence. 'I'll show him where his interests lie. Just get us together.' Her sublime self-confidence was back on top.

She was gone as quickly as she had come, but in a changed mood. Sheila walked her to the front door.

James looked at me. 'How much of that do you think she had planned when she arrived and how much was she making it all up?'

'I don't know and you don't know,' I told him.

Sheila said she had kept a cab waiting for her outside.

'She'll find it's cheaper to buy a new Daimler than to keep a London taxi waiting,' James said.

'I wonder when the last time was that one had to count her money,' Sheila observed sourly.

'I wonder when the last time was anyone put a bomb in a London taxi,' I said to anyone who was listening.

'Oh, she knows how to look out for number one, that little honey,' Sheila said, inspecting the teapot and taking it out to replenish. 'But she's more a bomber than a victim, if you ask me.'

James was uncharacteristically silent. Finally he said to me, 'Why should Charles Splendid walk away from just the star billing and big money he has always wanted, just like that?' He snapped his fingers.

'I know him better than you do,' Sheila announced loudly from the kitchen, letting us know she was still in this conversation. Then reappearing, swirling the teapot in her hand, she said, 'Charles would only give up that job if someone made him. He once said to me, if I'm not making the company blush, late at night, in bed, "I'll tell you something about me, Sheila. I'd rather have killed you than do without you once I decided to have you." '

I started to pour the new tea, but the leaves hadn't settled yet. 'I should have thought you'd get up at that point in the conversation and start walking as fast as you could out of there.'

'What, for that?' she said, amused. 'You've never been to bed with an actor, I can see that. They're great performers in bed.' She glanced slyly at her husband, who had decided to read the paper. 'Most of them,' she added with a wink.

'Why,' James intoned in mock solemn baritone tones, 'are we talking about the absent, late, great Charles Leonard when we could be talking about *my* forthcoming London production of Bloody Arden of Bloody Faversham?' He gave a whoop and threw his arms wide. 'Eh?'

'Will you still want Charles for Mosby?' Sid asked, not a hair out of place after we had all stormed in on him with

James's extraordinary story of his deal with Ashley.

'Of course,' the practical member of the family said.

Just as her husband was roaring, 'Of course not.'

'He's the best actor for the part,' Sheila said flatly. 'I don't care about his other problems.'

'If he's too ill to rake in the brass he'd be getting for this show, he must be as contagious as the bloody black death. I won't have him dead or alive.'

'We'll cross that bridge later,' she said to Sid, choosing to ignore James's ukase.

'Do you really want to do this TV thing, James?' his agent asked him suspiciously. He had a right to his scepticism. He knew that his client was as likely to have acted from anger as from intention. He'd be as good as his word either way, but Sid, I suspected, was fishing for an angle that might permit James to disengage himself from the arrangement if he showed any second thoughts now.

'I want to do *Arden*, for Chrissakes,' James barked at him annoyedly. 'For that I'm willing to sit up there on the screen and do my famous imitation of a man having a good time growing piles while a lot of rock stars with safety-pins through their brains bat their eyes at me and show the audience their arses.'

'It's acting, Sid. James is an actor, isn't he?' Sheila plainly didn't want Sid organizing any campaign to get James off the hook.

'An out of work actor at the moment, or about to be, as good as,' James added. I thought he was as uneasy about the whole idea as Sid was for him, but he was going to tough it out.

Sid sat back and looked at the options carefully before speaking, and when he did speak, it was very slowly, as though each word had to be measured as it was uttered.

'Charles called me this morning. He has fired Stan Giftos and he wants me to represent him.

'Where is he? What's made him quit the show?' Trust Sheila to get to the heart of it fast.

Sid did not alter his inexorable, measured, tone. 'I don't know and I don't know. I've spoken to Stan. He says that anyone who wants Charles for a client can have him.' In a side word of explanation to me he added, 'We're talking about ten per cent of very large earnings.'

He looked at Sheila and James. 'William Wisdom has something on Charles, that much is clear, and he is holding it over his head. Wisdom wants his show back. He wants it back the way you might want your liver back if someone cut it out of you. Between us, I know that man, and he wants Charles extinguished, blacklisted. Charles is suddenly a pariah with people who were fawning on him a week ago. If the Greek doesn't want him — and I don't like to disparage a colleague in this lilywhite profession, but Stan would take Attila the Hun for a client if there were a demand for barbarian acts — I'm pretty sure I don't. Do you? Still?'

James asked in honest wonder, 'What for sweet Jesus' sake can Wisdom, that fat-arsed twit, have on Charles that would put the frighteners on him that badly?'

We found out, starting immediately when Sid's secretary rang through to say that Ashley Fairly was in the outer office raising hell and demanding to see him.

She took one look at the three of us when she banged in. 'Jesus, you three again. What the hell is this runaround?' were her opening words to Sid. 'Giftos just finished telling me you're handling Charles now.'

'Have a seat, Miss Fairly,' he said in his politest academic manner. 'I think you know Mr James, Miss Edwards, and Professor Kelly.'

Formality is the greatest deflater of blown-up entrances the theatre provides. Ashley calmed, sat, and began again.

'Mr Dawkins, forgive my barging in on you like this,

but I am sitting on an adjournment of my Board, your bloody secretary won't put me through to you on the phone, and I came over here, keeping a lot of important people waiting, to ask you one simple question. And the answer just might cost FairCom one million pounds, so, goddammit, I want an answer.'

She was, again like the late young Buonaparte, very good at recovering a lost advantage.

'Miss Fairly,' Sid said evenly, 'it is of no interest whatever to me what your gains or losses might be. As a matter of common courtesy I shall answer one question for you if I can, simply so that you will have an example of good manners to study for your own possible future use, but I don't want you coming in here and shouting at me, and I won't have my employee cursed for doing her job properly.'

Sid wasn't bad at unarmed combat, either. Quieter, but more thorough.

She went white, this young whirlwind daughter of her father, who had breezed past his corpse to take control of a multi-billion dollar business and was revelling in it like a freebooter. She might, with her percentage of control on the executive committee at FairCom, have her vice-presidents cowed, but she understood what Sid meant and that she had no leverage on him.

Ashley asked her question flatly. 'Is Charles Leonard your client now?'

'No, he is not.'

She slumped in her chair and looked defeated. 'Shit. He's taken off for some bloody where in his plane and I can't reach him. I'm willing to buy whatever the bloody hell it is Wisdom is waving at him to frighten him off, and I want to tell him that. I'll pay for it if it will save my show. FairCom can't really afford any more scandal. Not the kind that gets right down to the level where the ladies who shop on High Street can understand.'

Thomas Bowie came in over her last line, the face of the outraged and despairing secretary behind him at the door.

I immediately recalled that I was still carrying Gerard's letter in my pocket, after having phoned Thomas earlier in the morning to say I'd bring it in to Scotland Yard.

'There's nothing you can buy now for a hundred thousand that you won't be able to get for fourteen p. in the afternoon papers, Miss Fairly.'

Ashley, the great interrupter, didn't like being interrupted. 'Who the hell are you? What are you on about?'

Sid was motioning to his secretary that it was all right.

I was borrowing Sid's lines to let him know what was going on. 'Inspector Bowie, I think you know everyone here except our host, Mr Dawkins. Inspector Bowie's assignment is to shadow me all over London. I'm beginning to expect him in my dreams.'

Thomas was still primarily interested in Ashley. 'Haven't you figured out yet, Miss Fairly, a smart girl like you, that your ex-employee William Wisdom has his own informer on your Board?'

'That bastard.' I could see her sifting the possibilities through her mind, looking for another head to chop.

'When you told your Board finally two hours ago that you were going ahead with a substitute format for your TV show, pending the eventual return of Charles Leonard instead of reinstating Wisdom, you made his response inevitable. He had just the one card, and he's played it.'

'What has he done?' She was all attention, like a chess champion watching a Knight's move to see what it meant for her Queen.

'I can't prove he's done anything. Someone—I underscore the person's anonymity to Scotland Yard—sent over a bundle of letters by special messenger to St John-

Stewart. I'd describe them as love-letters. From Sylvia Fairly to Charles Leonard.'

If Ashley had slumped before, she all but collapsed in her chair now. 'That idiot. That's what I thought. Why the hell didn't he sell them to me?' She looked at Thomas with interest for the first time. I found it hard to believe, but she seemed to be evaluating him, or some quality in him, for possible usefulness to her. 'What I need is a friend at bloody Scotland Yard.' She blew wisps of hair from her eyes disgustedly and leaned back in her chair.

'Charles was my teacher in Switzerland. He was a playwright nobody would produce then, and an actor with no parts, so he spent a year teaching Drama to sex-mad teenagers at a boarding-school. God, he must have laid fifty of us, all under sixteen. They finally gave him his papers to cool the place down.

'That was no scandal. At least, not one you could blackmail him with now. But dear Sylvia came over *in loco parentis* to see her exiled stepdaughter, all feverish with concern for my well-being. I knew that silly stud took her to bed too while she was there, I was positive.'

She shook her head at the folly of her elders. 'Wouldn't Lady Sylvia fall on her face for that tiresome gigolo? It's really too disgusting. God, I thought it was humiliating to have lost my virginity to him. But Stepmama had to go the whole hog, the grand affair, that silly bitch.'

Thomas added an apparently random comment. 'In one letter, written almost a year ago, she asked him to meet her down in Canterbury, in the cathedral. Her solicitor for the transfer of that Margate land down there was in Canterbury.'

'Then longen folk to goon on pilgrimages,' James recited in his best Brummy dialect.

'Geoffrey Chaucer,' Sheila said automatically, '*The Canterbury Tales.*'

'Jesus, could she get any tackier?' Ashley asked the ceiling.

'To talk about quote matters of great future interest to both of us, but requiring mutual risks, unquote,' Thomas concluded.

He leaned forward to get Ashley's attention again. 'I think that Charles might have decided that he wasn't going to get away with it after all. I think Charles conspired with your stepmother to kill your father, Miss Fairly.'

'Why should he?' she spat at him. 'Gordon was going to hand him that TV show on a platter.'

'Not before Sylvia got him to accept the idea of Charles doing it he wasn't. She talks at some length of her campaign to persuade him, in between the riper bits. When Charles finally did have it on a platter, he had to make good on his half-promises and hints to Sylvia, didn't he, to hang on to it?'

Thomas sat on the arm of the sofa wearily. 'Charles was the silent partner who arranged for his old pal Stan Giftos to give his faithful office slave and cousin Freddie Constantine over to Gordon Fairly to be his second driver, wasn't he?'

He grinned over at me. 'It was Neil who said to me one day when we were analysing this case at some length in another part of this city, "Why in hell doesn't anyone ever call him Freddie Jones or Freddie Smith? It's as if he didn't come from a real family, as if someone mailed away to a comic book for him." Remember that, Yank? And I thought about that. Constantine is Greek. Greek families are close, you know; they're like us Wops. So I started eating a lot of *trigone spanakopittes* and drinking a lot of *kokkineli*, and surprise, surprise, it all led back to him working for Stanley Giftos and being his goomba.'

Thomas was enjoying having the floor. I could see why he had once had an itch to act. He spread his hands in a mute Mediterranean gesture of appeal.

'You were the one who upset all the pieces, Miss Fairly, just as they were in place. You came steaming back from Jersey, where everyone was assuming you would stay forever, happily painting pictures and living the lesbian persuasion, and announce you're going to stick around and run your father's store.

'They were right back where they started from, weren't they? You and young David Chaldecott between you flushed Sylvia's plan for rescuing Dunham's and marrying Gerard Chaldecott right down the tubes. As for young William Wisdom, he wasn't so young any more, and his career of kissing Sir Gordon's rosy red to keep his job on the big screen was bust.'

Ashley unerringly saw how Charles had scuttled himself. 'Wouldn't that vain little prick keep his love-letters? God.'

Thomas nodded approvingly at her seeing the point. 'Not just from Sylvia, either. We went over to his place after we got the first batch. He must have a thousand of them, including some from fourteen-year-old girls, Miss Fairly.'

'Jesus, I sent him a poem once.'

'He saved it,' Thomas said reassuringly. 'Someone enterprising knew Charles well enough to send someone else to steal those letters, we suspect, and they ended up in Wisdom's hands—or someone's, we can't be sure whose, can we?'

Ashley said almost dreamily. 'If I had just taken the plane back to Jersey after Gordon was killed, they might have pulled it off. I'll be damned.'

'Yes, they might well have. Sinjin of Scotland Yard is very grateful to you, Miss Fairly. You're what the scientific boffins down at the lab call a catalyst. Take a relatively quiet state of affairs, add you, and you got not one nicely controlled explosion in the back of a motor-car, but several, all over London. I think the last one will be fatal for your old teacher when we land him.'

'You said once that, even with the two handymen to do the actual dirty work, you thought there had to be someone besides Sylvia behind it, didn't you?' I asked our beaming Inspector.

'I was positive. It was elementary, as they teach us to say in cop school.' He ticked the names off on his fingers. 'Sylvia, Steve, Freddie — not one of them had ever ridden in the back of Fairly's car. So they wouldn't know exactly how he dealt with his morning post when he got it, would they? Now Charles had been in the Daimler a dozen times, hadn't he?' He gave the same Italian shrug with his eyes shut that he used to explain why he was a sensational personality, in a Jungian sense.

CHAPTER 17

The final explosion in the case was fatal to Charles's career, at least. Unless they produce enough theatre in HM prisons so that he can keep his edge for the next twenty-two years, when he is scheduled to be released back into the world of professional entertainment again.

The two hired goons got ten years less, but enough surely to interrupt their plans for racing and gambling glory.

Sylvia buckled when they brought Charles back from France under warrant and he chose to spend most of his first press conference reviling her. I actually think she might have kept on shielding him, out of whatever obscure erotic loyalty, if he had simply had the wit to say that he still loved her and had only helped her for love's sweet sake. Her sentence was as hard as his.

She had planned it all with him, and she finally

confessed it all in detail. People have killed for less, certainly. In *Arden of Faversham*, to take an example at hand from the beginning, Arden's wife and her lover actually murdered him to gain control of a quite small estate down in Kent, near Canterbury. Those who remember the play from Hugh James's sensational London production of this past year will recall that the wife and lover hired two mindless villains to do the actual killing for them, But they were the real murderers, of course, and their motive was a few acres of fields.

Sylvia had convinced herself, as guilty people have been known to do, that Ashley knew all about her affair with Charles. She even suspected that Charles might have shown his ex-pupil some of her letters, so much did she know and trust him. All her sessions with me had apparently been designed to find out if Ashley had told me any of that.

The only ones to gain much from the whole horror story were Ashley and David Chaldecott. FairCom lost heavily at first, but was reorganized and rescued by getting out of the travel business and the entertainment business entirely except for the lucrative cable TV franchises they leased. Their shares have climbed steadily back up since the success of their African merchandising for Israel.

David Chaldecott is now Lord Marchmill. As Sid pointed out to me, Gerard really should have consulted his solicitor, or at least a specialist in heraldry. One can resign the use of a title, but Parliament made a law back in 1678 making it impossible for any mortal man to extinguish a title in the peerage created by the Sovereign.

Thomas and I had our last drink together in a Greek restaurant in St Martin's Lane, where he introduced me to the exotically named *kokkineli*, a surprisingly decent retsina rosé, once you fight your way past the first fumes of turpentine from the glass.

I told him at about ten p.m. that I knew of a mystery he might enjoy trying to solve. At two o'clock in the morning he was still cross-examining me about exactly how Lucy Goodman could have been Wat Harris and where he could read up on Shakespeare's connection with this Richard Field dwelling in Blackfriars.

'I think he did it, Neil. No, really, you're laughing, listen to me. I think Shakespeare killed her. Look, let's say she did write this play, and then . . .'

Shakespeare scholars are well advised to be alert for an all points bulletin from Scotland Yard concerning this matter.

Dolly Allen and I left for two weeks in Ireland the next morning. Her hair was pulled back and tied with a green flowered scarf. She still wasn't smoking, and she was starting to enjoy it.

THE BEST IN SUSPENSE

BESTSELLING BOOKS FROM TOR

☐ 58725-1   *Gardens of Stone* by Nicholas Proffitt $3.95
     58726-X   Canada $4.50

☐ 51650-8   *Incarnate* by Ramsey Campbell $3.95
     51651-6   Canada $4.50

☐ 51050-X   *Kahawa* by Donald E. Westlake $3.95
     51051-8   Canada $4.50

☐ 52750-X   *A Manhattan Ghost Story* by T.M. Wright
                                                  $3.95
     52751-8   Canada $4.50

☐ 52191-9   *Ikon* by Graham Masterton $3.95
     52192-7   Canada $4.50

☐ 54550-8   *Prince Ombra* by Roderick MacLeish $3.50
     54551-6   Canada $3.95

☐ 50284-1   *The Vietnam Legacy* by Brian Freemantle
                                                  $3.50
     50285-X   Canada $3.95

☐ 50487-9   *Siskiyou* by Richard Hoyt $3.50
     50488-7   Canada $3.95

Buy them at your local bookstore or use this handy coupon:
Clip and mail this page with your order

TOR BOOKS—Reader Service Dept.
49 W. 24 Street, 9th Floor, New York, NY 10010

Please send me the book(s) I have checked above. I am enclosing
$_____ (please add $1.00 to cover postage and handling).
Send check or money order only—no cash or C.O.D.'s.

Mr./Mrs./Miss _____

Address _____

City _____ State/Zip _____

Please allow six weeks for delivery. Prices subject to change without
notice.